*Gui[...]
with[...]*

Although Guinevere was young, she had seen many eligible bachelors, both from Leonesse and further abroad, Arthur of Camelot among them. She thought of him now, the fine, dark eyes, the expressive brows, the rich voice and mischievous smile. No man had ever kindled a spark in her being, except perhaps this one. That he was of her father's years concerned her little. She was accustomed to older men in her daily routine, indeed preferred their patience and maturity to the shallow exuberance of those of her own years.

"It is a great honor, indeed," she murmured to Oswald. "And I know that you are right. No more words, let it be done."

"You accept King Arthur's offer?"

Guinevere nodded, and her smile remained. "Yes, Oswald, I shall marry Arthur of Camelot."

Her adviser's face brightened with a look of intense relief, and his taut shoulders relaxed. He took her hands in his and squeezed them. "My dear child. I was proud to hold you in my arms in the hour of your birth. I shall be prouder still to see you wed."

Guinevere gnawed her lower lip, not so sure. "Poor Arthur. All the dowry I bring him is a land in danger. But I promise I shall love him dearly, Oswald."

"So you should, child."

"I could never marry a man without love," Guinevere said stoutly. "But Arthur has such gentleness in his eyes—I've never heard him raise his voice. He wears his power so lightly, and it is all the more strong because of that. I've never known a man like him, Oswald. How could I love anyone more?"

Wind rustled through the apple trees again, and a yellow leaf, in premature anticipation of autumn, fluttered to the ground at her feet.

FIRST KNIGHT

A NOVEL BY ELIZABETH CHADWICK

STORY BY LORNE CAMERON & DAVID
HOSELTON AND WILLIAM NICHOLSON

SCREENPLAY BY WILLIAM NICHOLSON

POCKET BOOKS

New York   London   Toronto   Sydney   Tokyo   Singapore

This book is a work of fiction. Names, characters, places and incidents are products of the author's imagination or are used fictitiously. Any resemblance to actual events or locales or persons, living or dead, is entirely coincidental.

An *Original* Publication of POCKET BOOKS

POCKET BOOKS, a division of Simon & Schuster Inc.
1230 Avenue of the Americas, New York, NY 10020

ISBN: 0-671-53532-3

First Pocket Books printing July 1995

10 9 8 7 6 5 4 3 2 1

POCKET and colophon are registered trademarks of Simon & Schuster Inc.

Printed in the U.S.A.

FIRST KNIGHT

Chapter 1

*I*t was midmorning when Lancelot drew rein on the crest of the hill and, gazing out over tawny fields of ripe hay, saw the village nestling in the valley beyond. His stallion, Jupiter, took the opportunity to graze, his bit making a musical jingle as he tore at the lush grass.

The sun warmed Lancelot's skin, the air carried the meadow scents of summer, and for a moment his eyes took on a faraway look and a half smile almost curved his lips. Then his thoughts changed direction. He stiffened and his right hand reached to the hilt of the sword at his hip. The grazing horse jerked up its head and sidled.

"Easy," he murmured softly and took his hand from the weapon to pat his mount's satin dark neck. "Easy, boy." And now his lips were grimly set. It had been so many years ago, so far away, and yet no matter how he tried to put distance between himself and the ghosts of his past, they still kept pace with him.

He gathered the reins in his fingers, taking control, and kicked his heels against Jupiter's black flanks. He would pay no heed to the beguilements of summer. Winter always followed, as he had bitter cause to know.

The village was crowded, for it was market day, and Lancelot had to weave his way between ox-drawn carts, open-sided wains, goosegirls and shepherds, housewives and farmers. Men haggled over a pen of spotted sheep. A boy with a goad strove to control a pink sow almost as large as himself, her heavy dugs nearly touching the straw-littered ground. A woman offered to tell Lancelot his fortune, but he declined with a bitter laugh. Another offered him more dubious favors, but he declined those, too, and finally dismounted outside the smithy.

The blacksmith's lad ceased pumping the bellows beneath the fire and came to take the stallion's bridle.

"Four new iron shoes," Lancelot said. "We've come a long way, and we've still a distance yet to ride."

The boy nodded. The smith glanced up from the forge where he was heating a sword blade in the coals. "Where are you bound, stranger?"

Lancelot smiled and leaned against the doorpost. "Wherever the road takes me, friend." His dark gaze followed the sway of a young woman's hips as she walked past with a basket of fresh silver fish.

The smith grunted and turned back to the task at hand. "Be about an hour," he said.

Lancelot nodded equably. "Suits me." He studied the bustle of the market-day crowds. A lively place, this, and every likelihood of drumming up some funds for his sadly depleted purse. By the time he had paid for four horseshoes, there would scarcely be enough left for a loaf of bread and a hunk of cheese.

A young man emerged from the crowd and approached the smithy. A fat leather pouch hung on his belt, and Lancelot eyed it sidelong.

"Is my sword ready yet, Weland?"

"Aye, Master Thomas, it's over there." The smith nodded toward a trestle at the back of his ship where several artifacts were laid out—mostly spades and hoes for the farmers; but there were a few spears, swords, and daggers for those who liked the security of a weapon in their house.

The young man strode eagerly to the trestle and laid his hand to the hilt of the blade he had ordered. Lancelot watched with tolerant amusement as the customer cut the air to test the weapon's balance and practiced several fancy but meaningless maneuvers. Men bought swords as expensive toys. The trouble was that most of them did not know how to play with them.

"A fine sword," Lancelot said, and ceased lounging against the doorpost to hold out his hand. "May I?"

The young man appeared somewhat surprised, but then shrugged and gave the sword to him.

Lancelot curled his fingers around the grip and made a few cutting motions himself. The sword responded well, but not as well as his own. A sound, ordinary weapon for a sound, ordinary man, of which Lancelot was neither.

"Do you fight?" he asked, returning the sword to

its owner. "Are you good enough to justify this blade?"

The young man reddened. "I can beat my brothers, and they're all older than me—can't I, Weland?"

"Aye, that you can, Master Thomas," said the smith, his eyes on his job.

"I practice all the time. I've been our village champion twice over."

"Ah, a champion." Lancelot nodded as though impressed. He cocked his head and gave Thomas a considering look. "Would you wager your skill with your new blade against me for the weight of coin in your purse?"

"Against you?" The young man looked Lancelot up and down. He saw a handsome man with an air of easy confidence. A fine sword sat in the scabbard on his hip, but there were no bulging muscles to accompany it, and his clothes were shabby.

"Think you're capable?"

"As capable as you are," Thomas said with spirit as he made up his mind. "What have you to wager?"

Lancelot laughed. "You would not want my purse!"

Thomas glanced over his shoulder at the fine stallion that the apprentice had tied up outside the smithy. "Your horse, then," he said.

Still laughing, Lancelot agreed to the bargain.

The two men stepped out in front of the forge, Thomas with his bright unscarred sword in his hand, Lancelot drawing his own from its wool-lined scabbard into the light. It shone no less brilliantly than the new blade and was all the more deadly for the patina of finger grip on the elegant hilt.

Weland left his smithying and stood with brawny arms folded to watch. As Lancelot and Thomas tested each other, circling warily on the dusty ground before the smithy, a crowd of marketgoers and tradesmen gathered to watch and shout encouragement.

"Come on, Thomas, show him. Prove yourself!"

Blade rang on blade in a high, metallic note. Lancelot parried with ease the blows that Thomas launched at him. Stepping and turning with the fluid motion of a dancer, he held the young villager at bay until a large enough crowd had grown, among them, several other potential victims. It was always best to appear to give your opponent a sporting chance if you wanted to increase the size of your eventual winnings.

Parry, parry, turn, cut, and parry. "Do you want to know how to win a sword fight?" Lancelot asked.

"How?" Thomas was panting now, sweat streaking his face. Lancelot was barely warmed up.

"Be the only one with a sword, of course." Lancelot came off the defensive and attacked. A twist of the wrist, a swift flick, and Thomas's new acquisition went flying through the air to land in the dirt. The point of Lancelot's sword lay in the tender hollow of Thomas's throat. "See," Lancelot said softly, "it's easy." Then he sheathed his sword and turned to the onlookers. "Give him a hand!" he shouted. "He fought well!"

The crowd applauded with enthusiasm in which there was a mingling of sympathy for the victim and admiration for the winner. Red in the face, Thomas stood up, retrieved his sword, if not his pride, and joined his friends in the throng. Lancelot jangled

Thomas's comfortably fat purse and scanned the watching faces.

"Winner takes all, my friends! A fine, heavy purse, this!" He tossed it, caught it, and gave a wink and a grin to a winsome young woman in the crowd. Blushing, she returned his smile and then lowered her lashes.

Lancelot's gaze moved on, probing, selecting. There was a giant of a man among the watchers, his muscles twice the size of the smith's, and a heavy sword hanging at his side.

"Once in a hundred years there comes a fighter so powerful, so fast, so fearless, that no man can touch him!" Lancelot declared boldly to his audience. When he was sure the words had sunk in, he added, "But while you're waiting for him to come along, you can practice on me!" Removing cloak and tunic, he folded them in a pile at the edge of the arena.

The tall young man watched Lancelot narrowly. The latter could almost see the thoughts traveling through laborious cogs in the villager's mind. He was weighing the odds and deciding that he had a good chance. A young woman stood beside the giant, pride glowing in her eyes. She touched his arm and stood on tiptoe to whisper in his ear. Other members of the crowd nudged him, urging him to step forward and take on the stranger. Lancelot smiled to himself and gestured broadly.

"As sure as the sun will rise tomorrow, somewhere there's a man who's better than me, and someday I'm going to meet him, and he's going to go away very rich. Could be here, could be today . . . Could be you!" He stabbed his forefinger directly at his intended victim.

There was no resisting such a challenge. The men propelled their enormous companion into the ring. The young woman beamed proudly. "That's my Mark," she told other women among the crowd. "Strong as ten men, he is."

Lancelot pursed his lips as his own height and breadth were engulfed and made puny by the bear-like villager towering over him. He let his gaze wander slowly up and slowly down his opponent. "Ah," he said, as if entertaining second thoughts, and shading his eyes, squinted skyward.

"The sun is getting high and it's hot for fighting," he prevaricated. "Perhaps we should leave it until another occasion."

"Coward!" one of the giant's friends yelled. "Call yourself a fighting man? Scared, are you?" More jeers and catcalls followed. Without speaking himself, the huge villager held out a silver coin to Lancelot. There was easily enough to shoe a horse and buy bread and cheese.

"Ah," said Lancelot again and grimaced as if torn between taking the coin and declining the danger of a fight with such a colossus. Then, appearing to have made a decision, he took the silver, put it in the pouch, and tossed it on top of his folded cloak and tunic.

"How good is he?" he addressed the giant's vociferous friends in the crowd. "He certainly looks as strong as an ox." Brawn being one thing, brains entirely another.

"Show him, Mark!" yelled a towheaded youth. "Show him how Lizzie bites!"

Mark grinned and drew his heavy sword from its sheath. Light glinted off the pattern-welded blade,

7

giving the weapon an air of sulky menace. Mark set both hands to the grip and, raising the sword on high, turned and launched a tremendous blow at a nearby timber post. The wood might have been butter the way the blade sundered it from top to bottom. The force of the blow scarcely registered a ripple upon Mark's iron-hard muscles.

"Ah," said Lancelot for the third time and rubbed his chin. "Impressive, my friend."

"Keep out of Lizzie's way, stranger!" yelled Mark's towheaded friend. "One kiss, and your doom is sealed!"

Lancelot eyed the sword. He had no intention of ever coming close enough to "Lizzie" to be kissed.

Mark withdrew his weapon from the split post and patted the brooding, bluish blade. "My Lizzie," he said affectionately.

"He named it after his mother-in-law!" some wag in the crowd shouted. The comment was greeted with shouts of laughter.

"Right," Lancelot rubbed the back of his neck and gave the appearance of being nervous. "Well, no need for Lizzie to work too hard. You don't have to kill me to win."

The young giant nodded. His eyes flickered to the crowd and sought the young woman who had been standing at his side.

"Go on, Mark!" she urged, her face aglow, "I know you can do it . . . only don't hurt him." She blew him a kiss, which the watchers appreciated greatly.

Lancelot drew his own sword and crouched upon the balls of his feet. "So you're Mark, are you?"

"That's my name," his opponent said gruffly, and copied Lancelot's stance.

"I'm Lancelot. Are you ready?"

Mark wiped his wrist across his mouth. "I'm ready," he growled.

"Then take me."

Mark advanced and tested the pressure on Lancelot's blade with his own sword edge. Lancelot smiled and obliged him, his wrist supple and easy. Uttering a roar that would have sent the village bull fleeing in shame, Mark attacked in full earnest, launching blow after blow at Lancelot. Lizzie was a blur in Mark's fist, but Lancelot's reactions were faster. Every single swipe that the young giant took cut nothing but air, and yet Lancelot seemed scarcely to move from his original spot. Panting, confused, Mark paused to gain his second wind.

"Are you sure you've got tight hold of your sword?" Lancelot inquired lightly. He could see that the young man was both baffled and irritated, and that his crude fighting skills would suffer even more as a result.

"Don't you worry about that." Mark scowled and launched another assault. Once more Lizzie fed on nothing but air while Lancelot moved with a dancer's fluid grace.

"Can I give you some advice?" Lancelot suggested innocently.

"What?"

Lancelot smiled. His voice was friendly. "Don't drop your sword like your friend did."

Mark's face darkened with temper, and he raised Lizzie on high to deliver a blow as powerful as that which had sundered the timber post. "I—will—not—drop—my—" he began to say through his teeth, but the sentence was never completed. Lancelot's blade snaked out, and in a motion too fast for the eye to follow, he twitched Lizzie out of Mark's grip and sent her spinning end over end through the air in a perfect juggler's arc. Lancelot's left hand shot out and caught Mark's precious sword, hilt first as it descended.

"What were you saying?" he asked.

The crowd burst out laughing, and applause rippled around the ring. Lancelot grinned at his audience, reserving a special smile for the attractive young woman who had earlier caught his eye. He flourished a bow.

Mark stood gaping at Lancelot, all anger banished by dumbfounded astonishment. "How did you do that?" he demanded to know.

Lancelot turned from the crowd and handed Lizzie to the still-panting, mystified young man. He said nothing, his expression somewhat wry now, a little guarded. People always asked him that, and it always needled through his defenses to the wounded place deep within him.

Mark swung to his companions, his arms outspread in appeal. "What did he do? Was it a trick?"

"It is no trick, my friend," Lancelot said quietly. "It is the way I fight." He sheathed his sword.

"But I want to know how you do it. Could I do it, too?"

Lancelot shook his head. "I don't think so."

"Tell me, I can learn!"

Lancelot sighed. The face staring down into his

was eager and pleading, open and innocent. How long it was since those traits had flourished in his own soul, and yet still too close for comfort. "You have to study the way your opponent moves until you know what he is going to do before he does it."

"I can do that." Mark nodded confidently.

"You have to know the one moment in every fight when you win or lose. You have to know how to wait for it."

"I can do that, too, if you show me!"

Lancelot's voice was suddenly expressionless. "And you have to not care, my friend, whether you live or die. Can you do that, too?"

Mark was silent. The eagerness left his face, and he shook his head.

"No," Lancelot said, and put his hand upon Mark's brawny forearm. "You live your life, and I live mine."

Lancelot collected Jupiter from the smithy, paid for the four new shoes with a coin from his jingling pouch, and repaired to the inn across the way in search of refreshment. There was a stable at the rear. A quick word and a charming smile for the plump landlady obtained him permission to use it. He removed Jupiter's harness, gave the horse a rapid but thorough grooming, and left him with a manger of hay and a bucket of water.

The inn, which went by the name of the Three Apple Trees as attested by the boldly painted wooden sign swinging outside, was bustling with hungry and thirsty marketgoers. The perspiring landlady, her husband, and their assistants could scarcely keep up with the demand for ale, cider, and the sweet, honey mead brewed from their own beehives behind the stable. Wooden platters of hot bread and glistening roasted meat wafted past Lancelot, making his stomach growl with longing. Swordplay, no matter how easy it looked, was hungry work.

He found an empty table in a shadowy corner at the rear of the room and sat down on the trestle bench. A huge but friendly mastiff wagged up to him and thrust its moist black nose into his palm. He fondled the dog for a moment, remembering the hounds he had once owned himself in another life. His favorite had been a huge wolfhound, which his family had viewed with considerably less enthusiasm, since it had the habit of shedding hair and slobber in vast quantities over everyone and everything. *His* family. If he looked over his shoulder, he knew that he would see them. The mastiff whined. On the trestle, the dirty pots clattered as a serving girl picked them up.

"What can I get you, sir?"

He looked up. It was the young woman he had smiled at in the crowd. Her blond plaits were tied back with a kerchief, her throat was bare, and the scooped drawstring neck of her gown revealed the beginning of an interesting cleavage. His thoughts scrambled with relief to gain a sure foothold in the present.

"What would you recommend?"

She cocked her head on one side, and a dimple appeared in her cheek. "Well, the bread's fresh out of the baker's oven next door. My mistress says that we've no more roasts, but there's a cider chicken stew if you've a mind."

"I've a mind," Lancelot confirmed, and his eyes gleamed, making the statement less than innocent.

She looked at him through her lashes and smiled. "Then I hope you've a good appetite. I won't be more than a minute." She whisked away into a back room, the dog following on her heels. Lancelot glanced around at the clientele. Most were farmers or tradesmen, stocky, red-faced men, resembling the fat, rosy apples that abounded throughout their countryside. Their wives were florid and buxom, too, some dark-haired, others as blond as the serving girl.

As out of place as himself among all these rustic working folk were two lean, grim-faced men who sat near the door, peering out at the bustle. They were dressed in dark woolen tunics and both wore broadswords in black leather scabbards. Their hair was cropped so close to their scalps that they looked like recently shaven flea victims. Even as Lancelot glanced their way, they paid up and swaggered out, fists clenched upon studded swordbelts. Several villagers gazed after them and muttered softly, nor was it Lancelot's imagination that the atmosphere was suddenly less tense for their leaving.

The girl returned with a wooden bowl from which rose a tantalizing steam of meat and herbs. She set it down before him together with a round, crusty loaf and a jug of cider.

Lancelot jerked his head. "Who were they?"

She sniffed contemptuously. "Men from across the border. They belong to Prince Malagant of Gore."

"Who?" Lancelot dipped a horn spoon in the chicken stew, blew on it, and took a mouthful. The taste was divine. He was no slave to his stomach; as far as he was concerned, food was fuel. More often than not, he had to catch or pick his own, but he was hungry, and whoever had cooked this had a magic hand.

The girl looked at him in surprise. "You have not heard of Prince Malagant of Gore?"

"Should I?"

"You are fortunate if you have not. His soldiers are always causing trouble in the villages. Since Lord Leodegrance died last year, they have become bolder. Malagant would like our homes and farms for his own."

Lancelot shrugged. Petty feuding, he thought; it was the way of the world, and no concern of his, except that it warned him to be careful on the road. He tore a chunk of bread off the loaf and dipped it in the stew. The young woman watched him eat, and when he made no effort to continue the conversation, she disappeared to attend to some more customers. Soon enough, however, like iron to a magnet stone, she returned.

"Do you like the stew?"

"My bowl speaks for itself." He mopped up the dregs with the last of the bread, and sat back.

"It's a special recipe of the inn. There's more if you want it."

He shook his head. "My horse would break his back if I ate another morsel."

Her eyes widened in dismay. "You are leaving?"

He said nothing.

"Surely you will stay the night at least. We have the room."

For a moment he was tempted, but the emotion was fleeting. To stay even for one night would increase his burden. Travel lightly, travel free and fast. "I cannot." Another coin from the pouch paid for the meal. He smiled at her to lessen the blow of his words, but it only made it the more deadly.

"What's your name?" he asked.

"Oriele."

He kissed her cheek. "Well then, Oriele, farewell," he said softly, and went toward the door.

From outside the inn he heard the sound of screams and the wet smack of a blow being struck. He stepped outside in time to see one of the black-clad strangers measuring his length on the ground. Above him stood Mark, his features red with fury.

"Try and steal my sword, would you?" he roared. "You're nothing but thieves and brigands. Get out of here—go back to your own land!"

Malagant's man staggered to his feet, clutching his midriff and wheezing. Out of Mark's line of vision, the other soldier reached to the scabbard at his belt and began to creep forward.

The brawl was no concern of Lancelot's, but he was not about to stand by and watch Mark get stabbed in the back. With whiplash speed he intercepted the would-be assassin, seized his wrist, and flipped him head over heels into the dirt. A swift twist and a wrench drew forth a howl of agony and a nine-inch steel dagger with a saw-notched hilt.

"I should do as he says," Lancelot advised his victim neutrally. "I doubt remaining here will be good for your health." He transferred the dagger to his left hand and drew his sword with his right.

Nursing his dislocated wrist, the brigand scrambled to his feet. "You'll be sorry," he said. "Prince Malagant will know how you treat strangers in this village."

His compatriot joined him. He was still clutching his stomach, and his stance was groggy.

"I see only thieves!" Mark spat. Emboldened by the sight of Lancelot's naked weapons, he drew Lizzie from her sheath. "You wanted to steal her. Perhaps you'd like her to kiss you first!" He took a pace forward, the sword brandished high.

The men of Gore retreated before the menace but still managed the bravado of words and threats. Once they had been marched out of the village, Mark sheathed Lizzie and held out his hand to Lancelot.

"I owe you my life."

Lancelot accepted the brawny paw. "There is no debt," he replied with a shrug. "It was a pleasure to tumble him in the dust." He released his grip and started toward the stables.

"You are leaving?" Mark uttered the same words as Oriele and looked as disappointed as a child. "Alda—that's my wife—Alda and I would be honored if you would be our guest tonight. It is the least we can do."

"Thank you, and I would be honored to accept, but I cannot. It is time I was on my way."

Mark followed him into the stall and watched him harness the elegant black stallion. "Well then, God go with you and grant you safe journey to wherever it is you are going."

His wish elicited a bitter smile from Lancelot. "May the road never end," he said, and swung himself into the saddle.

He rode out of the village and did not look back, knowing that if he did, he would see his ghosts watching him with patient, tragic eyes.

Chapter 2

*I*t was fine weather for cutting the hay, and all the villagers without exception were involved in the harvesting. Scythes flashed in the fields; men with pitchforks tossed stacks of newly mown hay into the wagons. Their wives and daughters delivered baskets of food to the fields. The fare was robust to suit the labor—meat pasties, cheese, bread, and apples. And to wash it down there were brimming leather bottles of weak ale and cider chilled in the village well. Bringing in the hay was always thirsty work.

From his vantage point on top of the great, half-completed communal stack, Mark paused to watch yet another wagon rumble into the village barn from the fields, and mopped his brow on his forearm. Hay seeds clung to his sweat-damp skin and chafed; his nostrils were full of the dusty, sweet scent of cut grass. This was the fodder to carry their animals through the winter. It had been a good year, the weather kind, and they were likely to have a surplus to sell for luxury items in the main town of Leonesse where dwelt their ruler, Lady Guinevere.

Mark glanced down to the barn floor where his wife was laying out food on a colorful woven cloth, and he smiled. Alda loved visiting Leonesse. Like any woman, she had a passion for plundering the traders' stalls, and she enjoyed nothing more than a good haggle. Perhaps he would take her there before the winter weather set in.

Lady Guinevere had ruled in Leonesse for a little under a year. She was only in her early twenties, about the same age as Mark himself, but she had been bred from the cradle to responsibility, and she possessed a wise if sometimes willful head on young shoulders. The people were as fond of her as they had been of her father, King Leodegrance. Her mother, the queen, had died young and no one much remembered her. The few who did said that Guinevere had inherited her fine features and graceful carriage. Mark had no such yardstick by which to measure his own opinion, but he thought that not only was she pretty and of heroic stock but she was also approachable and as tough as her father had been. His thoughts took a grim turn. She would need to be if this unrest continued along the borders.

Mark took the forkload of hay passed up to him by the man beneath and arranged it on the stack, shaking it out and pressing it down. While he worked, he wondered if the wandering swordsman Lancelot would make his way to Lady Guinevere's capital and replenish his purse at the expense of the townsmen. Mark had frequently thought about the stranger during this past week, and the more he pondered, the more puzzled he became. It was inconceivable that a man should not care whether he lived or died. Life was too rich a tapestry to treat in so threadbare a fashion. What had made this man Lancelot not care? Perhaps once he had cared too much?

Mark's ruminations were rudely curtailed by the sudden clang-clanging of the alarm bell from the village watchtower beside the barn. He turned quickly on the stack and gazed through the open doors, his eyes fixing on the slope beyond the hayfields.

Riders were thundering down toward the houses, an entire troop of darkly clad soldiers armed with daggerlike ripswords and one-handed crossbows. He knew that they could only be Prince Malagant's men—hard-faced marauders without a scrap of decency in their black souls. After that incident last market day they could be none other. He swallowed, his throat suddenly parched. Those crossbows might be short in range, but their iron bolts were killers. One hit and a man never got up.

Galvanized into action, Mark yelled down urgently to the women and children standing at the hay wagons outside the barn. "Raiders are coming! Get inside, hurry!"

Screaming in fear, the women swept up their offspring, abandoned their tasks, and ran for the cover of the great building. Mark slip-slid down from the top of the stack, his pitchfork still clutched in his fist. Alda, after one startled, frightened look at her husband, flung the food and the cloth back into her basket and scrambled to her feet.

"Close the doors!" Mark bellowed.

The men on the barn floor began hauling the great doors shut and slotting in the heavy oak beams to bar them fast. A golden darkness closed in, the only light coming from warped planks in the barn's timber side walls and the air gap in the gable end. The people within huddled together and listened with dread to the approaching thunder of hooves. There had been rumors of raids in other communities, but until this moment, they had thought their world safe. Now, feeling the vibration of galloping warhorses, hearing the panic-stricken bellows of the village cattle in their pens and the bleating of sheep, they realized how vulnerable they were. Sheep themselves before the jaws of wolves.

"Perhaps they will pass on by," whispered one of the men hopefully, and fingered the small eating knife at his waist. "It may be that they are just riding through."

"Oh yes, Edwin, they're riding through, all right," Mark said grimly. "And they'll leave naught but our bones behind. You saw what happened on market day." He wished he had brought Lizzie with him instead of leaving her at home. The only weapons at hand were eating knives and farm implements, and what use were they against swords and crossbows? A child whimpered and its mother hastened to silence it. Mark's gaze darted round the barn, seeking for additional sanctuary, and lit upon the floor.

He strode vigorously across the building, stooped at a place where the planks were sawn shorter, and began yanking them up. In a moment he had exposed a shallow space between the joists. By October it would be full of crisp red apples from the orchards that flourished so abundantly throughout Leonesse, but now, mercifully, it was empty.

"There's no time to lose!" Mark beckoned urgently to the others. "There's room in here for the women and children, at least. Even if they do come in friendship, and I don't think they do, it won't hurt to hide them until we're sure. Hurry, come on, pass me the lad!"

A woman handed her small boy to Mark, and he lowered him into the cellar, then helped her down after her son. The other women and children followed, looking over their shoulders in fear as the sound of the marauders' approach threatened ever louder. Alda clutched her husband as he lowered her down.

"Oh, Mark, be careful!" Her eyes were filled with anxiety as she searched his face.

He tried to smile. "Don't you fret, we'll be all right," he said with more conviction than he felt. "Keep your head down now. I'm going to lower the planks over you."

"And you keep yours down, too, you great ox!" she cried, and kissed him fiercely on the lips before relinquishing her grip and joining the others.

Mark lowered the boards over the space and stamped them down. His fists clenched, containing all his anger and fear, he strode across to the barn's broad wooden side and set his eye to a warped gap between the boards.

His village was a scene of panic, chaos, and carnage. The short crossbow bolts struck people down as they tried to flee. Animals ran amok, houses were on fire; flames licked at the foot of the watchtower, and the bellringer had been silenced, an iron bolt through his heart. "No, oh no!" Mark groaned to himself. His heart thudded against his ribs as if it would escape, and his body was saturated with cold, sick sweat. This was not happening, it was all a bad dream, the result of too much wine in the tavern last night.

The leader of the troops had drawn rein and was staring around the villagers' houses for any signs of life. He was hard-eyed and hard-mouthed with cadaver cheekbones. Clad from head to toe in dark leather, the very air around him seemed to shimmer with menace, or perhaps it was just the heat ripple from the burning buildings. The miss-nothing eyes came to rest on the great barn, and Mark's scalp prickled with terror as the marauder's gaze fixed directly upon the crack in the planks. Even though Mark knew it was impossible that he had been seen, he could not help but flinch.

A jerk of the leader's head sent one of his troop hurrying to investigate the great barn. The man rattled at the doors and pounded on them with the hilt of his ripsword, but to no avail. Inside, the village men tightened their grips on pitchforks and rakes and looked at each other, eye whites huge with fear.

The soldier turned to his master and spread his hands. "The doors are locked, Lord Ralf."

The leader turned his horse and studied the barn more thoroughly. A humorless smile curved his thin lips. "Burn it," he commanded. "Burn it down to the ground."

Inside the barn, the village men heard the words with horror. Before they could move, a flaming torch came flying over the tops of the doors where there was a wide gap beneath the eaves. It curved through the shadowy space to land high in the great stack of new-cut hay. Smoke wisped. Flame ran in delicate drips and trickles from the source.

Paralyzed by shock at first, the men now recovered the use of their limbs and ran to the stack, scrambling and struggling to grab the torch and beat it out. But the stack was steep and it was difficult to gain a foothold, and by the time they did, it was too late. The trickle had turned from a stream to a river, to a full-blown roaring red ocean.

Scared and dismayed, Mark stared at the burning stack, their entire hay crop for the year, and then set his eye once more to the gap in the wood. The whole village was aflame now, every home, workshop, and storeshed. And still he could not wake up from the nightmare. Smoke tickled his lungs and he smothered a cough. His eyes began to sting. Through a drifting gray pall, he saw a new group of horsemen gallop in to join the first troop. At their center rode a man upon a tall black stallion. His dress was plain, no different from that of Captain Ralf or the ordinary troopers, but the arrogant manner in which he gazed around and the swift deference with which he was treated revealed that his authority was absolute.

"Malagant!" Mark muttered, his eyes narrowing with hatred at the sight of the neighbouring prince who was the cause of so much misery in hitherto peaceful Leonesse. Malagant of the jet black eyes and even blacker heart. His own principality of Gore was bleak and barren, fit only to graze sheep. He had long coveted the fertile valleys of Leonesse, and what he could not have for the asking, he either took or destroyed.

The fire in the stack was spreading to other parts of the barn, sending out tributary fingers of hot yellow flame. Smoke thickened the air and Mark coughed again. He turned from the gap, seized a water bucket from the hay wagon, and hastened over to the planks covering the apple cellar. These he soused thoroughly, trickling the water evenly over the wooden slates. He dared not think that it was a futile act, that they might never emerge alive. He had to believe, and he had only himself to believe in. "We'll be all right, Alda," he whispered in a smoke-roughened voice. "Just hold tight."

There was a soft thump of acknowledgment from the underside of the planks.

When he turned from sousing the wood, he was appalled to see that his companions had panicked and were freeing the great timber beams that barred the doors. "You fools!" he bellowed. "Don't open the doors! Wait until they've gone!" His voice choked on the last word as he cast aside the bucket and began to run.

"We'll all be dead by then, Mark!" cried one man over his shoulder as he struggled with the beam. On the other end of it, the villager Edwin nodded agreement. "If we run, at least we've got a chance!"

Mark shook his head, "Don't do it!" he pleaded, but he reached them too late. The beams came down, and the doors blew open under the pressure of the hot air within to reveal a scene from hell. The village wore walls and roofs of fire. Coiled in a mist of smoke, a throng of marauders waited like reapers to beat the vermin out of the corn. The two men who had lowered the beams made a dash for their lives. A third villager, not quite so brave, ducked down behind the wagon and peered out from under the iron-shod wheels at the devastation outside. Mark retreated beneath the timber rack that held the great haystack in place and wedged himself in a far corner, seeing but unseen. His heart pounded as if it would burst from his body, and sweat trickled from every pore.

The two who had made a bid for freedom were joyfully chased by Malagant's horsemen. Whooping, uttering hunting calls, they rode them down and shot them with the lethal crossbow bolts. Edwin screamed like a snared rabbit, shuddered, and was still.

Mark squeezed his eyes shut and swallowed deep in his throat. No chance at all, he thought. When he opened his eyes once more, Malagant had halted his sweating stallion before the barn and was gazing up at the gush of flame that not long since had been a haystack. Mark tried to press himself further back, but a solid spar struck his spine, and he could go no further. The hay immediately above him was on fire now. Smoke tore at his throat and he suppressed a cough, tried breathing through his hands to filter the air, but with little success. The air around him was hellishly hot. It would not be long before his own turn came to die, either by fire or by arrow bolt. It came to him that the latter was probably the easier way to go, but his determination held him back. He would not make of himself a gift to Malagant's black marauders.

The other man in the barn thought differently and, bursting out from beneath the wagon, threw himself at Prince Malagant's feet.

"Please," he blubbered. "For the love of God, have mercy, my lord!"

Malagant slowly drew his own crossbow from his belt. His thin lips smiled, but his black eyes were devoid of pity. "God loves a winner," he snarled, and shot the man where he lay, the bolt ripping clean through his body. Malagant watched him die, his features impassive, then returned to the main business.

His men had herded the surviving villagers into a huddle away from their burning homes and livelihoods. Weeping women, terrified, whimpering children, angry but silent men, who were as frightened as their sons and daughters, for Lord Malagant was known to be pitiless.

Malagant stared down contemptuously upon them from the saddle of his sidling warhorse. And then he spoke, his voice loud and harsh, carrying like the cry of a raven, the bird of the battlefield and the ravaged land.

"Last night men from this village crossed the border and murdered three of my people. In reprisal, I have destroyed your homes. The borderlands have been lawless long enough. Know now that I am the law!" He punched one fist into the air, the knuckles showing a clenched bone white. At once his men responded, raising their swords on high and saluting Malagant with a single, bloodcurdling war cry.

Malagant wrenched his horse around and rode away from the devastated village toward the border, his men following him like a black banner. And this time the thunder of hooves was overlaid by the roar of flames.

Choking for air, Mark stumbled from his hiding place and ran to the apple store. With feverish hands he tore up the planks. "Alda!" he cried as if uttering a prayer or a talisman against the evil he had just witnessed. "Alda, Alda!" His voice broke, became a sob. He was terrified that they might have been smothered.

A child's retching cry reached him. Then he heard Alda sobbing his name, and next moment he had pulled her out of the cellar and into his arms. He clutched her to him fiercely for a moment but no more, for the barn was on fire all around them, and it was imperative that they escape.

"Mark, what happened?" she demanded as they helped the other women and youngsters out of the apple store and sent them running toward safety. One young wife uttered a wail and fell to her knees beside the body sprawled near the wagon. Her companions pulled her away, screaming and struggling, toward the safety of the open ground outside the barn.

"Malagant, that's what," Mark said through his teeth as he and Alda hastened outside. "He said that he did it in reprisal for raids we have carried out on his territory, but no one in Leonesse would do that. It's just an excuse to add our lands to his. He has coveted them even since the days of Lady Guinevere's father." He paused to cough and then spat to one side. His lungs felt as if they were full of burning cinders, and his eyes were raw with smoke. Small spark burns pocked his arms and made brown singe marks on his clothing, but at least he was still alive. His arm around his wife, he stared at the smoking, burning ruins that had once been their home, a thriving community full of laughter and life. Now it was nothing.

Alda was still holding the picnic basket in her hand. He took it from her, bundled half the food into the woven cloth, and slung a cider bottle over his arm, wincing as it touched a raw burn.

Alda stared at him. "What are you doing?"

"I'm going to Leonesse town. The lady Guinevere must be told what has happened." He drew her to him and gave her a hard, bristly kiss. "I'll be as swift as I can, I promise."

Alda bit her lip and nodded.

With one final glance at his village, dying with the flames, Mark turned on his heel and began striding out on the road that led to Leonesse.

In the peaceful gold of the afternoon, Lancelot was riding along a wooded ridge overlooking a valley through which wound a stream and a narrow white ribbon of road. Jupiter ambled along at a sedentary pace, his head slightly dipped and the reins slack on his black neck, and Lancelot half dozed in the saddle. Butterflies flickered in and out of the sun dapples through the trees, and birds scolded at the passing of man and horse.

Lancelot thought he heard a distant cry. It might only have been the call of a curlew, but it brought him upright in the saddle. Jupiter heard it too, for his head came up and his head turned with ears pricked.

Below them in the valley, a troop of horsemen

darkened the white thread of the road. They were riding hard for the thicker forests to the north. Lancelot watched them and recognized the dark armor that they wore. It would be wise not to tangle with them, he thought. He was not afraid of trouble, but neither did he deliberately go seeking it out. If the lands of Gore lay at the end of that road, then it was time that he changed direction.

On reaching the end of the ridge, he paused for a moment to think, and then turned Jupiter's head toward the southwest.

Chapter 3

After two days of hard walking, with one night spent under the stars and another in a friendly village whose people had given him shelter, Mark came to Leonesse. At midday, he rested briefly on a grassy knoll beside a fine stone windmill. There was half a loaf in his satchel, two boiled eggs, and the last of the ale with which the villagers had replenished his bottle. A fertile valley spread before his eyes, its fields a green and gold carpet of lush high summer. Sleek cows grazed in the meadows, and the haymakers were abroad with their pitchforks and ladder-sided wagons. Mark suddenly found his bread hard to swallow as he contrasted this peaceful scene with his own images of bringing in the hay. His mind's eye was filled with the vision of Malagant pointing and firing that crossbow, of flames higher than a house, of blood, destruction, and death.

He forced himself to chew and swallow, knowing that although Leonesse was in sight, there was still a fair distance to travel. His gaze followed the winding silver ribbon of the river Leon toward the timbered walls of the city. Access was by a narrow wooden bridge that linked the town to the fields. Mark had heard that there were plans afoot to widen the bridge so that supply wagons would have less difficulty crossing it, but there was no sign yet of any building activity.

Outside the palisade, many simple houses were clustered. Leonesse was no grand citadel such as Camelot, the capital of the kingdom to the west ruled by Arthur, the High King, but it suited the needs of its population, a town of farmers and country people, simple and honest. The gates, made of mature oak trunks, stood wide open and unguarded, and Mark was filled with fear and a sense of urgency. Did they not know how vulnerable they were to Malagant? If the warlord were to appear now with his troops from hell, he could occupy the land's capital and overthrow Lady Guinevere as simply as pulling the trigger on his crossbow.

Mark slung his empty water bottle over his shoulder, tucked his woven bundle cloth inside his jerkin, and strode on his way. She had to be warned, dear God, she had to know.

Inside the town of Leonesse, untroubled by tidings yet to arrive, a good proportion of the population was occupied in the traditional sport of pit ball, most as avid and vociferous spectators of the two dozen players. The game had been played time out of mind, and there were several octagenarians in the crowd who could remember past moments of their own glory on the town square pitch.

Shallow pits, five feet in diameter and two feet deep, had been dug at either end of the square. The object of the game was to kick the ball, made of a straw-stuffed pig's bladder, past the opposition and into the pit. The teams, identified by either red or black sashes tied around their waists, consisted of a dozen players a side composed of both men and women. The rules dictated that hands were to be clasped behind the back at all times and that only feet were to connect with the ball. Anyone using their hands in the heat of the moment was yelled back into order by the crowd. The game was rough, although not life-threateningly dangerous. The players constantly and deliberately barged into each other, and in consequence, there were a lot of falls and minor bumps and scrapes. These, however, all added to the spectators' enjoyment.

Among the scrimmage of muddy, kicking boots and pummeling, barging bodies, a young woman wove as effortlessly as a sharp needle drawing thread through cloth. Her face was radiant and fierce, her absorption total. Her teeth flashed in white laughter, and her green-hazel eyes sparkled with merriment. "Oh no you don't, it's mine!" she shrieked at a black-sashed opponent and dodged neatly around him before kicking the ball to a member of her own team. "Ned, over here!" The ball sailed, was caught on a boot, and propelled toward the black-sash goal.

"Forward, move it forward, reds!" someone bellowed.

"Look out, Richard!" the girl screamed, jumping up and down in frustration, her eyes full of battle light. While most of the men wore clumpy boots, her own feet were shod in dainty scarlet slippers.

"Clodhead, you've lost it!" groaned another of the red team in frustration as a black sash took the bladder and charged up the pitch in the opposite direction. The crowd erupted with excitement, chanting and roaring, shaking fists in the air. Spurred on, the young woman threw herself into the thick of the fray, determined to recover the ball and put it firmly in the black's pit where it belonged. Despite the fact that she was one of the slightest players on the pitch, she was surprisingly effective, for she was both fast and fearless. Her hair came loose from its knot and flew around her face in warm brown tendrils, and there was a streak of mud on one flushed cheek.

"No!" she yelled, "you're not getting it off me, just you dare—ouf!" The air was knocked from her as the man did indeed dare and succeeded. "Oh, you great ox, Jude!" she gasped, and stamped her foot. "Rally, red, rally! Don't let him get away with it!" And she plunged determinedly back into the melee.

Through a constantly shifting screen of players, the girl caught sight of two Elders approaching from the direction of the palace. She knew full well that they came looking for her and was filled with irritation. Could they not leave her alone until the game was finished at least?

They pushed their way through the crowd and made urgent beckoning motions. The ball was coming her way. She grimaced and gave them an "in a minute" gesture, hoping to put them off, then flung herself back into the fray. Her feet flashed nimbly and the ball was hers. "With me, reds, with me!" she shrieked in excitement. "Jem, where are you? Pass, pass—ouf!" A wallop from an opposing player sent her flying. She landed with a bruising thump. "Bully!" she shouted, and scrambled up, brushing mud from her dress. During the time it had taken her to fall and regain her feet, the Elders had fought their way to the side of the pitch with the same determination that their mistress had displayed on the field, and now stood before her, their expressions grave.

"Lady Guinevere . . ." began the foremost Elder. He had wispy silver hair and wore a long, gold-colored wool robe with a high, round collar.

"Yes, I know, Reginald," she said impatiently. "I won't be much longer if you can wait."

The Elder's lips tightened. "I am sorry, my lady, but I don't believe that this can wait." He clasped his hands before him in a wringing gesture. "There has been another attack, my lady, another border village burned to the ground."

At once the impatience melted from Guinevere's expression to be replaced by worried concern. She untied the red sash from around her waist and handed it to one of the women spectators. "Take my place, Ann," she commanded, without looking away from the Elders.

"Yes, Lady Guinevere." The young woman belted the sash around her waist and ran out onto the pitch.

Guinevere's manservant, Jacob, ran up with a linen towel in his hand. She took it from him with thanks and set off toward the palace with the Elders. "I suppose it was Malagant again?" She wiped her brow as she walked, her stride brisk and purposeful. The older men had trouble keeping pace with her.

"I am afraid so, my lady," said the second Elder a little breathlessly. "We heard the news just now from a fellow who survived and came to bring the tidings."

"Is he being looked after?"

Reginald gave a little shrug. "We offered him refreshment and comfort, but he would take no more than a drink of water and he seemed greatly agitated. He wants to see you, my lady, says all else can wait. I sent him to the apple grove courtyard and told him that we would find you. Oswald said he would talk to him in the meanwhile."

Guinevere nodded firmly. "You did right," she said. "A game of pit ball is nothing compared to the welfare of my people."

Without taking time to change from her muddied garments or tidy her hair, Guinevere went straight to find the villager and Oswald. The latter had been her father's trusted friend and chief adviser, and the same held true for herself. She was deeply fond of the old man and frequently leaned on the experience of his years. He was the grandfather she had never known, and his comforting support had carried her through the difficult days following her father's sudden death from an affliction of the chest.

When Guinevere entered the courtyard of the apple grove, she found Oswald deep in conversation with quite the largest man she had ever seen. He was dressed in the rough garments of a borderland farmer. His blue tunic and green breeches were scorched, and there were red burns dotted over his brawny forearms and broad, honest face. She saw from the way he was standing how weary and distraught he was.

As she advanced across the grove, the men broke off their conversation and bent the knee. Guinevere shook her head in consternation and, gesturing Oswald to rise, hastened forward and took the young farmer's calloused hands in her own.

"No, no, enough now, get up," she chided gently. "I know the reason for your journey here and how heartsick and weary you must be. You shall have all the succor you need." She looked into his dust-rimmed blue eyes. "Now, tell me your name."

"It is Mark, my lady . . ." His great paw squeezed hers, and his massive frame shook like a tree about to be felled. "Our homes are gone, and our hay store. Malagant burned everything. He . . . he says that we're outlaws, that we cross the border and raid his lands, but why should we want to cross into Gore? It's a barren, hostile place, nothing but sheep. And we are farmers, not fighting men." His voice wobbled with emotion.

"I know, I know," Guinevere agreed. "It's lies, all lies. He means to frighten Leonesse into submission, and these raids on your border villages are a means to that end."

The young giant stiffened as if a metal rod had been rammed down his spine. "You must not give in to him, my lady! Even if we are not warriors by trade, we'll fight, every last one of us. We'd rather die than see Malagant become Lord of Leonesse!"

Guinevere's own deceptively soft lips tightened in a stubborn line, and her eyes were stormy. "Don't worry, Mark, I'm not the yielding kind. One day soon Malagant is going to take a bite too big to swallow." She removed her hand from within his and turned to her manservant, who was standing discreetly but attentively to one side awaiting her order. He was sprucely dressed in a blue tunic and startling scarlet hood with a long tippet. Something of a dandy was Jacob, a martyr to the latest fashions, but his heart was in the right place, and he was devoted to his young mistress.

"Jacob," she said, "take this good man to the hall and give him food and drink and find him a bed for the night."

"Right away, my lady." Jacob bowed, the red end of his hood falling toward his neck like a turkey's wattle. Mark stared, mesmerized. Guinevere touched his arm, and with an effort, he forced his exhausted gaze back to her.

"This evening, when you have had a chance to refresh yourself, we'll pray together for your village and Leonesse. Go now with Jacob and have your needs seen to."

Mark bowed and kissed her hand. " 'Thank you, my lady. God keep you safe."

"And you," Guinevere murmured as Jacob led the villager away in the direction of the great hall.

"That's the third border village that Malagant's burned in a week," muttered Reginald, stroking his grizzled beard in agitation.

Guinevere sighed. In the apple groves a soft breeze rustled, echoing her breath. She stared at the trees, symbol of Leonesse, and thought how easily the bitter winds of winter would strip them bare. "What is it he wants?" she asked them. "To destroy the whole world perchance and become king of a graveyard?"

"He wants us to sign his treaty, Lady Guinevere," ventured the second Elder, his eyes apprehensive because he knew how his mistress felt about that particular piece of parchment.

Guinevere's upper lip curled scornfully. "He thinks that because my father is dead, no one can stand up to him!"

"The Elder shook his head sorrowfully. "My lady, even if your father were alive, I doubt that . . ." He paused, torn between telling her the truth and not wanting to hurt her.

His companion, although compassionate, was of a more practical and forthright nature. "If we do not give Prince Malagant what he asks, he has the strength to take it, my lady. It grieves me to say so, but we are powerless."

Guinevere flinched before the troubled gray stare. She knew that he was right; the people of Leonesse were peaceable farmers for the most part. What did they know of war? Her father might have been able to rally them, but perhaps only to send them to their deaths. "I will not yield to him," she repeated stubbornly and turned to old Oswald, who had been standing aloof beside one of the apple trees throughout the conversation. "Well, Oswald," she said a trifle impatiently, "you say nothing for one so wise."

Oswald gently shook his head. "You know what I think, child." His voice held the quaver of old age, but his eyes were steady.

Guinevere met them for a moment before dropping her own. "Yes, I suppose I do." The head Elder had done his best to impress upon her the fact that although Leonesse served her, she, in her turn, must serve Leonesse. It was the way her beloved father had governed his country, with heart and hand and generous vision. She wished desperately that he were here now, but he wasn't, and the responsibility was all hers to shoulder.

"Forgive me, my lady," said Reginald, looking uncomfortable, "but Prince Malagant must be answered. If he is made to wait, then perhaps he will burn another village."

Guinevere composed herself. Her jaw tightened. "He will be," she replied. "I shall decide this very day. Now, leave me, both of you." She held out a slender white hand. "Oswald, I want you to stay."

The two men bowed and, not without a little relief, departed. Guinevere paced the courtyard with suppressed agitation, then turned and faced the patiently waiting old man. "It has all come so quickly. I had hoped to have more time to consider."

Oswald studied her with the shrewd eyes of eighty summers and as many deep winters. "How much time does it take to know your own heart?"

"Oh, I know what I want." Guinevere gave him a sad smile and lightly touched the low bough of an apple tree where the fruit hung heavy but as yet unripe. "I want to marry and I want to live and die in Leonesse. But I can't have everything, can I?"

Oswald's brow furrowed and he stroked his beard. "Forgive me, child, but an offer of marriage from Arthur of Camelot is a great honor for you and Leonesse . . ." he hesitated.

Guinevere looked at him. She knew why he paused. Marriages were often made for political gain and reasons of bloodline, but Guinevere's father had always hoped that his daughter would marry for love.

Although she was young, she had seen many eligible bachelors, both from Leonesse and further abroad, Arthur of Camelot among them. She thought of him now, the fine, dark eyes, the expressive brows, the rich voice and mischievous smile. No man had ever kindled a spark in her being except perhaps this one. That he was of her father's years concerned her little. She was accustomed to older men in her daily routine, indeed preferred their patience and maturity to the shallow exuberance of those of her own years.

"It is a great honor, indeed," she murmured to Oswald. "And I know that you are right. No more words, let it be done."

"You accept King Arthur's offer?"

Guinevere nodded and her smile remained. "Yes, Oswald, I shall marry Arthur of Camelot."

Her adviser's face brightened with a look of intense relief, and his taut shoulders relaxed. He took her hands in his and squeezed them. "My dear child. I was proud to hold you in my arms in the hour of your birth. I shall be prouder still to see you wed."

Guinevere gnawed her lower lip, not so sure. "Poor Arthur. All the dowry I bring him is a land in danger. But I promise I shall love him dearly, Oswald."

"So you should, child."

"I could never marry a man without love," Guinevere said stoutly. "But Arthur has such gentleness in his eyes—I've never heard him raise his voice. He wears his power so lightly, and it is all the more strong because of that. I've never known a man like him, Oswald. How could I love anyone more?"

Wind rustled through the apple trees once more, and a yellow leaf, in premature anticipation of autumn, fluttered to the ground at her feet.

Chapter 4

*R*iding through the forest in midsummer was like traveling through a vast and luminous green cathedral. The canopy created Gothic arches and spans of fan vaulting with windowed tracery of this year's delicate new growth. A pageant of leaves fluttered to acknowledge Lancelot's passing on the road that wound its way across Leonesse. It was nigh on midday, and the warmth of the sun magnified the woodland scents, making them as intoxicating as incense. Butterflies flickered through the trees in glimpses of stained-glass colors, and the voices of wood pigeons cooed a husky, somnolent plainchant.

Lancelot rode easily in the saddle, his stirrups long, his spine relaxed against the cantle. It was a fine day and he was in no hurry to be anywhere. His hands lay loose upon the bridle, and his stallion, Jupiter, took advantage of his master's lazy control to stray from the center of the path toward a roadside pool that was fed by a clear, freshwater spring.

Lancelot emerged from his somnolence with a jolt. Jupiter's thirst called to mind his own. He saw that this was an ideal place to refill his water bottle and give his mount a few moments to crop the lush grass growing around the water's source. Dismounting, he let Jupiter drink his fill, and when the stallion had begun to graze, Lancelot himself crouched at the poolside and using his hands for a cup, drank of the cold, clear water.

He had appreciated no more than a few mouthfuls when a jangle of sounds alerted him to the fact that a sizable cavalcade was approaching along the road. The clink of harness and weapons, the thud of hooves and rumble of cart wheels sent birds scolding through the trees. The ground throbbed. Lancelot's entire body tensed, and his air of laziness was replaced by one of narrow-eyed concentration.

A pair of knights rode into view, their magnificent horses moving at a brisk trot, and behind them two more who carried bold banners of yellow silk attached to upright spears. They were dressed in light armor, suitable for escort duty and long days in the saddle, rather than the hard clash of battle and sharp encounter of the joust. None of the four wore helmets. Their cloaks and rich costumes spoke of their wealth and rank, their high pride in the way that they did not so much as deign to look at the dusty traveler standing by the spring. For all that, I could best any of them in a fight, Lancelot thought, somewhat irritated.

The sudden appearance, the brightness, and the rapid drumming trot spooked Jupiter, and he bolted up the wooded bank with a snort of alarm. Still the knights did not turn and look; Lancelot and his mount might as well have been invisible. He had the desire to run in pursuit and caper about in the road in front of them until he frightened their horses into bolting, but he restrained himself. There were many escorting soldiers and only one of him. Behind the knights rattled two carriages, each drawn by four sturdy dappled horses, their harness brightly caparisoned and small silver bells jingling in their braided manes. As the first carriage rolled past, Lancelot saw that there were three women inside. Two were serving maids, to judge from their garb, but the other was a lovely young woman of high degree, her features as pure and clear as the crystal stream from which he had been drinking. Her eyes were modestly downcast, and she did not look out of the carriage to see Lancelot's bold stare as she passed him by.

Behind the second carriage rode a troop of royal guards, four ranks of four. Not a single person in the entire cavalcade paused to give the time of day to Lancelot or even acknowledge his existence. He watched them ride on into the forest with a wry look on his face. His own blood was at least as noble as theirs—but he had learned during his years of wandering that it was not blood that conveyed nobility. The dust of their passing began to settle on the road. He wondered who the young woman was and where she was going, his curiosity roused for the first time in an age. Perhaps he would follow and see where the road led.

Uttering a soft whistle, he set his hands on his hips and faced the wooded bank up which Jupiter had bolted. In a moment, his horse came trotting through the trees, his ears flickering nervously. Lancelot caught up the trailing bridle and soothed his mount with soft words and a gentle hand. Jupiter nudged and butted him affectionately, and the man gave one of his rare, rueful smiles.

Then a low cry sounded from the direction of the trees ahead, and Lancelot looked up, his whole being suddenly still. It might just be the call of a bird startled by the approach of the cavalcade, but Lancelot thought not. It was the first time that he had heard that particular call, and yet he had been riding through the forest all morning.

Lancelot's decision to follow the troop became carved in stone at that moment. Forests harbored wolves, and frequently they were of the two-legged variety. Mounting up, he loosened the sword in his scabbard, but instead of taking the road, he directed Jupiter into the green darkness of the forest beyond the path.

The trees closed around him, and there was only a slight imprint in the grass at the poolside to show that anyone had recently been there.

Guinevere had been so lost in her own thoughts that she had not noticed the handsome man standing by the pool, nor even the pool itself. The dull forest light and the monotony of nothing but trees had led her to withdraw into herself. She was on her way to meet and marry Arthur of Camelot. Soon she would be a wife and a queen with new responsibilities and burdens. She was both apprehensive and excited, a difficult mixture with which to live.

She desired very much to be wed to Arthur. He, too, would be taking on burdens, not least that of threatened Leonesse. She stared unseeingly out of the carriage window, her expression pensive. The journey seemed to be taking forever, and there was too much vitality in her slender frame for her to be comfortable cooped up in this carriage. She had wanted to ride with the men, but Sir Kay and Sir Agravaine had said that it was too dangerous with Prince Malagant in his current mood. Sir Tor, ever a stickler for convention, had opined that it was not seemly for a bride of her status to ride among the troops like a man. Guinevere cared nothing for Sir Tor's declaration, but she had taken note of Kay's concern and had chosen to ride in the carriage with her maids, Elise and Petronella.

Ahead of the carriage there was a sudden cry of alarm. Guinevere was jolted out of her reverie and leaned to look out of the window, her eyes alert to the likelihood of danger. "What is it, Sir Kay?" she shouted.

The most senior of Camelot's knights had drawn his sword. His stallion plunged and circled, its eyes rolling to show the whites. Foam spattered from its open mouth. The road was blocked by a huge felled oak tree. It was not a casualty of the natural forest cycle, but had been deliberately toppled to bar the way.

"Could be an ambush, my lady," Kay said, his words rapid and anxious. "Put your head in, stay where you are!" He turned to the knights and the royal guard. "Protect the carriage, keep your eyes peeled on the trees!"

The knights and guards formed a defensive cordon around the two carriages and faced the pillarlike trunks of the close-growing beeches. The drivers of the carriages grimly drew their weapons. The horses, unnerved, skittered and whinnied, and the men cursed as they struggled to control them.

Inside the carriage Elise began to whimper with panic, her hand to her mouth. "Oh, my lady, what's going to happen? I'm scared!"

"Hush," Guinevere commanded brusquely. "Don't be such a goose!" She had little confidence that Elise would obey her. Although Guinevere dearly loved both her maids, their natures were soft and gentle, without the steel that burned in her own spirit.

"Look to the trees!" Kay bellowed, stabbing an urgent forefinger.

Darkly clad men were darting between the trunks, using them as cover to draw near to Guinevere's troops.

The defenders tensed and braced their weapons. Soldiers licked their lips, crossed themselves, spat. One man took a step forward. "Hold the line, soldier!" Sir Agravaine snarled at him.

"Yes, sir." The man reddened and stepped back.

"Here they come. Stand firm, don't let them through!"

The marauders, about twenty in all, burst out of the trees, yelling and howling to frighten the horses and slashing the air with their vicious swords. Their plain dark clothing was a sharp contrast to the gorgeous apparel of the knights as the two sides clashed and the first blows were exchanged.

This time the marauders were not facing frightened village farmers but professional knights. While not wearing full battle armor, they still possessed their weapons and their horses were trained to warfare. More than one attacker was struck down by a vicious kick from a powerful shod hoof.

"Hold the line!" Kay roared at the men as the defense grew ragged in one place. "Hold the line!"

Guinevere peered out of the carriage window at that precise moment and was seen as a likely target by one of the enemy. He pointed his crossbow at her and fired. Even as he pulled the trigger, he was cut down by Agravaine, and the bolt smashed into the timber frame of the carriage window instead of through Guinevere's heart.

"Keep your head down!" he bellowed at her before whirling away to deal with an assault on his right.

Inside the carriage her maids screamed and cowered, their hands over their ears. Guinevere remained where she was. Her heart was beating fast, and the bolt smashing so close to her had made her flinch, but she wanted to know what was happening and had no intention of joining her women or obeying the command of the knight.

The line was holding and their attackers were taking by far the worst of the punishment. She watched the flash of reddened swords, the thrust of spear and gleam of sweat-darkened horsehide. Her gaze fixed upon the dark garments, short crossbows, and ripswords of their attackers. She knew without doubt that these routiers were the same ones who had been raiding her border villages. Let them take what was coming to them now.

It was not long before the marauders decided that they had taken enough punishment, that their target was not as soft as it had first appeared, and they began fleeing for the cover of the trees. Agravaine, however, was not content to let them escape so easily. His fighting blood was up and boiling, while his sword arm was scarcely warmed.

Ignoring his own earlier advice to the men, he himself broke the line. "Follow me!" he roared. "After the scum, follow!" He spurred his horse and charged in vengeful pursuit of the fleeing marauders. Half the other knights followed his example, chasing into the forest, slashing and harrying.

The reduced cordon tightened around the two carriages. Guinevere shook her head in exasperation. Hotheaded fools, she thought.

And on the other side of the road, hidden among the trees, Malagant's captain, Ralf, turned in his saddle to the twenty mounted men waiting on his command and gave it with a short chop of his gloved fist. "Go!"

The attack troops swept down on the carriages and hurled themselves upon the remnants of Guinevere's escort. The fighting was suddenly hard and frantic. One man unslung the horn he carried at his side to recall the others, but he took a bolt in the chest before he could raise the mouthpiece to his lips. The clash and clang of weapons was all around the carriages, close, hard, and desperate. Guinevere's maids were praying, wailing to God to save them, but Guinevere thought that all too often God helped those who helped themselves.

Two of the marauders leaped from their own horses onto the lead horses of the woman's carriage. Guinevere screamed a warning, but no one heard her; and even if they had, could not have come to her aid, so hard were they pressed. Her driver was gone, shot down by one of Malagant's bowman. The two raiders wrenched the lead horses around and goaded them off the road, up the bank, and into the trees, where they lashed them to a reckless gallop down a deer path barely wide enough to let the carriage pass. Branches scraped the top and the sides. Once or twice the carriage actually struck a tree trunk, and the women within were bounced about like peas in an iron frying pan.

Elise screamed and screamed, hysterical with terror. Petronella was rigid, her eyes huge and frightened. Guinevere was frightened, too, but it did not make her helpless, rather the opposite. She knew that they would be shown no mercy and that their only means of survival lay in escape.

She struggled off her seat and, bracing herself, looked out of the window to see what lay in front. Almost immediately she had to duck back as she was nearly decapitated by a tree slicing by. But she had seen enough to realize that there was a gap in the trees ahead. It was a slim chance, but her only one, and seizing it in both hands, she threw open the carriage door.

Her maid's screams grew louder still as the door frame was snagged in the branches of a huge beech tree and torn off its hinges to clatter down on the path behind the wildly careening carriage. Guinevere seized Elise by the arm and forced her, crying and protesting, to the ragged opening.

"Roll when you hit the ground," she commanded, "And then run as fast as you can. Now, Elise, do as I say!"

The young woman had little choice, for although

Guinevere was slender, she was strong. A push in the center of her back sent Elise flying. She screamed as she tumbled from the carriage, but she did manage to roll when she landed and was able to scramble up and run for cover. Guinevere turned and took hold of Petronella.

"Save yourself," she told the maid. "It's me they want, Arthur's bride."

"No, my lady. Oh no, I can't!" Petronella sobbed, shaking her head and trying to back away. "No, I'll stay with you!"

"You think I'm staying here to be murdered?"

Guinevere's last word was drowned out by the sound of smashing, tearing wood, as a marauder upon the carriage roof ripped through the decorated covering with a murderous hand ax. Petronella shrieked, her eyes almost popping from their sockets with terror. Guinevere saw another small gap opening up in the trees and, knowing that they had no time to lose, thrust the woman out onto the road and prepared to follow her. But she was not fast enough. The trees defeated her, closing in once more and creating prison bars. Guinevere knew that if she jumped, she would be smashed against the trunks and every bone in her body broken. She drew her head back and clung in the open doorway, waiting her moment. The marauder was not waiting for his, but actively seeking it out.

The panic of the hunted prey seized Guinevere as she glanced around and saw a big boot drop down through the jagged hole in the roof, and then another one. Her heart thumped against her ribs and her knuckles whitened on the carriage sides. There was no sign of a break in the trees, not even a small one through which she might have taken the chance. If anything, the prison bars seemed to be growing closer together, melding into one solid wall with the speed of the carriage.

The marauder's body was easing through now. Guinevere gathered her courage, said a silent prayer, and leaped for the window ledge. Her fingers gripped and clung with the tenacity of her will. She glanced down at the ground, which was moving so fast beneath the crushing wheels that it almost looked like a river. If she fell, she too would be crushed. She felt a jolt as the man who had been on the roof now landed inside the carriage. Guinevere heard him curse and the thump of his footsteps across to the empty doorway. In an instant he would see her, and if he had one of the crossbows, she knew without a doubt that he would put a bolt through her heart.

Without stopping to think, for if she had done so, she would never have found the courage to take one hand off the sill, she snatched at the marauder, caught his shoulder, and unbalanced him. He teetered for a moment, and then, with a yell, he was gone. She heard the sick thud of his body striking a trunk and knew that there but for the grace of God went she.

She took a brief moment to recover her own balance, and then sought up ahead again, seeking for the elusive gap in the trees that would allow her to jump from the carriage and run for cover among the dense woodland. One appeared, a fleeting blurred glimpse. Guinevere bit her lip and threw herself clear. Her landing was soft, for the grass was moist and yielding and in a moment, with only minor bruises, she was able to rise to her feet and dust herself off. There were green stains on her gown, her hair was disheveled, and her hands were sore from clinging to the side of the carriage. Her body was trembling, her mouth was dry; but in essence she was unharmed, and her hazel eyes were fierce with anger.

She heard the thud of hooves and the cry of voices and through the trees saw three mounted marauders pounding toward her. Guinevere took off like a hunted deer. She could run fast and well—games of pit ball had honed her skill—and she was far more fit and agile than most young ladies of her breeding, but she was still not swift enough to escape from her pursuers, who were mounted and had a better eye view of the terrain.

If she could not outrun them, then she must outwit them. Guinevere dodged between two trees and, dropping to all fours, scrambled into the deep cover offered by some low-growing bushes. Panting, trying to hold her breathing quiet, she lay as still as a fawn and prayed as she had never prayed in her life before.

The mounted men crashed past her hiding place. She felt the vibration of the horse hooves through the ground. Her spine prickled, and she imagined the sudden thud-thump of a crossbow bolt entering her body. She raised her head and peered through her screen of leaves and whippy branches, terrified but knowing that it was better to see and know than to be killed while blind. The riders were turning back, scanning the terrain like wolves on the trail of prey. Guinevere dropped down again, curling herself up as small as she could. They were going to find her, she knew they were.

"Gone to ground," one of the horsemen grunted.

"She's not gone far," one of the others growled and dismounted. "Come on, we'll beat the vixen out of the bushes."

Two of the marauders dismounted and began to plow through the undergrowth, beating and slashing with their swords. Upon their belts their crossbows were hooked, immediately to hand. The third man remained astride, and sheathing his own blade, he took up his crossbow and loaded it with a fresh bolt.

Guinevere heard the arrow lock home and knew that it was intended for her. If she was dead, there was no heir of the blood for Lyonesse, and Prince Malagant could make good his claim. His men were heading directly toward her. In a moment they would beat her from hiding and everything would be finished.

Before they could reach her, Guinevere leaped to her feet and bolted from cover. Terror gave her feet wings, but behind her she heard the lumbering crash of the men and their whoops of delight as they gave chase. It was no more than the blood lust of predators scenting an imminent kill. The mounted man remained where he was, his manner almost casual as he took steady aim.

As his finger squeezed the trigger that would put out her life, Guinevere was seized roughly around the waist and dragged bruisingly to the ground. Above her head the crossbow bolt slammed into a tree trunk, tearing bark and wood instead of her flesh.

Her assailant's face was close to hers, and their limbs were entangled as if they were lovers. He had chiseled features, fine-grained skin, and eyes of a dark honey brown shielded by thick black lashes.

"Don't move," he whispered urgently.

Guinevere, who had been about to scream and struggle, desisted but held herself stiffly in his arms, ready to fight. The marauders could be heard crashing through the underbrush like a pair of wild boar. The man laid his finger to her lips once more in warning, and then, releasing her, rose to his feet and blocked the path of the oncoming soldiers, his sword drawn.

They both halted abruptly and stared in astonishment. "Who are you?" demanded one.

"Who cares?" sneered the other and raised his loaded crossbow to shoot. Lancelot's sword flashed and the crossbow was snapped out of the soldier's hand to curve through the air and land in the undergrowth where Guinevere lay. The ruffian's face grew dusky with fury. "You're dead!" he snarled, and jerked his head at his companion. Together they attacked. Lancelot met the first sword halfway with an explosive parry and delivered a clubbing fist blow to the marauder's face. Still in motion, he caught the second man's sword arm as it descended, and sent his weapon flying. The first soldier, still half stunned by the blow to his face, tried to strike Lancelot and missed. While he was attacking, his friend pulled a dagger from his belt and threw himself upon Lancelot, body to body. Lancelot felt the power in the man's arm in the moment before it surged into the thrust of the dagger. He turned to meet it, locking his own wrist. The marauder shuddered, and his stare widened, then fixed on nothing. Lancelot gave a twist and a wrench and felt the heat and wetness of blood upon his fingers. His victim fell off the sword blade, leaving its bright edge bloodied. A snarl on his face, Lancelot turned upon the remaining man, who fled for his life.

The blaze of battle died in Lancelot's eyes, but the embers remained hot. He stood like a stone, calm now, listening.

Guinevere, who had been both frightened and stunned at the sight of such effortless deadliness in battle, rose to her feet, her breath indrawn to speak. Without looking round, Lancelot held up one hand to silence her.

"What is it?" she whispered.

He shook his head and looked round. "There were three of them," he murmured. "I have dealt with only two. Where is the man on the horse?"

"I don't know, I didn't notice where he . . ." Guinevere's voice caught in her throat, trapped there by the hand that locked across her windpipe. Her eyes widened upon Lancelot in stark terror.

"Don't even breathe," her attacker said against her ear. She could feel the hardness of his body behind hers, smell his stale breath, and see in front of her his raised arm with the one-handed crossbow aimed directly at her rescuer. Guinevere struggled to swallow and reached stealthily for the trigger guard on the crossbow concealed in the folds of her skirt. If only she was granted the opportunity to use it before it was too late.

"You, drop the sword!" the marauder snarled at Lancelot.

An expression of savage contempt on his face, Lancelot stared death in the eyes. Then the look was gone. He gave a shrug and an easy smile and let his sword slip from his fingers as easily as a spendthrift pouring money down a drain. "All right," he said equably, "but can I have her when you've finished?"

Guinevere eyed him, not knowing how to take his words. Was he just playacting, or had he rescued her in order to have her for himself? There was nothing but self-interest in his face at the moment.

"You were after the woman?" the marauder queried suspiciously.

"Of course I was," Lancelot replied, and looked lingeringly at Guinevere, his eyes filled with frank desire. She looked stonily back at him, but her face grew hot beneath an exploration that was more intimate than touch itself. "Did you ever see anything so beautiful in all your life?" he asked huskily.

The marauder's glance flickered to Guinevere, but without turning her round, he could not see her face. "I don't know about that," he muttered.

"Don't tell me you don't want her!" Lancelot scoffed. "Soft skin, sweet lips." His voice drew out the words and made them a caress. "Young, firm body, clean, too."

Guinevere narrowed her eyes. Her captor swallowed jerkily and held her tighter to his body. She could feel the dampness of sweat on the hand that clutched her. "I have my orders," he growled.

"So?" Lancelot spread his hands. "Who's to know? Doesn't take long." He made a lewd gesture.

The marauder's eyes darted, checking to see if any of his comrades were in sight. There was no one and the woods were silent.

Lancelot rubbed his chin consideringly. "I tell you what, I'll hold her for you and then you can hold her for me. No one will ever find out, I promise." He continued to stare lecherously at Guinevere, but there was more than just lust in his eyes as they traveled down her body. Guinevere saw him stare at the bunched folds of her skirt. Almost imperceptibly, he nodded.

"I don't want any trouble," said Malagant's man, still hesitating, but his breathing was fast and uneven and his eyes glittered.

"Hah, this one's no trouble. Look at her! She's hot for it, all right!" Lancelot retorted crudely. "These highborn women, all they want is a real man." Once more he stared at Guinevere's thighs. She maneuvered the crossbow, readying herself.

The marauder felt her wriggle. "What's she doing?" he demanded breathlessly.

Smiling lasciviously, Lancelot reached out and slowly unbuttoned Guinevere's dress at the throat, his fingers lingering on her skin between each plucking motion. "See for yourself," he drawled. "Turn her round, look into her eyes. See what she's got for you."

The marauder was audibly panting now. He relaxed his lock on Guinevere's throat just enough to let her turn around. He stared at her, his eyes popping with lust at the sight of her clear complexion, pure features, and graceful, lithe body. He feasted upon the open buttons, his eyes drawn to her breasts.

"Oh, pretty, pretty," he said in a congested mutter. "What have you got for me, then?" Licking his lips, he leaned down to taste her lips. There came the muffled sound of a discharged crossbow and he jerked back, a look of pure surprise on his features before they took on the blank expression of death, and he slumped at her feet. Guinevere stood rooted to the spot, the crossbow pressed to her thighs and still tilted upward in its firing position. She stared at the dead marauder, not quite believing what she had done, not quite believing that any of this was happening.

"I killed him," she whispered, more than half to herself.

"You did what you had to do," Lancelot said with a brief nod. "He was going to have his pleasure and then kill you. There are the hunters and those who are hunted. You become either one or the other." The leering look vanished. Turning, he gave a low whistle.

A fine black horse came trotting through the trees and halted at the man's side with a gusty nicker of greeting. Lancelot seized the pommel and mounted in one lithe motion. Alert for sight of any stray marauders or reinforcements returning with the one he had seen off, he offered his hand to the lovely young woman he had just rescued. "Let's go," he said.

Guinevere looked up at him, wondering if she could trust him. There was a dangerous air about him, and he was like no man she had ever encountered before. Like a hawk, she thought, or a caged panther she had once seen at a traveling fair in Leonesse, the eyes trapped and hungry. She chewed her lip, overrode her qualms, and joined her hand to his. His grip was hard and warm as he swung her up behind him on the high saddle, made sure she was safe, and then urged the horse to a canter.

After a while, he slowed the stallion to a walk, and they rode through the forest. With only the birdsong for company, they might have been no more than two lovers abroad, intent on making a pleasure of the day.

"I do not know your name," Guinevere said to break the silence between them. Her arms were around his waist to keep herself secure on the horse's back, and she was aware of his wiry strength, of the feel of him beneath her palms, she who had never been close to a man in that sort of way before. She was disturbed by the pleasurable sensations that such closeness roused in her.

"My name?"

For a moment she thought that he was not going to answer, but at last he said, "It is Lancelot," and offered no further information so that they rode in silence again while she waited for more that was not forthcoming. Whoever he was, Guinevere thought, he did not want to tell her anything beyond his name.

"Why did you risk your life for me?"

"I didn't."

"They could have killed you," she contradicted.

"I'm not that easy to kill." He scanned the trees around them for signs of danger, and she sensed that he was indifferent, if not a little hostile, to her probing.

"Do you know who I am?" she asked.

"Who are you?" His voice was slightly bored, as if he was humoring a tiresome child. His attitude made Guinevere more haughty than her true nature.

"I am Guinevere, Lady of Leonesse."

He said nothing but continued to regard the trees.

Guinevere's temper began to rise at his attitude.

She was not accustomed to this cavalier treatment. "Well?"

"Well what?"

"Doesn't it please you to know that you've saved the life of a lady?"

He shrugged. "I'd be just as pleased if you were a dairymaid."

"A dairymaid could not reward you as I can," she said with a lift of her chin.

He drew rein and turned round in the saddle to face her. His eyes lingered upon hers, then dropped for the merest instant to the place where her buttons were still undone. "If she was as pretty as you," he said softly, "she could give me all the reward I want."

Guinevere gasped and slapped him across the face.

"What did I do?" he asked as if he did not know.

"You—you insulted me!"

Too late she saw the dark blaze in his eyes as he closed on her. And then she could not see at all as his lips covered hers and she was engulfed in the scent and taste of him—forest and horse leather, the bite of recent battle sweat, the man himself. A spark ignited and licked through her veins but was immediately quenched as he broke the kiss and drew away.

"Now I've insulted you," he said.

Guinevere was enraged at him and horrified at her own behavior in letting him get so far. She knew she was not handling the situation very well, but it seemed to be running away from her with the speed of a bolting horse. Seething with fury, she dismounted and rounded on him from the safer distance of the forest floor.

"How dare you!" she spat. "How dare you treat me like this!"

"You are not a dairymaid," he said, his tongue in his cheek. "If you were, it would indeed be different."

Guinevere whirled from him and set off at a rapid walk down the track. Lancelot touched his heels to the stallion's sides and paced him along beside Guinevere. And said nothing.

She was intensely aware of his presence and greatly unsettled. She could still taste him on her lips. "I blame myself," she said angrily. "I take it that you know no better, and you have done me good service today. I shall find it in my heart to forget the matter."

Lancelot's brow raised at this remark and he pursed his lips consideringly. If she sought to put him off, then she was going the wrong way about it. He thought her courageous, beautiful, and proud, a challenge impossible to resist, since women very rarely resisted him. He would seek out more than the misplaced charity of forgetfulness in her heart.

Guinevere halted at a fork in the track and looked both ways, a frown of indecision crossing her face. "Which way now?"

Lancelot glanced skyward beyond the green canopy of the trees. "Left, I would guess. I've never been in this forest before in my life."

"Then why do you guess left above right?"

Lancelot pointed upward. "Do you not see the scavenger birds? They're looking for small animals crushed by passing wagons. Toads, hedgehogs. Ravens follow the roads like gulls follow the plow." He did not add that they were also the birds of the battlefield that swooped to plunder corpses. "It isn't far now."

Guinevere stared toward the circling birds, and a small shiver ran down her spine. "Left it is, then," she said, and started forward once more.

Lancelot dismounted and walked behind her, Jupiter pacing at his shoulder.

"About this reward of yours," Lancelot said doggedly.

Her jaw tightened and her pace increased a little. "My men will pay you when we find my escort."

"I don't want money."

She looked back at him, exasperation in her eyes. "Don't you ever give up? You should know that I am on my way to be married."

"If you're on your way to be married, then you're not married yet," Lancelot argued in a reasonable tone. "If you're not married yet, then you are free." His interest deepened as he watched the emotions flicker over her face. That kiss had gotten to her, no matter that she was giving him the cold shoulder now. His own resolve deepened.

"I have given my word," she said with dignity.

"I don't want your word, I want you."

Guinevere rounded on him, her hazel eyes flashing with anger. "I am not to be had for the wanting, sir."

Lancelot smiled, and there was battle light in his own eyes. "Why not? If I want you and you want me—" He let the sentence trail off suggestively.

Guinevere sniffed and tossed her head. "You may find that your childish arrogance impresses servant girls—dairymaids," she retorted with spirit, "but it does nothing for me, except to make me think you a presumptuous fool."

Lancelot continued to smile. This was like playing at duels for money in market squares, except that this time he had found a worthy opponent. "I know when a woman wants me," he said. "I see it in her eyes."

"Not in my eyes," Guinevere parried with scorn.

"Look at me and say that," Lancelot challenged. Eye to eye, blade to blade.

She walked on as if she had not heard, her head slightly bowed, almost in the pose of a nun.

"You're afraid, aren't you?" Lancelot needled. The moment approached, the moment in the battle when you won or lost.

"I've nothing to hide." Guinevere kept her head down.

"Then look at me," Lancelot commanded.

Pursued to a point where she was at bay, Guinevere stopped and turned and met his predatory stare. Lancelot gazed into her eyes. They held all the colors of the summer forest—green and gold and brown—and he could have lost himself in them for a fortnight. As if to protect herself, she lowered her lids. The shadow of her lashes lay on her cheeks, and Lancelot thought he had never encountered a woman so beautiful in all his wanderings, nor such a challenge.

He leaned close and kissed her once more. Her supple, slender body remained quite still and her lips were cool and passive beneath his; nor did they warm. If Lancelot had hoped to disarm her and claim his prize, he was disappointed. He drew away from her with a slight hiss of breath and saw that her eyes were upon him again and that they were steady. Whatever her emotions, she had mastered them and could now look him in the eyes, her only betrayal a slight heightening of the color along her cheekbones.

"If there is any honor in you at all," she said contemptuously, "you will promise me never to do that again."

Lancelot shrugged. Thus far he was gaining little ground. Perhaps it was time to change his tactics. "I don't know about honor," he said, "but I will promise you this, my lady. I won't kiss you again until you ask me to."

"Hah! And that I never will!"

Lancelot drew the reins through his fingers. "When do you get married?"

"On the last day of summer."

He nodded and turned to Jupiter, fondling his muzzle, before swinging up across his back. "Then before summer's end, you will ask me to kiss you again," he said, and started to turn the horse around.

Guinevere's detached demeanor thawed and became the heat of indignation. "You insult me and then you abandon me. I truly see that you know nothing of honor!"

Lancelot pointed brusquely through the trees. "That's the road ahead, my lady. And that, I presume, is your brave escort, none of whom with all their 'honor' was able to save your life."

Guinevere followed the direction of his pointing finger and saw the knights of her escort spread out on all sides, desperately searching for her. Petronella and Elise rode pillion. Now and again they called her name in high-pitched, frightened voices.

"Thank God!" Guinevere cried and, gathering her skirts, started to run toward them. Lancelot watched her go, a curious heaviness in the pit of his stomach. He sat motionless on Jupiter, and it was all he could do not to dig in his heels and canter after her. His fists tightened on the reins, and his eyelids tensed as if to resist pain.

Then she stopped and looked back at him, and in her face he saw confusion and realized that he had indeed pierced through her defenses.

Two of the escort knights had now seen their mistress and with shouts of relief came hurrying toward her.

"Before summer's end," Lancelot repeated, and tipped his forefinger to his brow in a mocking salute.

The color mounted Guinevere's face, and turning from him, she ran on toward the safety of her escort.

Chapter 5

$\mathcal{T}$he sun was setting in streaming banners of orange and gold as Guinevere's escort and repaired carriage approached the border between Leonesse and Camelot. It was two nights since the attack in the forest, and Guinevere had succeeded in regaining much of her equilibrium. She had her life and her liberty, and Malagant had failed. Guinevere had not spoken to anyone about the man responsible for that failure. He troubled her thoughts enough without bringing him further to life with words. He had saved her life and escorted her to safety. He had insulted and harassed her; he had treated her like a kitchen wench. The memory of his physical presence disturbed her, and she shifted restlessly within the carriage and peered out of the window, fixing her eyes upon the passing scenery. She would think no more upon Lancelot the Wanderer.

The road now ran alongside a winding river, its water tinged by the sunset to a ribbon of beaten bronze. On the far bank, Guinevere could see many moving points of light like giant fireflies. As she stared, these resolved themselves into lines of flaming torches carried by two columns of mounted men. She completely forgot Lancelot and leaned out of the carriage to view this spectacle, her eyes shining with the reflections of sunset and torchlight. The columns of riders illuminated a long procession that was advancing down the road toward a wide timber bridge, the gateway to Camelot. Closer now, Guinevere could see that the procession consisted of royal guards, followed by knights accoutred in full armor, their colors the blue and silver of a starry night.

Beside her in the carriage, her old adviser, Oswald, had been dozing—the journey had been long and arduous for a man of his years, but he was wide awake now as she turned to him and laid her hand over his gnarled, dry knuckles.

"Your new country awaits you, child," he said with a sad but satisfied smile. "You are here in one piece, and you are soon to marry a strong and caring man. I could not wish more for you except great happiness, and I know that will grow as does your marriage."

Guinevere put her arms around Oswald and hugged him close. "If anything should happen at home—" she started to say, a quaver in her voice.

"I'll send word," Oswald soothed. "Never fear, my lady."

"Send Jacob. I want to know at once, good news or bad. Promise me, Oswald, promise me."

"I promise, my lady."

Guinevere broke from the embrace, sniffed away a single tear, and composed herself. A watery smile broke through and lit her face. "I'll never stop loving Leonesse. I'll return to you as often as I can."

"I know you will," Oswald said in a comforting tone.

The torchbearers halted on the far side of the bridge, forming an avenue of light from the river all the way back up the rising ground beyond. On the crest of the low hill, beside the high road, stood two tall, granite crosses, the spiral carvings upon them etched in the gold and black shadows of torchlight.

Guinevere's carriage rolled toward the bridge and came to a halt, the horses champing their bits and jingling their harness. Four of Camelot's royal guards dismounted and carried their torches across the bridge to illuminate Guinevere's path. The knights of her own escort dismounted too and stood at attention on either side of her carriage.

Jacob leaped down from his place beside the driver and opened the door. Guinevere gave a last smile to Oswald, gathered her skirts and her courage, and stepped out. Flanked by Camelot's torchbearers and by her four knights, she took her first steps on the bridge to the sound of loud brass trumpets. The sky was almost dark now, and the torchlight grew in strength. She could smell the pine pitch of the torches and feel the wavering streamers of heat. Head held high, moving with regal dignity, she crossed the bridge between Leonesse and Camelot and set her feet upon the soil of her new country.

The column of royal guards marched toward her between the lines of the torchbearers. With superb discipline, they stopped, turned, and formed a second inner pair of lines, and all in exact time with each other, not a footfall out of place or sequence.

Then came the knights and nobles of Camelot, dressed in their ceremonial robes of blue velvet, jewels winking on collars and headdresses. They formed a third pair of lines, leaving a corridor from the stone crosses all the way down to Guinevere.

First the trumpets had sounded, now came a low drumroll that echoed away to silence like slow thunder. Out of the silence, through the ranks of assembled courtiers, paced a tall, imposing man, his bearing charged with authority. His robe was of chevron-patterned royal blue silk, gathered by a belt with an ornate buckle and chappe. His silver hair was neatly brushed back and a close-cropped beard hugged his taut jawline. There was no vanity in the mature planes of his face, no concealment in his dark eyes. He was a man at ease with himself, a man who knew his own worth and set it neither too low nor too high.

He halted before Guinevere and, for a few moments, just looked at her. The beginning of a smile curved the somber mouth and lit in the fine eyes, and suddenly the face was younger than the years it held.

"Lady Guinevere of Leonesse, welcome to Camelot," said its king in a voice that was resonant, deep, and rich.

Guinevere thought that Arthur needed no drumrolls or trumpets to announce him. She sank in a deep and reverent curtsey before his royalty, which was as much of nature as of birth.

Arthur immediately bent down and raised her to her feet. "God be praised you are safe." He looked her over, and the smile faded slightly. "Nothing and no one shall harm you from now on."

"My lord honors me with his kindness," Guinevere murmured formally. She felt a little overwhelmed. It was like being wrapped in a warm, fleecy blanket at the end of an arduous journey. She freely drank of Arthur's calm strength.

Arthur raised her hand to his lips and kissed it. "Your coming brings me a happiness I had not dared hope for." His voice bore a husky note, which touched Guinevere with both fear and anticipation.

"My lord, you must not think too highly of me, or I'm afraid you will be disappointed."

Arthur smiled with wry humor. "You fear that, too? Well then, I shall take you as I find you, if you'll do as much for me."

Guinevere returned his smile. Lifting his hand to her lips, she kissed him in return, the gesture shy and mischievous at one and the same time. Delight sparked in Arthur's eyes before he turned to his attendants.

A guardsman stepped forward and stood to attention.

"Leonesse will want to know that you have arrived safely. John here will take any message that you care to send." Arthur gestured at the young man.

"My lord grants my wishes even before I speak them," Guinevere said, still smiling.

"Do you require a quill or parchment?"

She shook her head. "There is no need, my lord." She turned to the guardsman. "Tell my people that I'm come safe into my new country." She swallowed at the thought of her beloved Leonesse. "And tell them you saw my eyes filled with tears of joy."

"Yes, my lady." The young man bowed and departed to seek a horse. Oswald would bring the tidings to Leonesse in the fullness of time, but Arthur's guard would travel faster.

"Already a queen," Arthur said softly as he observed her dignity and the way she controlled herself despite all the emotional tension she was under.

A swift gesture sent his escort wheeling to form two parallel processions, and he led Guinevere toward the tall stone crosses, emblem of his kingdom.

Sir Agravaine walked close to Arthur's side, and the king turned his head to appraise the knight. There was a healing scar on his cheekbone and a minor sword cut on his hand. "We heard from your advance rider that you were attacked on the road," he said quietly so as not to disturb Guinevere.

Agravaine grimaced. "Yes, Sire."

"Malagant?"

"I am sure of it. The attack was too carefully planned just to be forest robbers. First they drew us off with common foot soldiers, and while we were engaged in pursuing them, they loosed their horsemen upon us."

Arthur grunted. "You should have known better after all the campaigns that we have fought."

Agravaine looked uncomfortable. "I know that, Sire. They seemed such easy meat . . ."

They were approaching the great stone crosses on the crest of the hill. Arthur made a small gesture, dismissing the subject. "We'll talk about Malagant later at the Round Table," he murmured. "At least Lady Guinevere has come to no harm, and we know to be on our guard."

Agravaine bowed and stepped back among the ranks so that Guinevere and Arthur approached the stone crosses alone. Arthur took her hand in his, and the smile returned to his eyes. "Come," he said, "let me show you your new home." He led her the last few paces to the peak of the hill. "I was still a boy when I first followed this road, climbed this place, and saw what was to become my city—Camelot."

He looked across the valley and as ever felt his heart move at the sight of the gleaming walls and turrets; then he looked down at his bride-to-be, eager to see her reaction.

Guinevere stood and stared, transfixed by a vision so beautiful that it almost seemed unreal. A wide lake lay silver in the light of a waxing moon. Rising out of the water on the far side, the towers of the city of Camelot glimmered with the light of a thousand torches. Reflected in the lake, the city seemed to float in midair, as if transported from the mythical land of Faery. Moonlight and fire. Silver and gold.

Guinevere stared at it, her hazel eyes wide with wonder. A small shiver rippled down her spine. "It is so beautiful that it almost frightens me," she whispered, and looked round and up at Arthur. He, too, seemed a part of the magic with his majestic silver hair and beard, and his shining blue silk robe.

"Yes," he said, his eyes tender upon her. "It is something I have felt, too, but I wonder why you say it."

Guinevere shook her head. "I was brought up to set no faith in finery. Beauty doesn't last, my father always said."

"Yes, but I remember the way he looked at you."

Guinevere glanced at her future husband, a question in her eyes.

"I remember him asking me if all fathers thought their daughters so beautiful," Arthur mused.

"He never said that to me." Guinevere had been her father's only child. He had cherished her, but without coddling her or encouraging vanity. He had always taken more pride in her skill at pit ball or managing a spirited horse than in her ability to dress and preen like a young lady of rank. "I suppose that beauty is in the eye of the beholder," she murmured, and stared once more at the sparkling, floating mirage that was to be her new home, half expecting it to disappear.

"Sometimes it is in the eyes of all beholders," Arthur said, and once more led her forward.

Down in the valley, the lake gleamed like dark glass in the moonlight, the lights of Camelot dancing in reflection on the water's surface. To the sound of brass trumpets, the royal procession crossed the long wooden causeway to the citadel. The road was built so close to the waterline that the carriages, horses, and men seemed to float across the water and become a part of the magical image.

From the heart of the city the cathedral bells rang out to welcome Arthur and his intended wife, the sounds as clear and silver as the night itself.

Guinevere was brought a splendidly caparisoned white horse to ride into Camelot. Her pale gown gleaming, she too became a part of the mirage as she and Arthur rode onto the causeway surrounded by the glorious blue and silver of the royal guard.

On either side of the causeway, Guinevere saw small boats bobbing up and down on the water, all of them filled with cheering townspeople holding torches and horn lanterns. The population was out in force to greet its queen-to-be. The top of the city wall was packed with cheering crowds, and there was much elbowing and jostling as individuals fought for a sight of Arthur's lovely bride.

The bride herself was feeling more than a little overwhelmed by the exuberance and delight of the folk of Camelot. It was one thing for Arthur to promise to take her as he found her, quite another for these people. Looking at a fairy-tale world from the top of a hill was not quite the same as living within it. But she had been trained in a strict school, and she knew the part she had to play. Arthur was watching her, and she could feel the intensity of his gaze, his need to know that she would be happy here. She smiled for him. I will be happy, she thought. He is so understanding and kind and wise. How could I not be happy with such a husband?

As she rode through the great gates, flower petals cascaded down from walls and balconies, showering her with their fragrance, and a gauzy golden banner unfurled, proclaiming her entrance to Camelot.

Chapter 6

$\mathcal{L}$ancelot broke his fast at a wayside cottage. In exchange for a coin, the goodwife gave him bread, still warm and fragrant from her brick oven, and sticky honeycomb from the straw hives in her small orchard. While Lancelot ate his food at a table beneath the trees, Jupiter grazed on the nutritious summer grass between the trunks.

Lancelot enjoyed the moment while it lasted. The goodwife came out of the house with her spindle and a mass of raw wool and tried to engage him in conversation. Lancelot answered her queries politely but volunteered no more information than was necessary, and finishing his food with thanks, whistled for Jupiter, mounted up, and rode on.

The woods were peaceful today, filled with nothing more sinister than sunshine and birdsong. Lancelot rode along at a leisurely pace, whistling softly through his teeth, no goal in mind. There was still money in his purse, and the goodwife had given him a parting gift of half a loaf and some homemade cheese. For today he was self-sufficient.

The woods petered out, yielding to fertile grasslands grazed by sleek cattle and larger, meatier sheep than the spotted ones of the border village where he had stopped to fight. The road widened and showed evidence of being frequently used. Down the center there was a ridge of tufty grass standing proud of well-worn wheel ruts; soon enough Lancelot came upon a carter, red-faced and towheaded, his wagon filled with cabbages, and sitting on top of them, a woman suckling a small baby. He answered their greeting, but chose not to ride alongside, and urged Jupiter to a trot until he had left them behind.

Other wayfarers continued to straggle across his path, some of them on foot, others in wagons or mounted like himself. There must be quite a large town in the vicinity, he thought, perhaps a market or administrative center. A river wound its way along beside the road, and there were boats and trading barges upon it, suggesting a fair-sized community. He pursed his lips. Although his pouch was nowhere near depleted, it would still do no harm to drum up a little trade. He could buy some oats for Jupiter and perhaps see about purchasing a new bridle, since the existing one was becoming shabby.

Up ahead he thought he heard a shout, and he tensed. Surely not another assault on a bright morning like this with no tree cover behind which to hide. He gathered up the reins, ready to command Jupiter, but the black stallion jerked his head and made a whiffling sound through his nostrils.

Hoofbeats drummed upon the road, galloping

hard, and a white mare thundered around the corner, her leading rein broken, her ears back. She swerved past Lancelot and Jupiter and pounded on down the track, a gleaming vision. The stallion pranced and turned, arching his neck, his tail carried high. He needed no encouragement to give chase.

The mare flew before them like a beast from out of the hollow hills, surefooted, ghost-pale, and with elvish fire in her hooves. Jupiter galloped in pursuit. At first he made no impression, but as he found his stride, he began to eat up the ground as effortlessly as the mare. She had already been running for some time, and her flanks were sweated up. The stallion's stamina was still at its peak, and he brought Lancelot alongside her. The man snatched for the reins and rode Jupiter in close to the smaller mare, forcing her to steady down.

"Whoa, whoa, my beauty," Lancelot cried as he leaned back in the saddle. The mare's head was drawn toward him. Foam spattered from her bridle onto Jupiter's damp black hide. Constrained by the stallion and Lancelot's sure hold, she slowed to a trot, and then stopped altogether, her sides heaving like a pair of bellows. Lancelot slid from his saddle and set about soothing the mare, breathing in her nostrils, making gentle noises, stroking her with his hands. Beneath his touch she became calm. Her eyes ceased to roll and her ears pricked up. Her skin twitched and shivered beneath his touch. Lancelot admired her. She was of eastern blood, a rich man's mount—if she was saddle-broken.

A sound made him look around. A horseman was galloping toward them—a young man with earnest, worried features and curly dark hair. He drew rein before Lancelot. "Thank you," he panted. "You've saved me a long ride. God knows where she would have stopped!" He swung down from his own mount with the lithe ease of a born rider. "A wood pigeon spooked her, and she just took off as if the devil himself was at her heels!"

Lancelot smiled and fondled her velvet-soft muzzle. "She's a fine animal. His voice held an admiration and gentleness far beyond that which he would have given to any human.

The young man nodded and pushed his hair off his forehead. "Fit for a queen," he agreed, adding wryly, "if she weren't so wild." He took the leading rein from Lancelot's hand and stroked the mare's silken silver hide. Then he looked at Lancelot out of shrewd blue eyes. "You know horses. I can see from the way you handled her just now."

"I have a small knowledge," Lancelot said with a shrug, as if it did not matter, although it was something that still mattered to him among all the other things that did not.

The young man extended his hand. "I'm Peter, the king's head stableman."

Lancelot held out his own hand and shook the other's in a firm grasp calloused by a sword hilt. "My name is Lancelot. Of which king do you speak?"

The young man's eyes had widened as he felt the pressure of Lancelot's grip and realized what the hard skin intimated. Now it widened still further. "Which king?" he said on a rising, incredulous note. "The King of course, Arthur of Camelot! This beauty here is supposed to be a gift for his new bride."

"His new bride?" Lancelot regarded the horse and

thought of the young woman he had rescued from the forest ambush. She and the horse would suit, he thought, and she had said that she was on her way to be married.

"Lady Guinevere of Leonesse," Peter qualified, thereby confirming the other man's thoughts. A pang went through Lancelot, swift and sharp as the cut of a boning knife. He had thought himself armored against anything that the world could throw at him, but the lady Guinevere had pierced his guard, his bright, hard exterior. Stay away, the reasoning part of his mind warned him; stay away and the wound will heal. But Lancelot had never backed away from danger or challenge in his life.

"Are you bound for Camelot?" the stableman inquired as he remounted and took a firm hold of the white mare's leading rein.

Lancelot hesitated for an instant, then shrugged. "Why not?" he said, and swung himself across Jupiter's back.

The two men rode along the track beside the river, then climbed the slope to the great stone crosses marking the boundaries of Camelot.

Peter glanced sidelong at his silent companion. "After all these years our king is taking a wife. There are those who swore he would never marry, but I knew better. He was just waiting for the right one, like we all do. There'll be some feasting today, I can tell you."

"Waiting for the right one," Lancelot repeated, and his lower lids tensed. "What if she passes you by?"

"What did you say?"

Lancelot shook his head. "Foolish thoughts

aloud," he muttered, and on the crest of the hill drew his horse to a standstill and stared at the city spread out before him. In bright sunlight the lake and turrets were blue, each reflecting the other and the sky. The walls shone a mellow silverish gold. The view was like something drawn out of a monk's illuminated manuscript, sturdy and delicate at one and the same time, and possessed of a profound spirituality. Once more, long-dormant feelings stirred uneasily within Lancelot and threatened to awaken.

From the city, floating on the air like fairing ribbons, he heard the distant sounds of revelry and celebration. Their new queen-to-be was being joyously welcomed.

The stableman eagerly set off down the hill, looked round for Lancelot, and saw him still motionless on the crest. "Come on!" he urged. "The party's already started; you don't want to miss it!"

Lancelot hesitated a moment longer, a swordsman unsure of his ground for the first time in more than fifteen years. Then, irritated at himself and the situation, he kicked Jupiter into motion and followed Peter down the hill toward the gleaming city.

The citizens of Camelot were celebrating the arrival of their beloved king's bride with gusto. The town square before the entrance of the royal palace was packed with people wearing their best clothes, in particular the famous Camelot blue, a cloth made by the city dyers using an ancient and secret formula of water plants from the lake and herbs from the fields around the stone crosses. The color produced was bright without being garish and possessed a luminescent quality, like a deep night sky imbued with starlight.

Children ran excitedly through the throng, pulling long, streamers of colored silk called dragon's tails, vying with each other as to who could swirl the prettiest patterns. Lancelot deposited Jupiter at a livery stable and made his way on foot through the jostling, good-natured throng. Trestle tables had been set out along the edges of the main square, and they groaned with platters of food—fruit, meat pies, jugs of ale. Bakers paddled hot loaves from brick ovens and the fragrance of fresh bread filled the air and mingled with the tantalizing aroma from the open fire pits where whole pigs were being roasted to a crisp, golden turn.

Lancelot stared around at the turrets and archways, stained glass gable windows, and fluttering blue and gold banners bearing the symbol of the stone cross embroidered in gold. On one side of the main square stood the palace, its huge studded doors guarded by two soldiers wearing the royal livery, their spears struck at attention. On the other was the cathedral, its doorway a magnificent series of decorated arches. Lancelot had never encountered such an impressive city, not even in the days before he took to wandering, when he had wealth and stability of his own, and despite years of ingrained cynicism and caution, he found himself moved to admire what he saw.

A single yell of alarm followed by the roar of the crowd drew Lancelot toward a crowd at the center of the square. He saw that people were gathered around a causeway built of timber planks. It was just wide enough for one man to pass along and was raised several feet above the ground. It stretched the entire length of the square, north to south. On either side of the causeway were upright wooden pillars, each one supporting a rotating vertical shaft, and from the shafts, suspended on chains at varying heights, were leather balls and pig's bladders, some stuffed with straw, some weighted with stones and studded with nails. Beyond the bladders, the causeway rose slightly and there was a second section that housed a deadly collection of outsize double-headed notched axes, maces, and various slashing, slicing instruments.

Lancelot's interest quickened, and he moved closer for a better look. He saw that the rotating pillars were driven by a system of cogs and shafts, which were powered by an immense weight housed in a scaffolding tower at the north end of the monstrosity. Cranking the weight to the top of the tower took the efforts of three strong men hauling on a huge drum winch.

A queue of foolhardy young townsmen waited to brave the machine. All of them wore heavy padding to protect themselves from being injured by the various missiles, although it would need more than padding to save them from the axes and blades at the far end, Lancelot thought. The cry that had drawn him to join the crowd had come from a challenger who had been sent flying into the deep straw spread below the causeway. The next man was already in position, waiting for the weight to reach the top of the scaffolding.

Lining the causeway, keeping the crowd at a safe distance, were a row of drummers in quilted blue tunics. Mastering the proceedings was a portly man with a voice that rolled across the crowd like thunder.

"Beat the gauntlet, meet the king!" he roared at the people, and gestured grandly. "Beat the gauntlet, meet the king. Come now, who's game to try?"

The drums rumbled. Lancelot folded his arms and remained where he was, but his gaze was both intent and intense. "What do you do with the remains of those who don't make it?" he asked of the merchant standing beside him in the crowd.

The man chuckled, his double chins wobbling. "No one's ever made it past them leather balls," he said. "The weapons are just for show. It's harmless fun. Furthest I ever seen anyone get was up to those last balls, and that was two years ago, the fishmonger's lad. Ran out of time he did—the weight reached the bottom of the scaffold."

Lancelot smiled. "Is that so?" he said, and leaving his garrulous companion, moved closer still to the gauntlet.

To the accompaniment of a tension-building drumroll, the challenger, a brawny lad with arms the size of hams, set out. As the weight descended, the pillars spun around, and the leather balls rotated at different speeds. Some came sailing round with slow, lazy menace, others whizzed like hornets.

The young challenger took the course at speed, leaping and ducking the flying balls with initial success. One small bladder caught him an offside blow, but it was not hard enough to pitch him into the straw. The crowd jumped up and down, egging him on, punching the air with their fists. "Go, go on, Simon, go! Look out!"

A grimace of deep concentration on his face, the brawny young challenger advanced to the second set of balls and bladders. He looked as if he were going to succeed his way through these, too, but then a low chain swept away his ankles, and a high ball thudded into his flank. A cry burst from him as he was hurled from the causeway to land in the straw, all breath driven from his body. One of the drummers struck a pair of cymbals as the challenger landed, and the crowd laughed and cheered.

Even before the victim had risen to his feet, another young man had leaped to the starting point and poised, one eye upon the weights in the scaffolding, the other upon the gauntlet. By now Lancelot was right at the front of the crowd. He studied the operation attentively, absorbing every detail of speed and position, mentally twisting, leaping, and turning to avoid each blow and pitfall.

On the dais before the palace doors, a row of trumpeters raised coiled golden instruments to their lips and sounded a fanfare that rang out clear above the noise and bustle in the square. The lad braving the gauntlet was distracted by the sudden sound. He looked up at the wrong moment, was caught by a bladder, and sent hurtling into the straw.

A colossal cheer went up, but it was not for the gauntlet's most recent victim. All eyes were upon the dais, and whispers of "The king and his bride" threaded through the crowd. Lancelot looked, his breath quickening with anticipation. The gauntlet was on the opposite side of the square to the dais, and Lancelot's view was impeded. He could see the man who surely must be the paragon King Arthur, but not the young woman at his side.

Old enough to be her father, Lancelot thought. He wanted to feel contempt, but he could not. The man was tall, his limbs were straight, and he carried no surplus flesh. Silver his hair and beard might be, but there was a charisma about him that made nothing of his years—whatever they might be.

The trumpeters parted and Arthur stepped forward to the edge of the dais, an exquisite young woman at his side. Suddenly Lancelot could see clear across the square, and his breath caught. He had thought the lady Guinevere beautiful in the woods, but now, on the arm of the man she was to marry, she was breathtaking. Her silver robe accentuated her figure, her hair was a glorious mixture of forest browns, and her face was radiant. But her loveliness was more than just skin-deep. Lancelot had known many pretty women, and none had left a lasting impression, their faces all blending into one. But he knew that it would take some time before he forgot the face of Guinevere of Lyonesse or the feel of her lips under his own in a border forest.

She was smiling, her eyes scanning the welcoming crowd. Lancelot willed her to look his way, but her gaze passed over him without recognition.

The great weight that drove the gauntlet had reached the ground, and the spinning chains were still, apart from a gentle trembling. The winchers set about winding the weight back up to the top of its tower. Lancelot's eyes briefly followed the rising lead ball and then returned to Guinevere because it was almost impossible to look anywhere else. The royal party had seated themselves on low-backed chairs at the edge of the platform, and it was obvious that they intended to stay awhile and watch the entertainment on the gauntlet. Arthur leaned close to Guinevere, explaining and pointing, and she nodded attentively, a half smile on her lips.

The gauntlet master climbed up onto the apparatus to set the weight descending, but before he released the locking bar, he bellowed encouragement to the crowd. "Beat the gauntlet, meet our lovely queen!" Then he turned to the dais, and a mischievous twinkle lit in his eyes. "Will you give the victor a kiss, my lady? Don't worry, no one's beaten the gauntlet yet!"

Enchanted, Guinevere laughed and turned to Arthur. He murmured something, a smile in his own eyes, and she nodded agreement at the gauntlet master.

"How's that, lads?" the man roared with increased vigor. "Beat the gauntlet and you win a kiss from Lady Guinevere, soon to be our lovely queen!"

Lancelot stared between Guinevere and the gauntlet with narrowed eyes and knew in his own heart and mind which was the more dangerous of the two. He also had no doubt that both could be conquered. A challenger came forward and was strapped into the protective padding. The gauntlet master unlocked the release bar on the weights. The chains and balls began to spin, and beyond them, the steel pendulums and axes sliced.

Lancelot made his decision and, pushing through the crowd, ran up the steps to the starting position, leaving the would-be challenger floundering with indignation.

"Hey, wait your turn!" yelled the gauntlet master. Then his eyes widened in alarm. "Not like that, you idiot! Get padded up first, else you'll break every bone in your body!" He gestured vigorously for Lancelot to come down.

Lancelot ignored him. Padding distorted a man's balance and made him more unwieldy. The gauntlet required a cat's grace, not the lumbering of an ox. He crouched at the start of the causeway and studied the whirling leather balls and bladders, committing every detail to memory.

"Get down! Are you mad? It will kill you!"

All eyes in the crowd turned to the gauntlet. So did those of the royal party.

"By the stone crosses, the man's insane!" Sir Kay declared, and took an involuntary pace forward, thereby blocking Guinevere's view. "He's not going to do it. No one would be so foolish. It's just a stupid jest."

But it wasn't, and Kay's mouth hung open as the challenger took his first step upon the causeway. Guinevere shifted in her chair, and Kay moved so that she was granted a clear view of the man foolish enough to dare Camelot's gauntlet unclad. Her breath caught, and her fingers tightened on the low armrests of her chair. Fortunately, Arthur was too busy staring at Lancelot himself to notice her response, and in another moment she had gained control of herself.

Lancelot advanced along the causeway, his gaze far ahead of his feet, and his feet moving in time and counterpoint with the machine. He did not rush, for to rush was to trust to chance and make mistakes. Every move had to be calculated. Think fast and go slowly.

The crowd fell silent and a tension gripped the

atmosphere. The first set of bladders was the easiest, and with precise timing, Lancelot swerved, jumped, and ducked his way out of trouble as neatly as a cat. But the first section was nothing, a mere child's game that most of the other players had won through, clumsy and padded though they were. Lancelot faced the punishing middle stretch where every previous challenger had met his fate in the straw below. Again he paused to assess and memorize. The four largest pillars hurled the heaviest balls and chains in intersecting circles, sweeping over the planks of the causeway in both directions, denying a secure foothold anywhere. A single blow from any one of these balls would smash bone on an unprotected body.

There was only one way to go to avoid the balls, and Lancelot took it. He poised, waiting his moment, and then launched himself sideways. He took an acrobat's grip on a horizontal spar from which two of the balls were suspended and let it spin him around until he was able to release his hold and leap for the spar on the next set of uprights. Once more he was carried around and farther along the causeway. Another leap and a swing, and he was dropping to the ground between the two sections, only the weapons between him and Guinevere's kiss.

She sat on the edge of her chair, her hazel eyes wide and her lower lip caught in her teeth. Lancelot did not look at her, although he knew fully that her attention would be upon him. A collective murmur had gone up from the crowd as he completed the first section. Now the audience fell silent again as Lancelot prepared to gamble his life on the fickle rotation of a blade. The drummers set up a slow drumbeat akin to the hammer of a war sword upon a shield as Lancelot commenced his dance with death. And a dance it was, the steps intricate but performed with such grace and timing by the men that they seemed simple. It was almost as though he was playing with the gauntlet, teasing it, daring it to catch him. A pause here, a curve of the body there, a crouch, a leap. Lancelot knew exactly what he was doing.

The crowd, beginning to sense that they were not watching a madman throwing away his life, started to clap in rhythm with the drums and encourage the challenger. There was a chance that he was going to win. Lancelot played to their expectations, their noise spurring him on, daring him to his limit. He increased the speed of his flirtation with the blades and pendulums, and in response, the people increased the speed of their clapping and the drums thundered faster than a racing heartbeat.

Lancelot stretched his arms, daring the final two-headed ax to slice him in twain, and ran seemingly to meet it. On the dais, Guinevere suppressed a scream and Arthur leaned forward in his chair. The wind of the ax's passing grazed the air above Lancelot's head, missing him by a hairbreadth, but he was through and whole. At the end of the platform he stopped and turned.

The crowd stamped and whistled, cheered loud appreciation. Arthur, Guinevere, and the knights of the royal guard had all risen to give Lancelot a standing ovation, too. He turned his eyes to the dais, to the woman standing there. Now came the fourth part of the gauntlet, and suddenly he was short of breath, when throughout the ordeal, he had had no trouble breathing at all.

"A kiss!" someone shouted among the cheers, "A kiss for the victor!" The chant was quickly taken up. "Kiss! Kiss!" Faces turned expectantly toward the dais.

Arthur beckoned good-naturedly to the victorious challenger. Lancelot stepped down from the gauntlet and crossed the square of cheering people to the royal dais. The king was smiling, delight and curiosity on his face. Guinevere's own features were blank, and she held herself stiffly, as if someone had thrust a broom handle down her spine, Lancelot thought.

In deference to Arthur, he bent his knee, but found himself immediately raised to his feet and his arm clasped in the friendship greeting. Arthur's grip was firm and strong, that of a man in the full surety of his prime.

"Extraordinary!" Arthur declared. "Unbelievable! What's your name, man?"

"Lancelot, my lord."

"Lancelot." Arthur said the word slowly, making it important. "We won't forget that name quickly." A broad smile on his face, he released Lancelot and gestured him to Guinevere. "Your prize, a kiss from the fairest lady ever to grace the earth."

Guinevere's face was pink as she stood before Lancelot. Hands clenched in the folds of her dress, she held up her face to be kissed.

Lancelot looked down at her, knowing the resentment that smoldered beneath her resigned exterior. He stooped slightly. "Ask me," he murmured, his voice too quiet for anyone else to hear.

Guinevere stared up at him. There were green flecks in the depths of her eyes, and small glints of gold. Just now the lids were slightly narrowed. "Never," she answered.

The crowd, waiting for Lancelot to claim his kiss, was growing impatient with their hero's hesitation, and in the same manner that they had clapped him on at the gauntlet, they began to chant "Kiss! Kiss!" in a pounding rhythm.

Guinevere's eyes flickered nervously. "Bend lower," she commanded.

Lancelot did so. "Ask me," he repeated into her breath. He could smell the jasmine in her hair and see the rapid beating of her heart beneath the silver silk of her gown. Utterly desirable and beyond his reach, but only just. So close that his fingertips could touch the air of her passing like the ax had so nearly touched him.

"Never," she returned, and her jaw was stubbornly set.

The crowd's chant was increasing in volume. "Kiss! Kiss!" The words became a cage surrounding the battle of wills between Lancelot and Guinevere. There was no escape.

Lancelot took Guinevere's hand in his. She had fine bones, but there was tensile strength in them, and her nails were trim and short without the manicured affectation so often sported by women of her birth. He kept his eyes on hers and spoke up loud and clear so that all should hear his words.

"I dare not kiss so lovely a lady. I have only one heart to lose." And then he raised her hand to his lips and kissed the back of it with a slow and courtly deference that concealed, except to himself and

Guinevere, the mockery. His gallant speech won laughter and cheers of approval from all concerned, both the highborn and the low, but his eyes never left Guinevere to acknowledge the crowd's approval, and there was no smile to be seen on her face or read in her gaze, which held the fierceness of a sword edge raised to parry a blow.

Arthur set his arm across Lancelot's shoulder. "Come, Lancelot," he said. "I would speak with you further before you go on your way."

Lancelot released Guinevere's hand and, after a final holding of eyes, turned his attention somewhat warily to Arthur. He wondered how much the silver-haired king had been told about that episode in the forest. From the way Guinevere was behaving, he guessed that she had said nothing, and that in itself was interesting.

Arthur led Lancelot through the heavy studded oak doors behind the dais and into a room handsomely appointed with fine tapestries on the walls and elegantly carved coffers, cupboards, and chairs. Lancelot stared around at the wealth. The understated way it was displayed revealed yet more about the majestic man regarding him now.

"Tell me," Arthur asked, "had you ever run the gauntlet before today?"

Lancelot met the shrewd gaze full on and shook his head. "No, never."

Although the king's hair and beard were the silver of his mature years, his eyebrows were still raven black and made his stare all the more arresting and charismatic. "So how did you do it then?"

Lancelot shrugged. The same question. It always came, whether it be from the wondering voice of a peasant farmer or the lips of the king of Camelot. "It's not hard to know where the danger is, if you watch it coming."

"But others have found it hard enough. You're the first one to do it."

"Perhaps fear makes them go back when they should go forward," Lancelot said. "The safest place is often closest to the blade."

The dark brows shot up toward the silver fringe. "And also the most dangerous. Can you stand here now and tell me that you felt no fear?"

Lancelot pushed his own untidy brown hair off his face and shook his head. "I have nothing to lose, so what have I to fear?"

"No home? No family?"

"No."

"Everyone has a background, a past," Arthur said. His brows had lowered and were frowning slightly now.

"I don't." Lancelot's reply held a note that was almost defiant, as though he were an unruly adolescent brought to task by an adult. He felt uncomfortable, almost lacking beneath Arthur's scrutiny. King the man might be, but he had no right to probe at what a man chose not to reveal.

"Well then, do you have a profession?" Arthur questioned in a reasonable tone.

Lancelot would have curled the fingers of his left hand around the comforting familiarity of his sword hilt, but he had left the weapon behind at the livery stable with Jupiter. "I live by my blade," he said, "and my wits."

"Ah, you fight for pay?" Arthur gently ran his forefinger through his beard.

"Yes, I fight for pay," Lancelot said tautly. He was growing tired of the interrogation, and his eyes flickered toward the door.

"No one paid you to run the gauntlet."

"It was of my own choosing. I knew I could do it, so I did. If a mountain exists, it is there to be climbed."

Arthur eyed him thoughtfully. "Well, Lancelot, you're an unusual man. I do not believe I have ever before seen such a display of courage, skill, nerve, grace"—he paused for effect—"and sheer stupidity."

This time it was Lancelot's turn to raise a brow. Arthur, it seemed, was a man who not only measured his words but dealt them out plainly if he felt the necessity. No one had ever called Lancelot stupid before. He found himself feeling resentful and angry, when usually such words would be water off a duck's back. Arthur, like Guinevere, had found a weakness in his armor.

Lancelot would have left then, but Arthur took him by the sleeve and led him forward, away from the door and the distant shouting of the feast day crowd. Lancelot stared around at golden stone walls and decorated columns, more rich tapestries showing hunting and battle scenes. As they walked, Arthur continued to speak.

"Here in Camelot we believe that every life is precious—even the lives of strangers. Your courage is worthless if it serves no purpose. Dying is easy. It is living that takes courage."

Lancelot made a slight sound of disparagement, but it was in defense. He did not want to listen to Arthur, because the older man was threatening the formidable defenses Lancelot had built around himself during the many barren years since his nineteenth birthday.

"If you must die," Arthur said, ignoring the sound, except to make his voice more forceful, "then die serving something greater than yourself. But I say it is better still to live to serve."

"I go my own way," Lancelot replied through stiff lips.

"No, you don't, you're lost," Arthur said forthrightly.

Pinned down, Lancelot struggled to maintain a calm, indifferent facade. "I see the king knows all he needs to know about me already," he said with a slightly mocking salute.

Arthur ceased pacing and, in a rustle of blue silk, turned to look intently into Lancelot's eyes, meeting depth for depth. "Not all," said the king. "But I can see the pride in you that asks nothing of any man and will bow down to none. And I see the anger, too, and the loneliness. It is a hard path you have chosen for yourself."

Lancelot did not answer, could not have done so had he tried, for Arthur had read him as if he were transparent, and he was still reeling from the shock and trying not to show it.

Without looking down, Arthur drew the sword from his belt and held it out to Lancelot, hilt first. "You're a swordsman. What do you make of that?"

Automatically Lancelot took the king's sword in his right hand, and although his mind was preoccupied, his body was so long attuned to the skills of weaponplay, that he immediately took up a fighting stance. The feel of a sword in his hand, and a very fine one at that, restored some of his equilibrium, as if the balance of his body restored the balance of his mind. Closely watched by Arthur, he tried the sword with his right foot forward, in the pose of a fencer, and then his left, in the more traditional stance that a knight would use when fighting behind a shield. He examined the finely wrought grip and the bluish razor-sharp edges that could easily slice off a limb in battle.

"It's very fine," he said, and looked Arthur up and down. He thought that despite the measured stride and silver hair, Arthur was probably still capable of fighting for his life if the moment demanded. But he wanted to hear it from the king's own lips. "Do you ever use it?"

Arthur gave him a wry glance. "When necessary. A sword is not a solution, but it helps if your enemies know that you have one and that you are not afraid to use it."

"It is too fine for me." Lancelot returned the weapon to Arthur. "I have a way of losing swords."

"I doubt that," Arthur said shrewdly. "A man who lives as close to the blade as you would never lose a sword." He sheathed his weapon and, walking on, opened the heavy studded doors at the end of the hallway. "Enter," he said to Lancelot, and made an ushering gesture.

Lancelot stepped slowly into a grand circular chamber fashioned of the same pale gold Camelot stone as the rest of the palace. Light flooded through two tiers of magnificent Romanesque arches to illuminate a stepped platform girding the room, and at its center, in the well, a huge round table divided into thirteen equal sections, and placed at each section a chair.

"The round table," Arthur declared. "This is where the High Council of Camelot meets. There is no head, no foot, everyone equal."

"Even the king?" Lancelot glanced at Arthur.

"Even the king."

Lancelot approached the table and slowly walked around it. The sections were arranged in alternating shades of pale gray and charcoal. At the very center stood a small brazier, flames licking over its rim and giving off a faint smell of incense. Ringing the brazier was an inscription deeply incised in silver gilding. "In serving each other we become free," Lancelot said aloud.

Arthur watched him narrowly. "Does that mean anything to you?"

Lancelot looked at Arthur and said nothing. How could he answer another man when he could not answer himself?

"That is the heart of Camelot," Arthur said before the silence could become drawn out, and gestured at the room's magnificent architecture. "Not these stones, these timbers, these palaces and towers. Burn all this and Camelot lives on, because it lives in us. Camelot is a belief that we hold in our hearts." He stared intently at Lancelot as if he were a miner examining a face of common rock for a seam of gold. Then he nodded. "You're not ready yet, are you? Well, no matter. You are welcome to stay in Camelot for as long as you choose."

Lancelot shook his head. "Thank you, my lord, but I think I shall be on the road again soon. Your city is magnificent, but perhaps, like your sword, it is too fine for a man like me."

Arthur pursed his lips and thought that he ought

to add stubborn to the list of qualities that he had seen in Lancelot. "And which road might that be?"

"Whichever one chance leads me to. I have no plans."

"You believe that what you do is a matter of chance?"

"Yes."

Arthur went to the entrance of his council chamber and pointed down the hallway. "At the end of this corridor there are two doors. One to your right and one to your left. How will you decide which one to take?"

Lancelot shrugged. "Left or right, it makes no difference. It's all a matter of chance." He knew that he was being obtuse and difficult, but he felt as if Arthur had backed him into a corner, and for Lancelot, it was a rare and disturbing situation.

Arthur gave him a long look. "Then I hope that chance leads you to the left, since that is the way out."

And to the right was the way in? Lancelot smiled grimly and, giving a slight bow of his head, turned to leave. He was already walking down the corridor when Arthur called his name. Halting, he turned warily round.

"It is just a thought," Arthur said. "A man who fears nothing is a man who loves nothing. And if you love nothing, what joy is there in your life? I may be wrong."

Lancelot stared at him for a long moment. Then he drew a slow breath through his teeth and turned away, taking the left door to freedom.

Chapter 7

After leaving the palace and a mental duel with its far too shrewd and astute king, Lancelot was stared at, commented upon, and congratulated by members of the crowd who had witnessed his daring feat on the gauntlet. Some even wanted him to repeat his performance so that they could marvel anew and try to decide how he did it. In the right mood Lancelot might have obliged, but just now he had a longing for solitude. He could not even bear the sight of the machine.

The people pressed gifts of food upon him and treated him like a hero. He looked at the raised platform in front of the palace doors, but Guinevere's chair was empty. And then he caught sight of her viewing the square from an upstairs gallery. Arthur was with her and their arms were linked. It was too much for one day, and Lancelot pushed aside the goodwill and headed for the stables and the quiet company of his horse—only to discover the eager young stableman, Peter, sitting on a bale of straw outside Jupiter's stall.

"If you're here to bask in reflected glory, you've come to the wrong place," Lancelot snapped. "I'm not good company just now."

Peter's open, generous features fell, but he was a good-natured type and slow to take offense. "I thought you'd want to celebrate. I know of a good tavern—it's just 'round the corner."

Lancelot shook his head. A drink might help him discover oblivion for a time, but the place would be full of people reliving over and over again his defeat of the gauntlet, and he only wanted to forget the entire incident. "Thank you, but no. I just want to be left alone. I . . . I have some thinking to do." He managed a smile.

Peter nodded. "I understand. Time to yourself, it's hard to come by. I should know. There are never enough hours in the day. Actually, the king sent me."

"Oh?" Lancelot stiffened, wondering what Arthur wanted now. If it was another private talk, Lancelot was not sure that he would obey the summons.

"He spoke to me in the stable yard, and I told him that I had met you on your way into the city. He says that he knows you are independent and that you choose your own road, but that you are welcome to stable your horse at the palace during your stay—if not yourself."

Lancelot said nothing and, entering the stall, stroked Jupiter's sleek black hide. The stallion whickered softly and gave him a loving nudge.

Peter eyed man and horse. "Camelot's stables are unsurpassed, and it would cost you nothing to keep him there."

Lancelot smiled, but the humor did not light in his eyes. "In terms of coin, no," he said.

Peter looked puzzled. "You could stay, too. There are spare beds in the grooms' quarters if you want to be near him."

Lancelot looked at the eager young man, the open, generous features. He knew that he ought to refuse. It was not only the horse he would be near but Arthur with his sharp perceptions—and Guinevere. She was sharp, too, and he did not want to be cut again trying to disarm her. Set against those drawbacks, Jupiter needed resting. They had been a long time on the road without respite, and superb though the stallion was, he had his limits. To pay no heed now was to pay later in the middle of nowhere if Jupiter went lame. The needs of his horse came first, and Lancelot capitulated. "Then thank you," he said. "I will be pleased to accept the king's offer."

Accompanied by Peter, the stableman, and Mador, one of his advisers, Arthur walked slowly down the row of stalls that lined one side of Camelot's impressive stable yard. The complex was built in the shape of a square with three sides devoted to stabling and the fourth to holding supplies and quartering the grooms. At the center was a white stone fountain surrounded by a thick carpet of golden gravel dredged up from the bed of the river Camel. Arthur's footsteps crunched on the stones and then stopped as he paused to look at a handsome strawberry-colored gelding standing contentedly within one of the stalls.

"The roan's good-tempered, Sire," Peter volunteered, noting the direction of Arthur's eye. "A good mount for a lady."

"Perhaps." Arthur nodded and moved on down the block, pausing to study each animal—a dun, two bays, a chestnut, a handsome, rangy black stallion. Arthur's eyebrows lifted.

"He belongs to the man Lancelot," Peter said.

"Docs he?" Arthur looked at the horse curiously, and it looked back at him in similar wise, its ears pricked and its nostrils flaring to drink his scent. Arthur stopped for a moment to fondle its muzzle and found the horse far more amenable than its owner.

Behind him, Mador cleared his throat. "Your marriage, Sire," he broached. "Naturally the people are overjoyed that you are to take a wife, and wish you every happiness—"

"Thank you, Mador," Arthur said graciously, and moved on to the next animal. The black hung his head out of his box and watched the men with interest.

"The people love her already for her beauty and her youth." He stole a look at Arthur, who did not respond, his attention fixed upon a rotund gray mare with black mane and tail.

"She's slow," Peter said, "but steady as a rock."

Arthur nodded absently. At his shoulder, Mador persisted. "Most of all, they value her loving heart. They say that she loves her country so much that she would give her life for it."

Arthur sucked his teeth. "Or her body?" he said in a neutral tone, and faced Mador.

His adviser seemed slightly taken aback. "My lord?"

"You think that she is marrying me to protect her people from Malagant?"

Mador shook his head. "Sire, I would not presume so far. From what I know of the lady, she is gracious and good. But there is something I would ask."

"What?"

Mador stirred his toe in the gravel for a moment, and then looked at Arthur. "Does Lady Guinevere intend to sign Prince Malagant's treaty?"

"That I do not know, Mador. If I did, I would tell you."

Mador nodded. "Have you told her that Camelot will fight for Leonesse, should it become necessary?"

"No, I haven't." Arthur heard Mador's sigh of relief and crunched forward to the next stall where a white mare was plunging and kicking in objection to being confined in a small space. "But I will," he added.

A worried look crossed Mador's face, but Arthur did not see it, for all his attention was upon the bucking white mare. "Ah," he said with satisfaction, "this is the one. Peter, my congratulations, you have an eye for a fine horse."

There was concern mingled with the pride in Peter's eyes as he accepted the compliment. "She's a beauty, Sire, eastern-bred, but there is a devil in her."

Arthur watched her circle in her stall, admiring the sleek lines and superb confirmation. "She is rather high-spirited," he confirmed, but there was a gleam in his eyes as he watched her cavort.

Mador cleared his throat again. "I think we should avoid any specific commitments, Sire."

Arthur swallowed his irritation at Mador's persistence. The man's concerns were the concerns of all the council, and he knew that he had no right to brush them off. "What could be a more specific commitment than marriage, Mador?" He turned to the young stableman. "Saddle her up, lad, and bring her out on the parade ground."

Peter gnawed his lower lip. "She's tried to throw me any number of times, Sire," he warned. "She's wild for to hold."

Arthur nodded, unperturbed. "That's all right, saddle her up."

"Yes, Sire."

With consummate skill and not a little trepidation, Peter maneuvered the frisking mare out her stall and led her away to the saddling enclosure. Arthur followed their progress and rubbed his chin.

"A marriage is one thing, Sire," Mador said as he, too, watched the lad and his charge, "but a military alliance is something else entirely. There does not have to be a connection."

Arthur ceased rubbing his jaw and swung to look at his adviser. Mador had not meant his words in the sense that Arthur heard them, but nevertheless the king was struck by the truth of their content. "Yes, you're right, and I will tell her that, Mador. Thank you. I can always rely on you for insight."

Looking slightly bemused, the knight bowed and left, bowing again at the stable yard entrance as he encountered Guinevere and her serving women. Guinevere was wearing a riding tunic of cream fabric, the skirts full and the top tunic split to the hips to allow ease of movement. Over the tunic, she wore a short huntsman's jerkin, and her soft, dark brown hair was fetchingly braided and coiled. Arthur's breath caught at the sight of her fresh beauty, and he hastened toward her. In the periphery of his vision he caught sight of Peter with the saddled mare, and beckoned to the young man.

"Show us how she goes!" he commanded, and joined Guinevere, a new lightness in his stride.

Peter saluted his king and mounted up. Scarcely was he in the saddle when the mare took off without warning, cavorting and bucking as if she had never had a saddle or rider on her back before. Peter rode her manfully and proved his horsemanship by managing to stay astride. Unable to throw him off, the mare hurtled off down the yard at a hard gallop, her stride sure and fluid. Arthur looked tenderly down at Guinevere's rapt expression.

"I bought her for you," he said softly.

Guinevere raised glowing eyes to his, the tiny green flecks in the hazel as bright as emeralds. "Truly?" Her smile was wide with joy. "I have never seen a horse so beautiful."

Secretly delighted at her response, Arthur pretended to be doubtful. "Peter thinks she is not a suitable mount for a lady."

Guinevere laughed and shook her head. "She is just the horse I would have chosen for myself."

"Yes, I know."

She tilted her head to one side, "How do you know?"

"At Leonesse, do you remember? Last spring when your father was still in good health and we all went hunting together? I saw the way you rode then.

You were fearless." The image filled his mind. Guinevere astride a bay mare, laughing with the pleasure of galloping wild, her hair unwinding from its plait.

"I think my father's word was *reckless,*" she said impishly.

"Yes, he was always sparing with his praise, but I know he valued his daughter above all things."

Guinevere sobered. "And he admired you above all men, my lord. I think he wanted this marriage more than anything in the world."

"He's not the only one," Arthur said in a heartfelt voice, and led her into the center of the schooling ring near the marble fountain. "So much space, we could almost be alone." He smiled, glancing around at the servants who hovered on the perimeter—within sight, perhaps, but well out of earshot.

Guinevere looked up at him through her lashes. "You have secrets to tell me, my lord?" Her tone was playful.

Arthur restrained himself from tilting her face and kissing her soft, young lips. They were not yet his to claim. "No secrets, just a question to ask," he said and drew a deep breath. "Do you truly *want* to marry me?"

The flirt was gone. Guinevere gazed up at him with wide, startled eyes. "My lord, I—"

Before she could say anything else, Arthur overrode her, determined to have his say for richer or poorer. "You do not have to marry me because your father wanted it or because your country needs it. Camelot will protect Leonesse whether you marry me or not."

She was silent. He watched the color mount her

cheekbones as she searched his face, and held himself back from crushing her in his arms. He intended to give her the choice of freedom, not clip her wings.

Guinevere's eyes were bright with moisture. "You don't know what it means to me to hear you say that. All the world thinks that I am marrying for—for the advantages you bring me."

Arthur's heart sank. "So you want to be released from our betrothal?"

Vigorously she shook her head. "No, my lord. I want to marry you. Not your crown or your army or your golden city. Just you."

Arthur swallowed. "Am I enough?" he asked.

"If you love me, then, yes," Guinevere answered gravely.

They stared at each other. Then Arthur cleared his throat and held out his hand. "Do you remember this?"

Guinevere looked at the scar that ran across the back of Arthur's hand. It was still recent enough to be pink, but had faded from its original angry red. "Of course I do." She gently traced the line of the wound with her forefinger. "You hurt it on a thorn bush in the hunt. I had not thought that it would leave such a scar."

"It was just a scratch, but it bled like a war wound."

"I remember."

Arthur laughed shakily. Her touch was like a burning brand thrust amidst dry kindling. "You took my hand in yours and wiped away the blood with the sleeve of your dress."

Guinevere smiled and continued to gently stroke

the line of the scar. "The sleeve still carries the stain."

Arthur's senses spiraled. Hot chills ran down his spine. "I never thought until then how sweet it must be to be loved by one woman. But in that moment, for the first time in my life I wanted—" He broke off with a short laugh. Here he was a man with gray hair, and the years to match them, behaving like a callow youth. He could scarcely believe it of himself.

"Wanted what, my lord?" Guinevere asked softly.

"Ah, what all wise men say doesn't last. What cannot be promised or made to linger any more than sunlight. But I don't want to die without having felt its warmth on my face."

Guinevere was silent, not knowing how to respond to such an intense and poignant declaration. She did love Arthur; he was made in the same mold as the other men in her life she had deeply respected and admired—her father and Oswald. She would have chosen none other to be her husband, and yet her affection for Arthur was gentle, perhaps unable to match the intensity she saw in his eyes.

"Marry the king, Guinevere," Arthur entreated, "but love the man."

She raised her chin a notch, determined that he should see none of her doubts, for they were foolish. "I only know one way to love, my lord, and that is with my body, heart, and soul." She raised his hand and kissed the scar. "I kiss the hurt that brought me your love."

Before Arthur could respond, Peter rode up to them, the white mare snorting and prancing. With some difficulty, he reined her to a halt and swung out of the saddle.

The moment of intimacy vanished like the sunlight that Arthur had mentioned, but the warmth yet remained. "Take her," he said with an open gesture. "She's yours."

"My lady, be careful," Peter cautioned.

Guinevere merely smiled at him, and going to the mare, grasped her bridle, and began softly murmuring to her. The horse tossed her head up and down a few times, gave a single kick, and then settled to enjoy Guinevere's petting.

Peter looked on with an open mouth and scratched his curly head. "God save you, my lady. You certainly have a way with horses," he declared admiringly.

Guinevere glanced over her shoulder at him, her face radiant with delight at her new possession. "Does she have a name?"

Peter shook his head. "No, my lady."

"Then I shall call her Moonlight, to remind me of how I first saw Camelot." She gathered the reins and prepared to mount.

"Let me fetch a lady's saddle," Peter said quickly.

"There is no need." Without even leading her to a mounting block, Guinevere swung across the mare's back like a Mongol archer, revealing to the young groom that she was a young woman of uncommon equestrian skills. Almost before her feet were in the stirrups, she was urging her new mount into a canter. The mare half reared once or twice, forehooves pawing, and then settled down beneath Guinevere's expert handling. Guinevere forgot everything except the power of the beautiful white mare beneath her, every fiber of her being taken up in the experience of the ride.

Peter whistled softly. "She's a rare beauty, Sire."

"Yes," Arthur nodded.

Peter looked at his king from the corner of his eye. "And so's the mare."

Arthur laughed softly to himself.

Chapter 8

Lancelot had just finished attending to Jupiter when he heard a clatter of hooves in the stable yard and the shout of a groom. With a parting slap of Jupiter's black rump, he went to see who was arriving in such a hurry and found himself transfixed by a vision. She sat astride a snow-white mare, her brown hair blown back from her brow and tumbling in an unruly braid to her hips. Her lips were parted, and her face flushed from the exhilaration of the gallop. She looked as if she had risen straight from a lover's bed.

Concealed within the shadow of the stable, Lancelot stared and knew the torment of desire. It was self-inflicted, he knew. He need never have accepted the offer of stabling for Jupiter; they could have been on the road by now. And yet the freedom of the road was no substitute for the glorious sight tantalizing him now. He had told Arthur that everything was chance, that the road did not matter, but he knew in his heart that it was not true. It was not chance that had led to his decision to stay.

Guinevere dismounted from the saddle with casual, almost masculine ease; and the groom who had come running at the sight of her entrance reached for the reins. Immediately the mare began to frisk and jitter. Her eyes rolled and she launched a kick at the man.

"It's all right," Guinevere said with a smile. "I'll take her in myself. I want her to get to know me."

Looking relieved, the groom bowed and departed. Guinevere kept a firm hold on the reins, but with her free hand soothed and patted the mare, making sure she was quiet before leading her into a vacant stall. Lancelot followed Guinevere. Besides wanting to admire her wild beauty, he was curious to know more about her. It was not given to every young woman of her rank to be so familiar and confident with horses, especially high-spirited hellions like that mare. Perhaps each was at home with the other's temperament. He grinned at the thought and leaned against the stable door to watch Guinevere tend her mount. She unbuckled the saddle girths, then paused to make a fuss of the mare, whispering words into an attentively pricked ear. The horse responded by nuzzling Guinevere's cheek and snorting gustily. Lancelot was impressed. Many people were good with horses, but few had the ability to strike up an immediate rapport. Guinevere whispered to the horse again, and Lancelot found himself wishing that she would do that to him.

"What are you saying to her?"

Guinevere whirled around with a gasp of surprise.

When she saw Lancelot, hot color flooded her face, emphasizing the green and gold flecks in her eyes. "It's our own private language," she said, and then, gathering herself, acting as if she did not care about his presence, she resumed attending the mare, whispering in her ear and receiving another nuzzle.

Utterly enchanted, Lancelot left the door and entered the deeper intimacy of the stall, going to stand at the horse's other side.

"Careful," Guinevere warned. "She doesn't like strangers."

"I am not a stranger," Lancelot said and stroked the mare with a gentle hand. Then he, too, cupped a white ear and made a soft sound. The horse responded by thrusting her muzzle down into his hand and nudging him. "See?" He looked at Guinevere and smiled.

Guinevere's own lips curved despite her intention to keep them straight. Once more she spoke to Moonlight and received a gentle nuzzle. Lancelot did the same. The horse both separated and united them. Guinevere looked at his tanned fingers upon the silvery white hide, and it was almost as though it were her own body he touched. A shiver ran down her spine. Lancelot's gaze was a slow, hot smolder, and she knew that she must keep her distance or else be burned. Lancelot murmured again in the mare's ear, and Moonlight nuzzled him once more, lipping at the coarse brown fabric of his jerkin.

"All right, what are you saying to her?" Guinevere's tone was light and bantering, acting as a shield.

Lancelot smiled and the creases at his eye corners deepened. "You first, my lady—as is your privilege."

Guinevere hesitated for a moment, and then capitulated. If anything would ease the tension between them, the sweet, comical whiffling noise she used to Moonlight would. Lancelot's quizzical smile became an open grin.

"Now yours," she commanded, tapping her foot.

He pursed his lips and responded with a similar sound, its tone a little deeper, and then he laughed. So did Guinevere. Then, shy, more than a little afraid of him, she turned away, intending to remove the saddle.

"No, please, let me." Lancelot took the saddle from her, lifting its weight with ease. He was neither a large man nor heavily muscled, but he possessed a wiry strength, and catlike sureness of limb that served him better than brute force. Guinevere set about unbuckling the bridle instead.

"I didn't expect to see you again so soon, and in Camelot." She darted him a not altogether friendly look.

"I didn't expect you to be marrying its king," he retorted.

Her lips tightened. Why could he not have taken his reward in coin and ridden away? It was what any ordinary man would have done. But then, she was beginning to realize that he was not an ordinary man. "You seem to have made quite an impression on him."

"Oh?"

"You were the main subject of conversation at the evening feast last night. You interest him."

"He wants to save me from myself." Lancelot

rubbed the mare's sweat-salty back where the saddle had rested, and gave her a piercing look. "He doesn't know, does he?"

Guinevere busied herself with Moonlight's tack. "Doesn't know what?" her tone was offhand, a little defensive.

"That you and I have met before. For all you say I was the main subject of conversation, I doubt that you enlightened him."

Guinevere flushed at his barb. "If you want me to tell him of your service to me, then I will."

He looked her up and down and slowly smiled. "No, it can be our secret."

Guinevere's embarrassment deepened, for she could see that the word *service* was ambiguous and might refer to more than just her rescue from Malagant's brigands. Her jaw tightened and she held her ground. "I have no secrets from the king."

"Of course not."

Guinevere opened her mouth to snap at him but checked herself. It was what he expected. He was deliberately baiting her, working upon her temper to make her more vulnerable. Well and good, she would not fly to his lure. "So," she said in a tone of polite interest, "how long will you be staying in Camelot?"

This time it was he who opened his mouth, then changed his mind between the thought and the word. "I have no plans—what makes you ask?"

"You know I am very grateful for your help in the forest. But I think it would be as well if you were to leave."

He eyed her across the mare's withers, his gaze disconcerting and direct. "Why?"

Guinevere felt her face grow hot again. A knot of confusing emotions was growing and tightening within her. "Because of the way you look at me," she muttered. "And you know it full well."

Lancelot tilted his head to one side. "How do I look at you?"

"As if"—she caught her breath—"as if everything were possible."

"Everything is possible," Lancelot said in a reasonable, matter-of-fact voice. His utter confidence silenced Guinevere. How did she deal with a man like this, short of commanding his arrest and having him thrown out of Camelot and her life? But how could she do that when he had saved her from death at great peril to himself?

"You know very little about me," she said, and this time there was a look of pleading in her eyes. "But I think . . . I hope . . . you wish me to be happy."

A strange expression crossed his face, almost of pain, she thought.

"Yes," he said warily. "I wish you to be happy."

"You say that everything is possible, but that is not so. I have made my decision. It is carved in stone. I will marry Arthur."

"And that will make you happy?"

Guinevere sighed at him and, leaving Moonlight to her feed and water, went to the stable door. "If I marry Arthur, how could I not be happy?" She spoke with determination. Lancelot did not reply, but she was powerfully aware of his presence behind her and of the brooding stare that plucked at the doubts she had so carefully buried, exposing them once more to the raw air of daylight.

Chapter 9

*N*ear the great stone crosses that marked the boundary between Camelot and Leonesse, a shepherd was grazing his flock of spotted sheep and contemplating the wispy veils of cloud high in the blue when his dog whined and laid back its ears, its tail cringing between its hind legs.

Alerted, the man turned and looked to the road beyond the crosses, where Camelot's writ did not run. Beneath his feet the ground was vibrating. His long-sighted gaze narrowed on the horizon, and in the summer haze he saw a dark mass of horsemen approaching like a black thundercloud. They were not the royal guard of Camelot, for no such party had been abroad recently except to fetch the lady Guinevere to her wedding, and they had been back for almost two weeks. Nor could it be troops from Leonesse. That country possessed nothing so intense or fearsome.

The shepherd crouched down behind a rock and whistled his dog to his side. The sheep ceased their grazing and, with baas of alarm, galloped away from the roadside. The troops drew nearer, and from his hiding place, the shepherd saw that they were clothed in the dark armor that had become Prince Malagant's symbol of oppression and terror. Not that Malagant had ever attempted anything on the lands belonging to the High King, but the shepherd had heard enough tales to shrink in dread as the troop crested the hill by the stone crosses. There were at least a hundred hard-faced warriors, and all of them armed to the teeth.

Prince Malagant himself rode at their head, a tall, thin-faced man, black of hair and eye to match his garments. He had noticed the cowering shepherd and his dog, but he withheld the command to destroy. Camelot was still an unknown quantity, an unknown strength, and he was not prepared to test it until he had satisfied himself that he was the stronger.

He slowed his horse and his troops slowed, too. Then he drew rein and held up his gloved fist in a halting motion. Camelot lay spread out before him like a victory feast presented to a ravenous man. He gazed upon the silver lake, the pale gold turrets and crenellations shining in the sun, the blue slate roofs and the fluttering banners proclaiming Arthur's residence and authority. "Camelot," Malagant growled with pleasure, and a thin smile slashed across his face. As he and his men pressed forward onto the causeway, the hammer of hoofbeats mingled with the ringing of the city's cathedral bells.

Within the bell tower of Camelot's magnificent cathedral, monks pulled upon the striped ropes to ring the hour of noon over the city. The enormous bells heaved from side to side, and the clappers swung within their dark caverns. Up on his hill, the shepherd, still queasy from his near encounter with Malagant's troops, heard the chime clear and true. In the city square, people ceased their conversations or market haggling to wait until the bells had marked the time.

Within the royal palace the noontide clamor also marked the opening of a session of the High Council. The doors to the Round Table chamber were opened by two guards, and a fanfare was sounded to announce the arrival of the eleven knights entitled to a place at the famous table. Monks from the cathedral who served as scribes and functionaries took their seats on chairs that were set upon the raised dais running around the perimeter of the circular room. The scribes had large wax tablets and wooden styli upon which to make notes, should any proclamations be ratified.

Each knight stood before his allotted segment of the round table, his sword facing him hilt first. Arthur was the last to enter, Guinevere on his arm, her serving women pacing behind. Arthur tilted his head to murmur to Guinevere, and with a nod and a smile for him, she left his side and walked gracefully to take her place upon another section of the raised circular dais where a royal chair worked in silver filigree gilding had been set out for her.

Arthur paused before his own seat and looked around the table at the gathering of eleven knights—twelve including himself. The thirteenth place was empty, no sword laying upon its section, no man standing beside the ornate carved chair. This was Malagant's place, or had been until he had quarreled with the High Council last spring and flung out, vowing that they were all soft-minded fools. As yet his position remained open, for Arthur had hoped that the rift could be healed. Now, knowing what he did, he had resigned himself to the fact that it could not. The position would be filled when he found a man suitable.

One last time Arthur intended it to serve for Malagant, indeed he had openly invited the man to this session of the High Council, but it seemed that his former comrade and confidante had chosen not to attend. It was not chance, but choice, Arthur thought grimly. Lancelot was wrong.

The last note of the noontide clarion faded to echoes, and as silence fell, Arthur raised his voice in the simple customary prayer that always opened a session of the High Council.

"May God grant us the wisdom to discover the right, the will to choose it, and the strength to make it endure."

"Amen," declared the knights in unison. Everyone sat.

Arthur looked around the table at the men who were his bodyguards, his companions, advisers— and friends. No man could be more fortunate. On that thought his gaze flickered to Guinevere, and a warmth kindled at his core. One moment she was controlling a half-wild white mare, the next she was as dignified and as regal as a queen, both images overwhelmingly beautiful.

She returned his glance with a smile. Smiling

himself, Arthur addressed the knights. "My friends, as you know, I shall soon be married and—" He had to stop as one and all the men banged the table with their fists in a traditional soldier's salute of approval.

"About time, too!" Sir Patrise cried. "At one time we despaired that you would ever come to it!"

Still smiling, Arthur waited until the noise had died down, then continued. "We have had our share of war in the past, but now I look forward to quieter days. But first, there is one more matter to be resolved. I had hoped that—" He paused and stared toward the door as they all heard the sound of approaching footsteps, hard with the jingle of spurs. Arthur felt twin surges of relief and anxiety. Malagant had come after all.

Rising to his feet, he signaled two servants to open the round chamber doors. A tangible ripple of antipathy ran around the men seated at the table when they saw Prince Malagant standing upon the threshold backed by an escort of his dark-clad soldiers. Malagant himself was elegantly but starkly dressed in his black armor. He would have been a handsome man, were it not for the sneering line of his mouth and the acquisitive glitter in his black eyes. His features were powerful and clean, his black hair short-cropped so that it clung to his skull like a shadow.

"Admit our guest," Arthur said, clothing himself in cold dignity. "Prince Malagant is here at my invitation, and he has my protection." A swift glance in Guinevere's direction showed him that she had stiffened in her chair and that her knuckles were white on the carved armrests. If looks could have killed, then Malagant would have been smitten dead where he stood, the king's protection or not.

A cynical smile on his lips, Malagant entered the chamber, gesturing his lieutenants to remain outside. He bowed to Arthur, then turned toward the dais and inclined his head to Guinevere, his face wearing a mask of suave charm.

"May I congratulate the king on his forthcoming marriage?" Malagant said courteously.

Ashen-faced, Guinevere returned his look, her eyes burning, but she retained enough control not to speak.

Malagant swung away and strode across the chamber, his footsteps echoing, until he reached the empty chair and the swordless section. "I see my place has not been taken yet," he commented. "Once a knight, always a knight."

"You left the council of your own free will," Arthur responded coldly. "If your place is still empty, it is because I intend to choose your successor with great care."

Malagant lifted his shoulders. "We must each of us follow his own road, my lord. And my road had farther to go than yours."

"And where does yours take you, Malagant?" Arthur said, and although he was trying to keep his tone on the level, a note of hostility crept in. "To Leonesse?"

Malagant seemed unaffected by Arthur's challenge. The half smile never slipped from his face, and his own voice remained unchanged—reasonable and smooth. "Leonesse is my neighbor, and I would like to say my friend. I have offered the

Lady of Leonesse a peace treaty to benefit us both. I await her answer."

One of the clerks rose from his chair at the side of the room and handed Arthur an embellished parchment. "The treaty, Sire."

Arthur took it without comment, but Guinevere could not hold silent any more.

"You call burning villages an act of friendship?" Her lips curled back from her teeth in what was almost a snarl.

Malagant inclined his head to her, a slightly pained expression on his face, as if he were being greatly wronged. "I am afraid in this instance I do, my lady. Since your honored father's death, your country has grown more lawless by the day. Thieves and murderers roam the land. Travelers take their lives in their hands when they cross Leonesse." His voice increased in strength, reaching everyone seated in the great round chamber. "Lawlessness is a disease that infects all it touches. Yes, I have burned it out where I've found it, and yes, I call that an act of friendship."

"There is no lawlessness in Leonesse!" Guinevere retorted in fury. "You lie, you are the poison!"

"Forgive my ignorance, my lady, but were you yourself not attacked on the road here?" Malagant spread his hands in a gesture of appeal to the other men present as if saying, *"Look at this hysterical woman. She is not fit to rule."*

Guinevere gritted her teeth. "You know very well who attacked me!"

"I have made it my business to know. My men have hunted the bandits down and justice has been done. The iron fist is the only language that such

124

men fear and respect." He clenched his own fist and raised it to illustrate the point.

"Justice!" Guinevere exclaimed, and a shaken laugh was drawn from her. "You know no law higher than yourself!"

Malagant ignored her and instead bowed to the king. "I learned all that I know from a great teacher."

Arthur did not respond to that particular remark, for his attention had been on the treaty in his hand. A frown between his dark brows, he said aloud, "Armed forces to be given access to all Leonesse . . . troops to assist in the enforcement of law in all Leonesse . . . ?" He looked to Guinevere. "Do you want to sign this?"

Her jaw quivered. "I'll never sign it." She seethed.

Arthur put the treaty from him. "There's your answer," he said coldly to Malagant. "She says no."

The prince looked scornful. "She's very brave now that she's to be married to the High King." He folded his arms and paced over to Arthur. "So tell me, my lord, is Leonesse to come under the protection of Camelot?"

"Is Leonesse in need of protection?" Arthur countered. Although he remained outwardly calm, inside he was simmering with a rage as red as Guinevere's.

Malagant gave Arthur a man-to-man smile that pushed Guinevere even further toward insignificance. "Come, I'm here to settle this business in friendship. We both know that Leonesse is too weak to stand alone. Let us say—half each. The lesser gives way to the greater. And what nation is greater than Camelot, the land of justice, and the hope of mankind?" The timbre of his voice might or might not have been mocking. He held out his hand to Arthur, swordsman's blisters hard on his palm. "Shake upon my offer, and we all live together as friends."

Arthur did not take Malagant's hand, and his eyes were filled with disgust. "You offer me what is not yours to give."

Malagant continued to smile, but the expression was frozen on his face without warmth or meaning. His hand remained outstretched, and he appealed to the gathering of knights seated around the table. "You all know me. I rode with you for more than fifteen years. You know that I'm a man of my word. Don't make an enemy of me. I mean no harm to Camelot."

"You would eat the world if you could," Guinevere muttered beneath her breath.

Arthur glanced at her briefly before answering Malagant in a voice of quiet but powerful conviction. "You know the law we live by." Reaching to the center of the table, he ran his hand over the silver letters incised there, walking slowly around until he faced Malagant once more. *"In serving each other we become free.* Now tell me, where is it written in this room *'Beyond Camelot live lesser people—people too weak to protect themselves—we do not need to care about them, let them die'?"* Arthur stared hard into Malagant's black eyes, but the man did not flinch. Arthur's voice grew husky with the fury he was striving to control. "I tell you now, if we abandon them, their blood will run to our very doorsteps, and the smoke of their burning will sting our eyes until we, too, are weeping."

Malagant gave an indifferent shrug, as if Arthur's words were no more than drops of rain on a waxed warshield. "Other people live by other laws, Arthur," he retorted softly, "or is the law of Camelot to rule the whole world?"

"There are laws that enslave men and laws that set men free. Either what we hold to be right and good and true is right and good and true for all mankind under God, or we're just another robber tribe, and all our wealth is plunder, and all our glory a hollow show."

Malagant shook his head, the curve of his lips threatening now. Danger stalked the room as a palpable entity, and men tensed in their chairs, glancing at their swords. "Your fine words are talking you out of peace and into war."

Arthur planted himself solidly in the face of the danger as he had done so many times before. For Malagant, there would be no easy way to his desires. "There is a peace that is only to be found on the other side of war. If this battle must come, then I am ready to fight."

Immediately, Agravaine shot to his feet, his blue eyes bright with fervor. "And I!"

"And I, too!" shouted Patrise at his side.

Within moments, the entire complement of knights in the round chamber were upon their feet shouting their allegiance to Arthur, throwing down the challenge to Malagant. Guinevere also rose, pride shining in her eyes, and with gratitude that they were willing to do this for her and the people of Leonesse.

Malagant stared around the gathering and smiled bitterly. "The great Arthur," he sneered, "and his great dream. Say your prayers tonight, my brave friends. No dream lasts forever." With that parting sally, he turned and strode from the chamber, his lieutenants clattering after him.

Chapter 10

Striding through the great castle toward its armory, accompanied by his chief advisers, Arthur turned to Agravaine, who matched paces at his side. "What's the status of the army?"

Agravaine, in his position of constable, was able to pronounce the reply without pause for thought. "Two battalions under arms, my lord, two in reserve."

Patrise, walking just behind them and slapping his gauntlets in his hand as though he were striking Malagant in the face, snapped out a command to a guard captain. "Double the watch on all the gates immediately!"

"Yes, sir!" The man hurried away, his armor glinting in the early dusk.

Mador, the most cautious of Arthur's knights, strove to put his own opinion across above the tumult of the call to arms. "Sire, I don't believe that Malagant wants war with Camelot."

"He wants war," Arthur contradicted grimly. "And he thinks he can win. Agravaine, arm the reserves. A dog that bites an armored man breaks its teeth."

"Yes, sir." His eyes bright with the battle light that conflict always brought to them, Agravaine addressed one of his adjutants. "All battalions full alert. Weapons check in two hours."

Mador gnawed his lip. "He wants Leonesse as a buffer between your lands and his, I . . ."

"He wants Camelot," Arthur snapped. "He always has since the day he came to my court as a stripling youth. You have seen how he repays me. And even if it were true, and he desired Lady Guinevere's lands as a buffer, why should the people of Leonesse have to pay the price?" His stride was short and choppy with the strength of his anger.

Knowing when to beat a strategic retreat, Mador stepped back among the ranks.

Arthur returned his attention to Agravaine. "How soon could Malagant launch an attack?"

"There is no army within five days' march of Camelot at the moment, Sire."

Arthur nodded. "I want scouts sent into Leonesse and all troop movements reported immediately."

"Yes, Sire." Agravaine turned to relay the information to one of his captains.

Kay suddenly appeared at Arthur's side, almost running to keep up. "Sire, what about your wedding? Should it be canceled until after the crisis?"

Arthur hesitated for the briefest instant and then shook his head. "No, Kay, the wedding goes ahead. I would not have Malagant claim even so small a victory. But let it be kept small. The celebrations can wait." His expression became rueful. "My quieter days must wait for a while, eh?"

Guinevere was waiting for Arthur as he emerged from checking the castle armory. She was pale, and there was a slight puffiness around her eyes that suggested she had been weeping in private, but she had herself well under control now. Arthur gestured his men to wait and took her to one side.

"I am sorry that you cannot have the grand wedding that is your right," he apologized. "But later, when it is over, we will . . ."

"I do not care for that!" Guinevere interrupted, her voice as quiet as his own, but filled with passion. "I would go to my marriage in a woodland glade clad in naught but rags if I knew the bridegroom was you! It is I who am sorry that I have brought you to this pass."

Arthur shook his head and gently touched her flushed cheek. "It would have come to this anyway, sooner or later. You need have no guilt, my love. There is only one man to blame, and everyone in Camelot knows his identity." He set his arm around her shoulders and gave them a squeeze. Beneath his hard warrior's muscles and sturdy bones, her frame felt as fragile as glass, but he knew that she possessed a deceptive, tensile strength that enabled her to control a willful eastern mare, and she had courage and spirit to match his own. "All will be well," he murmured. "And I do not say that just to comfort you. I know it in my heart."

Guinevere drew away from him and managed to smile, her head held high for the benefit of the knights standing to one side. "I know it in my heart, too," she said.

And so, instead of preparing for a magnificent wedding, Camelot girded itself for war. Patrols rode out daily and the border guard was doubled. Armorers, fletchers, and weaponsmiths found themselves working all hours under the sun—and the moon. Every man in Camelot was armed at the very least with an ash spear bearing a winged crossbar for ripping away enemy shields. Swords were cleaned and oiled, ax heads sharpened with handheld grindstones. Tall tales of former conflicts were told by fathers and grandfathers around the evening fires. Supplies were stockpiled, and horses commandeered from the countryside.

Lancelot observed all of this bustle from a distance and thought about moving on. Jupiter had been rested for three weeks now, and his hide was glossier than polished jet with all the grooming and concentrated feed. Time and past time, Lancelot told himself, to pack his few belongings into his saddlebag and ride away. And yet he found himself reluctant to do so. Always before, the urge to travel on had been too great to ignore, but this time a pull equally as strong was being exerted in the opposite direction. An inner voice told him that perhaps it was time to stop wandering—to stop running, and face the past in order to gain a solid foothold in the future.

He had not approached Guinevere since their last encounter in the stables, although he had watched her from a discreet distance as she exercised her mare or went among the people of Camelot, boosting morale, winning their hearts just as easily as she had won his. Lancelot had seen her frequently with Arthur, too. He had seen the way of their relationship and knew that it would endure. Each possessed what the other craved in a partner. Arthur needed a wife who was young enough to bear him children and yet mature enough in outlook to be a queen and rule beside him. He also needed Guinevere's youth and beauty to refresh his spirit and gladden his eye. Guinevere's need was the security of an older man's love and protection. A younger man's arms were not so safe.

"Deep thoughts?" queried Peter, the stableman, entering the groom's quarters and sitting down at the trestle.

Lancelot shook his head and smiled.

The young groom reached to the loaf and knife on the table and cut himself a thick slice of bread, which he smeared with honey from an earthenware pot. "There's no more news of Malagant yet. Perhaps he's thought the better of tangling with the High King."

"I hear that he was once one of Arthur's elected knights."

"A long time ago," Peter said through a mouthful of bread. "And a fine warrior he was, too, the best swordsman in the kingdom. But he preferred to go his own way. He wanted his word to be law and did not see why he should bow to the decisions of the Round Table."

"So he was dismissed?"

"Oh no. He left of his own accord before that could happen, but there is bad blood between him and the others. The High King has tried to make peace, but if it comes to war, he's not afraid to fight."

"I know, he showed me his sword."

"Did he now?" Peter looked at Lancelot with interest. "It's famed throughout Camelot. There are as many stories told about that sword as there are about Arthur himself." He stuffed the last morsel of bread in his mouth and dusted his hands. "Are you going to offer your services to him?"

Lancelot placed his hand over his own sword hilt. He could see what the young stableman was thinking. Here was Lancelot, the stranger who had defeated the gauntlet, a craftsman of the blade with a fine black stallion at his command. It was inconceivable that he would not offer to fight for Camelot in this time of peril.

"He hasn't asked me," Lancelot said, and rose to his feet before the conversation drifted into deeper water.

"And if he did?"

Lancelot went to the door. A sarcastic reply was on the tip of his tongue. He could feel Peter's eyes boring into his spine like a hot spear. "I don't know," he said, and stepped out into the early summer dusk.

Ignoring the stable yard, which was busy with the comings and goings of soldiers and grooms, he made his way toward Camelot's ramparts in search of solitude. The problem with living among so many people, he told himself, was the demands they made upon you, crowding your mind until it was impossible to think your own thoughts. On the road with Jupiter, his mind was free to contemplate the natural landscape, to wander with only the impositions of his own discipline. Here, in Camelot, there were too many codes, too many expectations.

Apart from the regular guards on patrol, the city ramparts were silent as dusk fell over the city and candlelight began to glimmer in the houses below. The comforting aromas from cooking fires wafted skyward in thin blue trails of smoke, and the first stars pricked glittering holes in the luminous sky. Lancelot absorbed the calm of the dusk and began to feel less agitated. Tomorrow, he thought, tomorrow I will leave Camelot and let Arthur and his bride have their happiness . . . as I once had mine.

Far away across the lake, his eye rested casually on a rowing boat softly sculling across the water. There was a lamp on its prow, and by its light, he saw that the man at the oars wore a distinctive scarlet hood with a long liripipe. Lancelot's gaze fixed upon the piece of apparel with no small degree of curiosity. A man who wore such a garment certainly intended for the world to know his name. He wondered if he was indulging in a spot of night fishing, for now and then he ceased rowing to pay out a length of rope or line. If fishing was the man's sport, then he would be lucky tonight. Time and again Lancelot saw ripples at the surface, as if of large carp.

Guinevere was seated at the table in her chamber, writing a letter to Oswald by candlelight, when she was disturbed by the entrance of her maid, Petronella. The young woman's gray eyes were wide with concern, and her manner was agitated. Behind her, Guinevere glimpsed the guards whom Arthur had assigned to guard her chamber door lest Malagant should try to harm her.

"Petronella, what is it?"

"My lady, it is Jacob," the maid said in a frightened voice.

Alarmed, Guinevere put down her quill. "Jacob? Where?"

"He's been sighted at the north water gate. One of the guards is a Leonesse man, and he recognized Jacob's hood."

Guinevere jumped to her feet and snatched up her cloak from across a chair. "Something's happened to Leonesse, I know it has!" she cried as she swept it around her shoulders and fastened the clasp. "Pray God we're not too late!" She hastened to the door, flung it open, and hurried toward the turret stairs, the startled guards in rapid pursuit.

Guinevere ran down to Camelot's north water gate, which was protected from enemy entry by a vast iron portcullis, its winding gear housed in the towers flanking the doorway. Panting, her escort followed her under the portcullis and out onto the steps of the landing stage. Flanking the steps were two stone plinths, and braziers of fire burned upon these, giving light and warmth. There were torch sconces either side of the portcullis, too, illuminating the dark water with shimmering patterns of gold. The sentries already on duty there saluted her and stood to attention. Guinevere barely acknowledged them, all her concentration on the approaching rowing boat and the familiar figure with its bright scarlet hood.

"Jacob, Jacob, what is it? What's happened?" She stepped as close to the water's edge as she could without wetting her soft indoor shoes, and peered into the darkness.

In the boat, the rower's reply was muffled in the depths of his hood. He busied himself maneuvering the boat toward the mooring post at the foot of the stairs. Frantic with anxiety, Guinevere reached out her hand to help him up.

"Please, for pity's sake, tell me. What news of Leonesse?"

The rower raised his head, and his hood slipped back, revealing a face of hard cadaver planes, the visage of a brigand and deceiver, not her trusted, beloved Jacob. Guinevere cried out and pulled back, but it was already too late. Malagant's man had grabbed her hand, and with a swift wrench, he toppled her into the boat, landing her like a fish. Guinevere kicked and struggled, but to no avail. Her abductor had the tough muscles of an active fighting man, and he was twice her weight and strength. She screamed for help, unable to believe that this could be happening in the heart of Camelot, where she had thought herself safe.

All around the boat there were thin hollow reeds poking out of the water. These were breathing conduits for more men. From beneath each one rose a darkly clad swimmer. Shouting the alarm, the sentries and soldiers ran to Guinevere's aid but were intercepted by the swimmers, who were armed with crossbows and ripswords. The clash of weapons, the screams of injury echoed across the night. Camelot's guards floundered in the water, were dragged under by their armour, or were run through on the steps of the landing stage. The gold reflection of torchlight shattered and churned on the surface of the lake.

Upon the ramparts, Lancelot stared at the chaos below. At first he was frozen by surprise but rapidly regained his faculties. The fools, he thought. Could they not even protect her when they had all the advantages? He saw the white flurry of Guinevere's gown as she fought her attacker, and he heard her desperate cries for aid that was not forthcoming. The rower was striving to hold her; at least he could not make good his escape while she occupied his hands so thoroughly. But the man did not have to set his hands to the oars. The rope over which Lancelot had earlier puzzled, thinking it a fishing aid, now snaked up out of the water and drew taut against the knot on the prow. Dripping with jewels of water, it tracked a path across the neck of water to the far bank of the lake. A team of powerful carriage horses had been harnessed to the free end, and now they were whipped into gallop. The rowing boat raised its snout and plowed a furrow of white water across the lake. Fast, faster, tearing away from the landing stage and the fighting that still continued. There was no one to stop Guinevere's abduction.

Lancelot hoisted himself onto the top of the rampart. His palms were scraped by the stone, but he did not notice, for the blood was coursing too quickly through his body, singing in his ears. He poised upon the top of a crenellation and gazed down sixty feet to the polished black water below. The rowing boat passed in front of the section of wall on which he stood. Gauging his angle, as he had gauged himself on the gauntlet, Lancelot sprang upward and outward from the battlements, and dived like a fish eagle. Cold night air parted and streamed past his body, arrowed palms, dipped head, straight legs. He hit the lake with a small explosion of displaced water and, for a moment, continued going down. Black coldness enveloped him, embraced him, desired him to stay, but he kicked for the surface, and broke free in a spray of crystal droplets, his breath coming in short gasps from the shock of the sudden cold. For a brief instant he trod water while his body adjusted to the change in temperature. Torchlight rippled on the water, showing him that he had calculated his position well. He was in front of the rowing boat, just a few strokes away from the taut rope. It also revealed that he had no time to lose.

Drawing a deep breath, he swam to intercept the rope, seized the rough, wet hemp, and closed his grip hard about it. It was like riding a wild horse. He was torn through the water at speed. His face went under, he accidentally inhaled and broke the surface choking, spluttering, and spewing water. The rope burned his fingers; he could feel the welts rising across his palms despite the fact that they were toughened by swordplay. He gritted his teeth and hung on. If he could defeat the gauntlet, then he could defeat a rope and a rowing boat.

Hand over hand, enduring the burn of the water-heavy hemp, he made his way toward the boat and cursed the fact that he had no knife in his belt with which to cut the rope. It would have been easy then. As it was, Lancelot fought the drag of fast water against his legs and the bucking of the small craft and reached the prow. He released the rope, gripped the wet, dark wood, and prepared to haul himself on board.

Guinevere's abductor had both hands occupied in trying to keep her subdued. She kicked and fought, bit and screamed like a fishwife. He was hard-pressed not to use his fist on her. Only the knowledge of what Prince Malagant would do to him if she was harmed prevented him from doing so.

"Curse you, be still!" he panted, sweat springing on his brow.

Lancelot lifted himself, water streaming from his hair and garments, making him look like a merman. The hooded man glanced up then, alerted by the rocking of the boat. His hands were needed to keep Guinevere pinned down, but not his feet. A foot flashed out and a hobnailed boot slammed down across Lancelot's knuckles. Lancelot snatched his hand away, the pain a white-hot blur. He lost his momentum and sank back into the water, but his left hand still had a grip on the boat's side. The abductor kicked again, determined to dislodge him. This time he just missed as Lancelot changed hands, but it was an unequal battle, one that Lancelot for all his courage and resourcefulness could not win.

The hooded man's boots hammered Lancelot's fingers so hard that he could no longer keep hold. His abused hands refused to curl and grip, and the boat surged away from him, its wash bouncing him about like a cork on the tide. Treading water, his hands numb, he watched it draw away from him toward the shore. A white flurry of gown revealed that Guinevere was still struggling against her abductor.

Lancelot could have given up then, swum back to Camelot, and been praised as a hero for trying, but his defeat only made him the more determined to have Guinevere out of their clutches. And this time, it was not just for the sake of the challenge but for Guinevere . . . and for himself. As he struck out for the shore, following in the rowboat's wake, he felt anger and fear, emotions long suppressed in the depths of his mind but now rising to the surface in small bubbles of revelation.

He did not trail the boat all the way to its destination but hauled himself onto the grassy shore a small distance away. To have swum to dry land where the craft beached would have meant instant death, for armed men and horses were waiting to greet the hooded man and his hostage. Guinevere was manhandled out of the boat, and Lancelot saw that her wrists had been tied. His anger increased, burning white-hot and dissipating the nocturnal chill of the lake water. He headed for the tree cover above the bank and vanished into its lofty darkness.

Across the water from Camelot's north gate came the sounds of shouting and panic. The attack force, its task accomplished, disengaged and set out across the lake, swimming toward the tethered horses waiting on the other bank.

Guinevere was bundled across a saddle and hemmed around by dark-clad soldiers so that there was no means of escape.

"Well done," Ralf said to the man with the scarlet hood. "You will be rewarded for this."

The man bowed his head in acknowledgment and peeled off the head covering. "I was given a few difficult moments crossing the lake," he said. "Someone jumped clean off the ramparts into the water and tried to stop me. I fought him off, but he was a persistent swine. Could still be about somewhere. I'd tell the lads to keep their eyes peeled if I were you."

Ralf narrowed his eyes. "I do not need to be told

how to do my job," he said coldly, and dismissed the man. But when he had gone, Ralf detailed two men to remain behind and wait for the swimmers. "Guard the horses," he said brusquely, "and keep your eyes on the water. One of them might not be ours."

"Yes, sir."

Ralf swung into the saddle and joined the crowd surrounding Guinevere. "Come," he said, his eyes preying upon the slender young woman, her dark hair streaming in disarray over the white linen of her gown. "Let us take our royal guest to a court befitting her beauty."

The horses thudded into motion, the night sky reflecting on their dark hides.

The two remaining soldiers walked down to the lakeside and stared out across the water to the ripples of their own men, then searched the nearer ripples for signs of larger movement. Behind them, the horses quietly cropped the grass, the only sound the soft tearing of their teeth and the jingle of their harness.

From the cover of the trees, Lancelot watched Malagant's men. Their hands nervously gripped their sword hilts, and their voices were gruff with tension. As well they might be. Across the water, Camelot would be thronging like an ant's nest poked by a stick, and soon enough riders would be crossing the causeway in search of the culprits. A frog plopped, and the soldiers half drew their weapons. Lancelot's gaze flickered to the grazing horses. The nearest animal was about the same size as Jupiter. Almost beneath his breath, he made the soft nickering sound that he had made to Guinevere's mare.

The animal raised its head and pricked its ears in his direction. Lancelot slipped stealthily from the cover of the trees, untied the grazing rope, and swung himself into the saddle. The horse sidled and sidekicked once, then responded to the tug on the bit and turned. Lancelot kicked its flanks and slapped the reins down on its neck, and it broke into a gallop.

The two soldiers whirled around from observing their frog ripples and, with shouts of dismay, ran to their horse lines. The black stallion that Lancelot had stolen was the personal property of one of the guards, and he was furious as he untethered another horse and mounted up.

"I'm going to cut out his heart and nail it to Camelot's doors!" he cried, and punched his spurs into the substitute's flanks.

Riding faster than was prudent over dark terrain on a horse he did not know, Lancelot heard the thunder of hooves in pursuit and the rasp of weapons clearing scabbards. His enemies might or might not outrun him, but whichever way, the pounding gallop would founder his mount and foil his hopes of rescuing Guinevere. Besides, Lancelot had always preferred to be the hunter, not the hunted. There was a leather sheath on the saddle from which protruded a sword hilt. Lancelot controlled the reins with his left hand, and with his right, reached down and drew the weapon forth. It was a reasonable blade, a little crude, but it would serve his purpose.

The men in pursuit were closer now, goading their horses to match the pace of Lancelot's. The leading rider came up alongside. Lancelot turned in his saddle, met the blow launched at him with a parry, and guided his own horse with his knees and thighs so that it worked with him, aiding his sword arm. Trees flashed past, blacker shapes in the starlit darkness. Lancelot ducked beneath a sweeping cut that would have taken off his head had he been slower. He had the advantage of speed and lightness, but his opponents had the benefit of leather armor and numbers. Two to one on a forest path at night should have been a foregone conclusion, but then Lancelot had never played by the odds or the rules.

His horse was no better than theirs, but his horsemanship was, and the same went for his sword. He held them at bay, blocking and parrying. Then, as he took their measure, he came off the defensive and attacked. The man who played with his sword in marketplaces for money was not playing now. Neither of his adversaries stood a chance. The blade flashed and then bit clean through armor and flesh. The first soldier died, his sword only half raised to the parry position. His companion had time for a single cry of denial before he, too, folded over his saddle and then fell from his mount with a dull thud.

The riderless horses kept pace with Lancelot for a time, flitting between the trees like racing spirits, their stirrup leathers thumping against their flanks and their breath snorting hard. Then they took their own way, and Lancelot was alone. He eased his own blowing mount to a slow trot, wiped the bloodied sword on the saddle cloth so that it would not become rusty, and returned it to its sheath. Now all he had to do was trace Malagant to his lair and snatch Guinevere from out of his jaws.

Chapter 11

$\mathcal{T}$aken?" Arthur demanded of the white-faced Sir Tor. "Taken where? Explain yourself, man!"

Sir Tor was flanked by two companions for moral support, but that did not make breaking this news to Arthur any easier. "A boat came to the north gate, Sire. Lady Guinevere was tricked into going down to the landing stage in the belief that a trusted manservant of hers from Leonesse had brought urgent news." He grimaced. "Only the man in the boat was one of Malagant's spies, and he snatched her away."

Breathing hard, Arthur glared at the hapless young man. His chest felt as if it was going to explode. "I do not believe this," he whispered hoarsely, clenching and unclenching his fists. "Wasn't she guarded? How could she not be safe in the heart of Camelot?"

"It all happened too suddenly, Sire, and it bears the stamp of careful planning."

Arthur glared at Tor as if he loathed him. Tor looked miserably back and then lowered his eyes.

Arthur swallowed on his fury. Hurling recriminations was not going to get her back, and the morale of his knights had taken a serious mauling as it was. "Then our own planning was not careful enough," he snapped. "Patrise. Bring Patrise here. I want him now!"

A servant departed on the run.

Arthur paced the room like a caged beast. He paused beside a wine flagon, stared at it as if he did not know what it was, and as a servant hurried to pour him a drink, turned away and paced back to the knight. "Which way was she taken?"

"Into the forest, Sire. They had horses waiting on the far bank."

Arthur cursed beneath his breath and pushed his fingers through his short silver hair. And from the forest into the heart of Malagant's territory, which was mostly an unknown wilderness.

There was a perfunctory thump of a fist on the door, and Patrise entered the royal chamber, his chest heaving with the speed of his run up the stone stairs in half armor. Hard on his heels came Agravaine and several other knights, all of them on their mettle.

Patrise strode up to Arthur and bowed. "I have scouts out already, Sire, and the mastiffs with the keenest noses have been taken from the kennels and set on the trail. Give me a battalion of guards. Give me the men, Sire, and I'll get her back."

"No, that would be playing into his hands. A battalion is just the right size morsel for him to cut up and swallow on his own ground. Take a full brigade, Patrise."

"Yes, Sire!" Patrise saluted and left as rapidly as

he had arrived. Arthur met Agravaine's somber blue stare with an anguished one of his own.

The knight cleared his throat. "He'll not harm her, Sire. She's too valuable to him alive. My guess is that he will try to trade her for what he wants."

Arthur gnawed viciously on his thumb knuckle. "That's what I'm afraid of."

Agravaine swallowed and said nothing more, for there were no words to comfort Arthur's pain. The High King knew the stakes all too well.

"I would give my life for her, Agravaine," Arthur said softly. "But what if he asks for more than I can give?"

And again, Agravaine had no answer.

The walls seemed to be closing in upon Arthur, compressing his emotions until they were concentrated to a level where he felt he would explode. He could not bear the looks of pity and concern cast at him by his servants and retainers; he could not bear the burden of being so helpless.

"If there is news, send someone to find me," he said to Agravaine. "Otherwise, let me be." He headed toward the door like a swimmer with bursting lungs striving toward the surface.

"Where will we send to?" Agravaine asked, not unreasonably.

"The stables or the garden, somewhere that does not hem me around," Arthur said without looking around, and increased his pace.

Once out in the courtyard, the stifling sensation eased and so did the panic. He breathed deeply and stared up at the starlit sky, knowing that somewhere Guinevere would be seeing the same stars. Surely, surely, Malagant would not harm her. But as he gazed toward the distant pinpoints of light, Arthur was sure of nothing but his fear for her. Once he had thought himself complete, a man whole and mature. Now all he knew was that he was a mass of fragments, bound together with such fragility that one more blow would scatter his particles irrevocably to the four winds.

The stable yard was momentarily quiet. Scouting patrols had already ridden out, and the guard's horses were housed in another complex beyond the inner one. Arthur passed the marble fountain where he and Guinevere had stood and talked of duty and of love while the young stableman had saddled a pure white mare. He remembered the touch of her lips upon his knuckles, the smile in her eyes, all her bright, young radiance. He groaned aloud and strode on across the courtyard, but his anguish strode out with him. The top door of the mare's stall was open, and she was moving restlessly within, as if she sensed that something was wrong. When she saw Arthur, she swung her head over the half door and nickered to him. The man approached her and drew comfort from stroking her warm hide even while the thought filled his mind that Guinevere might never ride her again. In the stall next door another horse moved restlessly, and in a moment, Lancelot's handsome black stallion came to look out. His jaws busily working on a wisp of hay, he pricked his ears at Arthur. The white mare nickered again, and the black responded with a similar sound.

"Where is your master?" Arthur asked the horse, and stroked the velvety dark muzzle. "We need men of his daring and courage this night."

A footfall on the gravel behind him made Arthur turn rapidly to face Peter, the stableman. "Am I to have no peace?" he demanded.

Peter lowered his gaze and shuffled his feet. "I'm sorry, Sire. I came to look at Jupiter here, make sure he was all right, being as Lancelot is not back yet. He always checks his horse before he retires. I'll return later."

Arthur exhaled slowly and took control of himself. The lad had as much right as he to be here, probably more. "No," he said with a swift gesture. "Stay, tend the horse."

The young groom bowed and went to the black's stall. After a moment he said hesitantly, "We were all grieved to hear about Lady Guinevere. God pray that she comes home safe."

Arthur nodded briefly, thanked him, and made to walk on, but then paused and looked at the groom and the fine black horse, "Do you know where Lancelot has gone?"

Peter shrugged. "No, Sire. He often wanders off alone."

Arthur gave a pained smile. It was easier for a shabby stranger to find solitude for his thoughts in Camelot than it was for the High King.

Peter hesitated again, drew breath, then shook his head and continued attending the horse.

"What is it?" Arthur asked sharply.

"It might be nothing, Sire, but when Lady Guinevere was taken, there was a rumor that a man dived off the city ramparts and tried to stop the boat. Nothing's been heard or seen of him since—it might not even be true. I was just wondering if that man was Lancelot." Peter stroked Jupiter's silken neck. "He's never late when it comes to tending his horse."

Arthur's heart began to beat faster. "And if it was Lancelot?"

"Would the man who defeated the gauntlet drown?" Peter responded. "If he has not returned, then surely he must be on Lady Guinevere's trail."

Arthur shook his head. "There is too much danger in pinning hopes upon wishes and rumors."

"That is why I was loath to speak, Sire."

Arthur gripped the young stableman's shoulder. "And I was too quick to ask," he said wryly. "I would rather live with danger than with despair."

The cold, white glint of stars and the weak luminescence of a crescent moon was all the natural light that the riders had to illuminate their road across the border into Gore, and so they carried torches in order to maintain a hard pace. Through the dark forest they rode with their prize. Her hands were tied before her with thick cords, her loose hair streamed about her pale face, and Ralf fancied that it wore an expression of fear.

Indeed it did, but that was not the only emotion roiling in Guinevere's breast. Rage and hatred also had their places. They kept her spine stiff, her jaw taut. They held her tears at their source and filled her with a grim determination not to yield so much as a lowered glance to Malagant when she came before him.

His troops hemmed her around, making escape impossible. Horses rode flank to flank with her own. A marauder guided her mount with a leading rein.

She was well and truly at their mercy, but she would not acknowledge it to their smug faces.

After several hours of riding, they came to a place where the track forked three ways. Guinevere was tiring now and glad of the moment's respite. Her spine ached from the constant jolting, her legs were chafed by the saddle, for she was only wearing her light indoor clothes, and her wrists were burning where the cords scored into her flesh.

Ralf snapped out some brusque commands, and the troop divided into three groups. "One for each track," he said with false pleasantness to Guinevere. "Just in case someone is following."

She gave him a look full of haughty disdain, and he responded with a sneer and kicked her horse so that it plunged forward on his chosen trail and jolted her hard against the saddle cantle. Guinevere stifled a cry, and although she did not utter it, her bitten lips were testament enough.

If someone was following, she thought, then they needed guidance now if they were to be her salvation. She raised her hands, as if trying to ease the bite of the cords, and worked at the neck seam of her linen gown. During her struggle in the boat, it had been slightly torn, and she was able to rip it further and fray off a small piece of embroidery. This she let fly from her fingers. The wind fluttered the scrap of cloth back down the track, and it snagged in a bush close to the three forks. Guinevere, not knowing where it had landed, continued to pluck at her gown, tearing off small strands and fibers and scattering them abroad in the hope that someone would decipher the message.

As dawn approached, the terrain changed. The

forest thinned and gave way to windswept uplands scarred with outcrops of black rock. A bleak land, not given to comfort or warmth. Guinevere thought that it was small wonder Malagant desired the softer, fertile valleys of Leonesse and Camelot for his own if this was his inheritance. She shivered and wished that she still had her cloak, but the garment had been torn off during the fight in the boat.

Her captors approached a craggy hill, and in the faint dawn light she saw the black outline of a massive fortress. The sight filled her with foreboding, but she kept her head high, refusing to show her fear and, glancing around, memorized as much detail as she could. At first, the approach to the great black castle seemed deserted, but as she came closer, she saw flickers of movement. Sword steel glinted, drawing her eyes to a shadowy figure crouched in a crevice of rock. Opposite him was another guard with a spear and shield. Then, as if the first sight had trained her eye, she detected another, and then a fourth. Far from being deserted, the castle approach was heavily guarded, and by silent, camouflaged men. This was surely how the entrance to hell must appear, Guinevere thought as the riders halted and she was pulled down from her mare by Captain Ralf, his face as hard and grim as the landscape. She tossed her hair away from her face, the gesture defiant, but in truth, her heart was shrinking in terror.

Ralf was tense, too; she could sense it in his fierce grip on her arm as he led her through a beaded curtain of dripping water and down a long, dark tunnel carved out of the rock. The black walls glistened with moisture in the illumination cast by sputtering pine-pitch wall torches. Down and down, as if into the throat of a primeval beast. Then she entered its belly as the tunnel opened out into a great underground chamber, hewn from the dark slate stone of the inner hillside.

Ralf halted and held her still beside him. By the light from more torches and crowns of fire burning in wrought-iron braziers, Guinevere stared around at the bare, grim walls. In contrast to Camelot, there were no hangings or tapestries to add color and keep out drafts. The dank air had a musty smell, permeated with resinous overtones from the pine-pitch torches. There was straw on the floor, and what little furniture there was, was crude, ugly, and purely utilitarian. Was this the state of Malagant's soul? She was in more danger than she had ever imagined. The silence became drawn out, and still Ralf neither moved nor spoke but stared straight in front at nothing. Guinevere's unease increased. She rotated her wrists, seeking ease from the binding of the cords, and quelled the urge to speak out just in order to break the heavy atmosphere.

In the deep shadows at the end of the chamber, a darker shadow moved and took on human shape. Torchlight glinted on steel and black leather. "Welcome to my palace, madam," said Malagant in a smooth voice, and advanced into the dim orangey light with the slow purpose of a man relishing the moment.

Guinevere watched his approach and maintained a frozen dignity. She would not let him see how frightened she was.

With eyes as black as the stone of which his stronghold was built, Malagant stared her up and down as if she were a beggar wench masquerading as a lady. His gaze lit upon the torn and frayed neckline of her white linen dress. His fingers followed his eyes, and Guinevere could not help but flinch from their touch upon her skin. She noticed that his hands were beautiful—slender and long-fingered, with a quick grace—and was profoundly disconcerted. Her fear and revulsion redoubled.

"What's this?" Malagant demanded. "Your dress is torn. Ralf!" The snapped command half over his shoulder, brought his adjutant to his side.

"My prince?"

"I gave orders that the lady was not to be touched."

Ralf's eyes darted. "My prince, I didn't . . ."

A massive backhand blow from Malagant's clenched fist floored the captain.

Appalled by such casual violence, Guinevere gazed with fresh loathing upon Malagant as he turned back to her with a smile.

"Your dress is spoiled, madam," he said softly. "And you, almost a queen." Once more he reached to the neck opening of her gown, using both hands now. For a moment he rubbed the fabric between finger and thumb as if feeling its understated richness, and then with a sudden, savage burst of pressure, he tore the gown clean in two from seam to seam. Guinevere gave an involuntary scream, and then tightly clamped her lips so that no further sound would betray her. All that lay between her modesty and Malagant's greedy eyes now was her thin, sleeveless chemise, a garment of the finest pleated linen that clung upon the curve of her firm, young breasts.

"Ralf!" commanded Malagant again, and snapped his fingers.

Dazed, blood trickling from his broken nose, Ralf staggered to his feet. "My prince?"

Malagant gestured at the torn gown lying at Guinevere's feet. "Did you do this?"

"Yes, my prince," Ralf said with unhesitating obedience.

Smiling, Malagant turned back to Guinevere. "This is what Arthur doesn't understand. Men don't want brotherhood, they want leadership."

"You are mad," Guinevere whispered, her face full of revulsion.

The smile never wavered on Malagant's face. "It is Arthur who is mad, not I," he said and, raising his hands, gave a single, sharp clap. At once, soldiers stepped out from every side as if created from the shadows beyond the glare of the torches and braziers. "Mine to command," he said. "Arthur has no power like this." There was relish in his tone, and now he raised his voice so that it would carry to the gathering of warriors.

"I think, under the circumstances, the lady may be released from her bonds." He drew a knife and held it out before him, a sharp hunting dagger, the hilt bound in black leather. "If she so wishes, of course." Malagant made no move to cut the cords at Guinevere's wrists, just held the blade before her eyes, making her understand that any move made would have to be hers. Much as she wanted to spurn him, Guinevere realized that to do so would only be cutting off her nose to spite her face, so to speak. She returned his calculating stare with contempt and, stepping up to him, placed her crossed wrists above the knife blade. With one decisive, downward tug, she severed the cords upon the blade edge and shook them to the ground, where they lay like dead snakes. Then she stepped away from the scent of him, from his bitter, black lust.

Malagant raised his eyebrows, impressed despite himself at her continued defiance. Other women would have been gibbering at his feet long since. He gestured toward the darkness of a tunnel mouth beyond the braziers. "Come," he said. "I would not leave you standing in an outer chamber when there is so much more to see."

Guinevere had seen enough to last her a lifetime, but the choice was not hers. Malagant impelled her forward, and she walked with stiff, reluctant steps. The tunnel sloped downward into the bowels of the earth, its walls slick and black like polished jet. Malagant commanded two guards to light the way with burning torches, and positioned another pair of men behind. "Just a precaution," he said pleasantly to Guinevere. "I doubt that you'll be running anywhere."

When she said nothing, refusing to rise to his bait, he began to tell her about the sunken fortress that was the heart of his domain. "The ancients of Gore say that this was once the greatest castle ever built. Now look at it. Grass grows in the halls where kings feasted, and peasants cart away the mighty walls stone by stone to make shelters for their pigs." A scornful smile twisted his lips. "Such is glory."

Guinevere's eyes were stretched wide to absorb what little light was reflected from the torches. There was an overbearing musty smell, and she wondered how men could bear to live here. Surely it was not their pleasure? She supposed that Malagant kept his soldiers by paying well and punishing hard. And the wherewithal to pay them came from lands such as Leonesse and Camelot. She flickered a sidelong glance at her captor. "What do you mean to do with me?"

Malagant shrugged. "I shall keep you here until Arthur becomes more reasonable."

Her eyes flashed. "He'll not trade Leonesse for my life. I'd rather die. Arthur knows that."

The smile remained on Malagant's face. "Self-sacrifice is really very easy," he said. "It is having to sacrifice someone you love that puts your convictions to the test. I think you will find that Arthur will come around to the merits of compromise."

"Never!" Guinevere spat. "He is too much of a king to yield to such as you!"

Malagant arched his brow. "He is also an old man, growing fond in his dotage."

"And ten times the man you will ever be!"

The smile died on Malagant's face, but he maintained his control. "I commend your spirit, Lady Guinevere, while being disappointed at your foolishness."

The tunnel opened out into another underground chamber, much larger than the hall. Guinevere could not tell its exact dimensions, but the light from the torches touched neither wall nor roof, and although she knew she was deep underground, she had the feeling of echoing space all around her. Every sense stood on edge. Guinevere knew that if she screamed, the reverberations would never cease. Above the steady drip-drip of water in the blackness, there came another sound—the low moan of someone in pain and despair. It raised the hairs on Guinevere's nape, and she had to stifle her own whimper of fear.

One of Malagant's soldiers gave his torch to his companion and hurried over to a winch handle set in the wall. Near to the winch stood a large iron weight. Attached to its top was a heavy ring from which the links of a huge chain disappeared into the darkness above. As the torchbearer wound the winch, his muscles straining with effort, the weight began to rise. The chain clanked and swung. There was a harder, grinding sound as something else began a slow descent from the inkiness of the roof space.

Malagant took Guinevere's arm in a pincer grip and drew her forward. She found herself looking down over the edge of a vertical drop, and gasped. For all she knew, the pit went down forever amen. The moaning sound she had heard earlier was issuing from its depths, and now that she was closer, she could detect a broken sob in the voice below. Her head swam, and despite herself, she swayed in Malagant's grip.

The smile was back on his face now, confidence and relish in his eyes. "This is known as an *oubliette*. It's French for a place of forgetting."

Guinevere shuddered. Malagant took a torch from the soldier, who held two, and tossed it over the side. It fell, end over end, flaring down and down, until it struck the bottom, fifty feet below. It did not extinguish as it landed, merely sputtered, and then burned all the more brightly as the molten pitch coating oozed along the torch shaft. The light it shed cast a terrible sight up to Guinevere. Sprawled upon the floor of the pit were human corpses—some nothing more than white bones, others still wearing rags of rotting flesh. Rats scurried among the remains, red-eyed, fat, and sleek with gorging. Crawling upon the heap of carrion was one man, barely alive. He reached up stick-thin arms, raw with sores, and moaned at Guinevere and Malagant. The latter merely smiled, and Guinevere knew for certain that she was in the grip of a madman. What if he lost his patience and threw her down there? Dear God, it did not bear thinking about, or she would soon be mad herself. She averted her gaze and looked up instead to where the heavy weight was disappearing into the blackness, and in its place, a long timber walkway was descending. The torchlight illuminated dusty oaken planks bound together by ropes and enormous nails, crude and solid. With a thud it landed before herself and Malagant, one end secure, the other reaching out over the *oubliette*.

Malagant took another torch from one of his adjutants and prodded Guinevere forward onto the bridge. "This way, if you please, madam," he said in a softly courteous voice, more chilling than an outright brusque command. Trying not to show him how terrified she was, Guinevere stepped out onto the planks. The bridge swayed, and she had to brace her feet to prevent herself from falling over.

"Have a care," Malagant said behind her. "It would be a great pity if you were to slip."

"I could not say the same for you."

She heard his snort of amusement, and then again he pushed her forward. The other end of the causeway brought her to a square stone platform built out from one wall of the great pit and about ten feet deep. Guinevere stepped off the timber planking onto the cold solidity of stone flags and found herself facing a blank wall. She turned to look at Malagant, but he had only followed her as far as the end of the bridge and showed no intention of stepping off onto the platform. Instead, he gave a signal to the winchman, and as the soldier turned the handle, the walkway rose up and slowly began to swing around.

"Your quarters, madam," Malagant said, the humor still glinting in his eyes. "No bars, no gates, no locks. Just walls of air." The walkway carried him around, back across the pit to the other side and the tunnel entrance. Beneath him, the dying prisoner moaned once more as the torch Malagant had thrown down guttered and extinguished.

"I'm sorry about the noise," Malagant said over his shoulder with mock courtesy. "He'll be quiet in a day or two."

"His company disturbs me less than yours," Guinevere responded, and held her head high, refusing to let him see her terror. He walked on, as if he had not heard, and in a moment, as the torchlight and the footsteps receded, she found herself alone in the dripping dark, with only the despairing cries of one of Malagant's dying victims for company.

Chapter 12

Lancelot had neither torchlight nor familiarity to guide him on the trail of Guinevere's abductors, but he did have the instincts of a hunter and more than fifteen years of experience upon often dangerous roads to guide him. Added to that, the gelding he had taken was bound to have a nose for the comfort of its stable. He spoke to it as he rode and watched the flicker of its ears in response. It did not have Jupiter's fire or intelligence, but it was a sound beast of amiable nature and keen to please.

Riding hard, one ear cocked for sounds of pursuit, the other for any indication of the troop in front, Lancelot came to the fork in the track. A soft curse issued from between his teeth. "Which way now?" he asked the horse. It seemed inclined to take the right fork, but Lancelot was not so sure. Perhaps the road to his mount's stable was not the same road that Guinevere's captors had taken. There were hoofprints gouged in the soft mud of all three pathways, and no indication of which was which.

Lancelot narrowed his eyes, trying to see more clearly in the darkness. Dawn was encroaching from the east, but it would not be light for a couple of hours yet. The horse circled and plunged while Lancelot deliberated. From the corner of his eye he saw something pale fluttering in the long grass bordering the left track. A flower, he thought at first, but then decided it was the wrong shape. Keeping a tight hold on his mount's bridle, he dismounted and led him to the object. It was a torn scrap of linen with a tiny piece of embroidery on one edge, as felt by Lancelot's fingers rather than seen by his eyes. "Well done." He saluted an absent Guinevere with triumph and pride. He closed his fist over the scrap of fabric and leaped back into the saddle, his energy renewed.

The horse plunged and turned one more time, then Lancelot kicked his flanks and urged him to a canter down the left branch. Within a quarter of a mile, Lancelot came across another scrap of fabric snared in a low bush; and caught in a tree were more fibers and three filaments of long hair. He knew, even without benefit of daylight, that their color would be a bright brown, burnished with glints of gold.

Lancelot rode on through the forest and the night gave way to a soft, summer dawn, the sunrise flushed with banners of pink cloud, warning of rain later on. The trees thinned and then petered out entirely. He halted his tired horse in the final, scanty cover and stared out over rugged hills, hazed with the green of coarse grass. Before him, the road ran along a rocky shoreline and wound its way up the side of a craggy promontory pointing out to sea. On the crest of the crag towered a ruined castle, fashioned of black, jagged rock. It resembled, Lancelot thought, a rotten tooth waiting to be pulled.

He dismounted and loosely tethered his horse to a low-lying branch. The animal lowered its head to investigate the sparse grass at its hooves, and Lancelot went forward on foot. The daylight continued to brighten, making his path easier, but the castle remained as black as a silhouette. There was no sign of anyone guarding the approach, the only sounds the whistle of the wind around the sharp rocks and the pounding of the sea on the shore, but Lancelot knew that he was being watched and that weapons were trained upon him with deadly intent.

"You can come out," he cried aloud, spreading his hands and gesturing around. "I'm unarmed and alone."

For a moment there was no response, but Lancelot did not doubt that he was right. He smiled to himself when the first guard stepped out of concealment, a crossbow trained upon the intruder's breast. Others emerged, all replicas of the first with their short-cropped hair, leather armor, and primed crossbows. Lancelot faced them calmly, displaying no emotion whatsoever. It was the way that Malagant behaved with them, and they were accustomed to that kind of command. "Now," said Lancelot, "take me to Prince Malagant."

"What's your business?" demanded the guard who had first broken cover. The crossbow jerked in his hand.

"My business is none of yours," Lancelot replied.

"It concerns Prince Malagant and no one else. Matters will go ill with you if you do not bring me to him."

The guard narrowed his eyes, his finger tensed on the trigger. Lancelot eyed him impassively, and the man's nerve broke. "This way," he growled with a rough jerk of the weapon, and led Lancelot toward the curtain of droplets screening the black mouth of the entrance.

Malagant was sitting at a table near a brazier, breaking his fast on cold lamb, bread, and wine, when Lancelot was escorted out of the tunnel and into the first chamber.

Malagant ceased chewing and stared at the shabby stranger that his guards were ushering before him. The man wore rough breeches and leather leggings that had seen better days. His shirt was of undyed gray homespun, his tunic a similar fabric in brown, and the man himself looked as if he had endured a night in a city's back alleys.

"Who are you?" the Lord of Gore demanded, in a tone that implied he was less than impressed, and continued eating.

"A messenger from the High King," Lancelot said, and flickered a glance around the hall, absorbing detail.

Malagant grunted. "You travel fast."

"Needs must . . . when the devil drives."

The black eyes glittered. Malagant addressed his guards. "He came alone?"

"Yes, my prince. We have searched him, too. He is unarmed."

Malagant ran his tongue around the inside of his mouth. "What's your message?" he asked Lancelot.

"I must know that the lady Guinevere is unharmed first."

"She's unharmed. You have my word."

Lancelot restrained himself from saying that he would rather trust the word of a snake. "I must see her with my own eyes."

"My word is not good enough for you?" Malagant's voice became softly ominous, and beside Lancelot, the guards tensed.

Lancelot shrugged. "I'm a common man, sir. I don't have much use for words. If I can't eat it, drink it, or mount it, then it's no good to me."

Malagant stared. "No one talks to me this way," he whispered, a vein pulsing beneath his jaw. He stabbed a finger at one of the guards. "Cut his throat."

Almost before the words had left Malagant's lips, the soldier had seized Lancelot's hair, forcing back his head. From the sheath at his waist, the guard drew forth a long hunting dagger and laid the razored edge to Lancelot's throat. Lancelot felt the cold burn of the blade—the safest place to be, so he had once told Arthur—and stared into Malagant's frigid black eyes with a complete lack of fear.

The guard, a cautious man, stayed his hand, awaiting Malagant's confirmation of the order, and was rewarded for his prudence with his own life as Malagant changed his mind. "No, let him go. He has a message for me from the great Arthur himself, and I would fain hear it before I commit his body to hell."

The guard released Lancelot, giving him a small push to show that he was still under their control, and returned his knife to his belt.

Malagant waved his hand. "Go on then, fool, see her for yourself." The hand became a pointing finger directed at the two guards. "Take him to the pit, then bring him back here. It'll give me a chance to finish my breakfast in peace." He cut a chunk from the loaf and resumed eating.

The guards led Lancelot out, and Malagant chuckled to himself. "Eat it, drink it, or mount it." He shook his head.

Lancelot, not liking the word *pit* at all, departed with the guards. One man led the way, bearing a torch, while his companion followed behind Lancelot, a primed crossbow at the ready. The tunnel down which they took Lancelot was deep and black. Their footsteps echoed hollowly, and the flame shimmered on wet obsidian walls. Lancelot's rapid gaze absorbed as much as possible. He noticed dark tunnel mouths connecting to the main one and saw the torchlight's reflection on the steady trickle of water curving and flowing away into the darkness. A veritable labyrinth, he thought, the question being was he now at its center or its beginning?

Behind him, the guard was breathing down his neck, and he could almost feel the man's finger twitching on the trigger of the loaded crossbow. Lancelot lengthened his stride slightly, but his eyes remained as watchful as ever. The leading guard rounded a curve and suddenly stopped. Lancelot halted almost on top of him. There was a sudden smell of cold air and space, but it was not pleasant, for there was a fetid taint, too, as if of something rotting. The torchbearer lowered his brand to show Lancelot the sheer drop beneath their feet.

Lancelot stared.

"Lord Malagant's *oubliette*," said the second guard, a hint of relish in his gravelly voice. "He don't suffer fools lightly."

"I am not a fool," Lancelot said absently, for he had looked beyond the gaping maw of the pit, and his mind was distracted by what he saw on the other side. She was standing there, illuminated by a faint shaft of daylight so that she looked almost like a vision. Her loose hair streamed down to her hips, and she was dressed only in her chemise of pleated linen. The shaft of light and the white garment emphasized her pallor and filled Lancelot with emotions of tenderness and fury. If Malagant had been present on the ledge just then, he would have seized him and cast him down into the void. At the sound of voices, Guinevere had turned, and she looked across the abyss and met Lancelot's gaze. Her eyes widened, and for a split second he thought that she was going to cry out to him and thus give the game away, but she controlled herself. A small shudder rippled through her, and she rubbed her arms as if cold, then held them defensively across her breasts.

"You see her?" demanded the torchbearer.

"I see her," Lancelot replied somewhat grimly.

"That's what you wanted and what Prince Malagant ordered us to show you. Let's return."

"No," Lancelot said. "I wanted to see that she was unharmed, and I cannot tell from here. Indeed, to me it seems that all is not well with her. Why is she wearing naught but a petticoat?"

The guard had had enough. "You're coming back with us," he growled. "Lord Malagant will tell you all you need to know."

"No."

The second guard raised his crossbow and pointed it directly at Lancelot's throat. "You heard him, move."

"Go ahead," Lancelot said softly, "shoot."

The man hesitated. His eyes darted to his companion, seeking support.

"Do you have orders to kill me?" Lancelot asked. "I think not. It will go hard with you if you put a bolt through my voice before I have had a chance to deliver my message to your illustrious prince."

The first guard drew his sword. "Grab his arm, Jos. We'll drag him back and see what Prince Malagant has to say."

The second guard removed his finger from the crossbow trigger and pushed the weapon into his belt in order to free his hands for the anticipated struggle. Lancelot moved with the speed of a striking snake. His fisted left hand shot out and punched the first guard's sword arm high on the bicep. The man's fingers opened of their own accord, and the weapon flew up in the air. Lancelot's right hand was waiting and closed hard on the hilt. Almost in the same motion, he launched a slicing blow at his astonished victim. The expression of disbelief was still on the guard's face as he crumpled at Lancelot's feet. A crossbow bolt whizzed past Lancelot's ear and rebounded off the slick black wall behind, then skidded along the floor with a metallic screech. The second guard cast the empty crossbow to the ground and, drawing his sword, ran at Lancelot. Lancelot leaped, adroitly avoiding both the dropped torch and his attacker. The soldier's blow went impossibly wide, unbalancing him, and as he staggered, Lancelot ran in beneath his guard, seized his wrist and, with one sharp tug, sent him toppling over the edge of the pit. There came a falling, agonized scream, a heavy thud far below, and then silence.

Breathing hard, Lancelot checked that the guard on the ground was dead. He did not want a hand snaking out to grasp his ankle and send him the same way as the second guard. Then he picked up the torch and stared across the void at Guinevere. Her gaze met his, full of fear, but equally full of courage and determination.

"Go to your right," she commanded, in a low, urgent voice. "There's a handle in the wall—turn it."

Lancelot moved swiftly and lightly to her bidding. He knew that they had very little time, that Malagant would be expecting him and the guards back in the main chamber and would send others to investigate in very short order. He found the winch handle protruding from the wall just as she had said and, wrapping his hands around it, started winding.

A clanking, grinding sound filled the chamber, echoing and resounding, sending out shock waves through the listening orifice of the tunnel. It was a summons that was bound to bring Malagant's men running, and probably Malagant himself.

"Keep turning!" Guinevere urged. "It's the only way off this platform!"

Cursing beneath his breath, Lancelot increased the speed of his winding. Down from the darkness above his head came a heavy timber walkway, a swinging bridge, suspended from heavy chains and looking a little like a nightmare extension of Camelot's gauntlet.

When the end of walkway came within reach of Guinevere's outstretched arms, she clutched it, intending to guide it down to the base of the platform. But as she did so, a patrol of Malagant's soldiers burst from the tunnel, swords drawn. In the poor light it took them a moment to realize what was happening, and a moment was all that Lancelot needed.

"Hold on!" he bellowed to Guinevere. Then as the guards charged along the ledge toward him, he abandoned the winch, swung the walkway around, and hurled his end with all his strength. It rotated on its central chains, sweeping through the air at head height, and smashed into the guards. They had no chance to avoid the heavy planks, and it toppled them screaming into the pit. At the same time, the rotation brought Guinevere onto the ledge where Lancelot stood beside the winch handle. She released her grip and dropped down beside him.

"Are you all right?" Lancelot asked brusquely. The question was neither sympathetic nor solicitous; he wanted to know if she was capable of rapid flight. Guinevere did not disappoint him. She nodded in a businesslike manner, her body already in motion. Pausing only to grab the pine-pitch torch still sputtering on the door, Lancelot was with her.

Together, they ran from the pit chamber and out into the main tunnel that led back to the main hall.

"There is no way out," Guinevere said urgently. "We cannot win past Malagant's hall. He has guards everywhere."

"Who said anything about winning past Malagant's hall?" Lancelot replied. "You are wrong about there being no way out. See these tunnels?"

He pointed to the dark mouths in the black walls. "See the water running? If it can get out, then so can we." He took her hand and led her into the channel that housed the stream. "All we have to do is follow."

"This is blind faith," Guinevere said, a slight shake in her voice that might have been amusement or fear.

"It is good fortune," Lancelot contradicted, and there was a tremor in his own voice.

They followed the stream ever downward through the glistening black rock. When they arrived at another fork, he chose the one down which the water flowed. There was more of it now, racing and tugging around their feet with little rills of white water. Behind them, distorted by echoes and the very shape of the tunnels, they could hear Malagant's men shouting and the clump of their heavy boots as they ran in search of their quarry. A small, involuntary sob of fear was drawn from Guinevere.

"It will be all right," Lancelot reassured, not sure at all. He always gambled to win, but the odds in his favor were not so certain this time. "Hurry, it can't be far now."

The water surged and gurgled at their feet, guiding them on downward through a maze of tunnels, some so narrow that they had to go in single file, others wide enough for them to run abreast; and run they did, until they were breathless. And still the sound of pursuit rang in their ears, loud with the promise of capture for Guinevere and certain death for Lancelot.

They rounded a sharp corner and were brought up

short by the disastrous sight of a dead end. The tunnel ended in a circular chamber that rose up and up like a wide chimney into darkness. Lancelot held the torch on high, but it showed him only dark rock walls, too wide apart and too smooth to be climbed. And of what lay above that, the torch was too weak to show. In the center of the chamber was a deep, ground-level well into which the stream they had been following flowed.

Lancelot stared up at the chimney, seeking a way up and finding none. Guinevere stood looking down into the well, and now she called him over, her voice quick with excitement.

"Look into the well! Can you see light?"

Lancelot strode to her side and peered down. Beckoning beneath the water, not far down, was the unmistakable greenish gleam of daylight, pale as fine glass.

The footsteps and the voices of their pursuers were closer now. Lancelot looked over his shoulder, and then at Guinevere. "Can you do it?"

Her chin was determined, and although there was fear in her eyes, there was also fire. "Yes," she said. "I would rather die than become Malagant's prisoner again."

Lancelot nodded, and dropping the torch into the well, filled his lungs and jumped after it, kicking to submerge himself. Guinevere drew a deep breath for courage, and followed him.

The water closed over their heads with an icy shock as they made for the translucent glow of daylight. Through a semidark greenness they swam beneath an underwater arch and came into the brighter light beneath the opening. Sunlight was streaming down, diffusing through the water, guiding them up to its beams on the surface.

But Lancelot and Guinevere were unable to reach them, for blocking their exit were the bars of a solid iron grid, and the grid was underwater. Lancelot and Guinevere exchanged desperate glances. They were perhaps a minute away from drowning.

Lancelot turned vigorously and followed the stone wall back into the green semidarkness, abandoning the light. Black stars fluctuated before his eyes and his lungs were tight, bursting with the need to inhale. A final kick and thrust was all that was left in him, but suddenly the tunnel enlarged, allowing a small air space between the water and the arched stone roof. He broke the surface and drew great sobbing lungfuls of air. Guinevere broke up beside him, choking and spluttering, but she had only swallowed a little water, and in a moment, she was all right. Treading water, they looked at each other while their deprived lungs recovered.

"Are you all right to go on?" Lancelot asked when he could speak.

Guinevere nodded. "As long as there is breath in my body," she said with a spark of humor.

Her reply, the way she could make a jest even in these dire circumstances, filled Lancelot's heart to bursting. He had never known a woman like her, probably never would again. She was so close, and yet so out of reach.

"There has to be another way out," he said, and dived once more.

They made their way along the tunnel, swimming from air pocket to air pocket, pausing every now and again to rest for a few moments so that they would not grow too tired. The tunnel changed, growing wider, and they found themselves swimming among weed-covered timbers and stone pillars. Once this had probably been a great undercroft, Lancelot thought, a vast storage hall beneath the castle, probably for cargoes brought in from the sea. He glanced over his shoulder and saw Guinevere swimming resolutely behind him. In her white chemise, her long hair flowing behind her, she looked almost like a mermaid. They were said to lure sailors to their doom. Certainly she had stolen away his heart, and with such ease that he was still reeling.

As Guinevere swam between the weed-covered pillars, following Lancelot with a faith she had never put in anyone before, her foot struck some object and almost became trapped. Kicking vigorously, she turned to look and saw a loosely assembled suit of armor. The kick from her foot vibrated through the metal, giving it the semblance of life. The helmet's visor sprang open and a skull grinned out at her, its eyes sightless pits. *Here is death,* it seemed to say. *Malagant's promise.*

Terrified, filled with revulsion, she hastened to keep up with Lancelot, her promise of life.

It became evident, as they continued, that they were being carried along in an underground river. Lancelot was heartened by this, for he knew that all rivers flowed to the sea, and that it surely could not be long before this one met its destination. Beyond the weedy pillars of past glory, they rounded another curve and immediately were cast into a turbulent, swift-flowing current. They were snared in its grasp, tumbled and buffeted over and over, faster and faster. It was then that Guinevere and Lancelot realized that they were being hurtled toward a wide hole in the castle wall, a hole into which the torrent bearing them surged with devastating force.

Lancelot was swept into the whirlpool first. The turbulence hurled him against the stone side, and pain crashed through his ribs. The force of the water sucked him down toward oblivion. Summoning all his strength, he braced his body across the gap, making of himself a barrier so that neither he nor Guinevere could be sucked into the maelstrom beyond. She crashed against him like a piece of flotsam, and he dug his heels against the rock sides of the channel and hung on grimly.

The water pounded at them, roaring in their ears, furrowing over their bodies. Guinevere twisted to one side and managed to pull herself back from the brink. Lancelot mustered his own reserves, and when he saw that she was succeeding in inching her way back against the current, he twisted aside, too, and followed her. Slowly, painfully, they fought their way into calmer water. The cold waves ceased to thrust at them and just pulsed gently.

They surfaced beside a stone walkway in yet another wide underground tunnel filled with water. Exhausted by their struggle, it was all they could do to cling to the stone side of the walkway while they regained their breath.

Lancelot glanced at Guinevere. He did not have the strength for speech, but he could see that she was all right. She returned his look, unable to speak herself, unable to do anything but take in great gulps of air.

Reassured, Lancelot turned and looked the length

of the walkway. There was an archway at the end through which light poured. In a moment, when he had recovered enough, he would drag himself out of the water and investigate. All sense of orientation had gone amidst the twists and turns, the fight to live, to breathe. His ribs ached where he had been smashed against the side of the tunnel, and he knew that when the numbness of the water's cold wore off, he would notice numerous small cuts and abrasions. And Guinevere would be the same. He turned to her again, intending to speak, but before the words were uttered, they both heard the ring of footsteps and the excited cry of voices. A troop of Malagant's guards came running along the walkway, crossbows primed. There were far too many of them for Lancelot to have fought off, even had he been fresh and ready for battle.

"They're here, I told you so!" yelled one of the guards to his companions, and discharged his weapon at Lancelot. The bolt zipped into the water close to Lancelot's head, and others followed in a deadly rain. Lancelot met Guinevere's eyes. The same thought channeled through their minds and was exchanged in a split second. Nodding to each other, they both took a deep breath, let go of the walkway, and submerged.

More bolts shot into the water, but Lancelot and Guinevere were gone, swept along by the current, back toward the churning whirlpool in the side of the mountain. If this was death, then so be it.

This time Lancelot made no attempt to resist being sucked down into the dark hole. Feet first, he was dragged into the vortex, Guinevere swift behind him. One after the other, they hurtled down a wide pipe, its stone sides worn smooth by years of containing the torrent. Around bends and down sudden falls they tore at an ever-increasing speed, struggling for breath in the racing water, faster and faster.

Their tumbling journey was brought to a sudden halt as Lancelot's feet struck an iron grid fixed across the chute. This was where the water made its exit into the air, for below and beyond, he could clearly see bright daylight. Once more, Guinevere crashed into him. Her weight bruised his shoulders; the water cascaded over both of them, making breathing a series of precarious, snatched gulps. Lancelot slammed his feet against the grid. There was nowhere else to go. They could not swim back against this current, and their strength was ebbing. He kicked on the grid as hard as he could and felt it give a little. He kicked again, and one of the rusty retaining bolts snapped off.

"Go on!" Guinevere shrieked above the rush of the river. "Go on!"

He drew back both legs and bucked out with all his power. The grid jerked free and disappeared in a welter of foam. He and Guinevere were catapulted forward and shot out of the aperture. For a moment they were suspended in a tremendous white rainbow waterfall that shimmered out from the rocks in the morning sun, a contrast of silvery spume against hard black stone, and then they were falling eighty feet into the sea below.

Cold salty water closed over their heads, and they welcomed it as freedom. Even if any of Malagant's men had followed them this far on their tortuous journey, they could not have survived this final baptism. Their heavy warrior's garments would drag them straight to the bottom and anchor them to death.

Guinevere and Lancelot broke to the surface like seals, smiled at each other out of the mystery and triumph of still being alive and free, and struck out for the nearby shore.

Chapter 13

The horse was one-paced, but he had an unflagging stamina. Even though he had been ridden hard throughout the previous night, and had not seen the inside of a stable for nearly two days, he bore the weight of Lancelot and Guinevere with equanimity and raised a game canter.

Guinevere clung to Lancelot, her arms around his waist, her cheek pressed to his saturated tunic. The motion of the man in tune with the horse was comforting. Each sure, strong stride took them away from Gore and toward Camelot. She counted them in her head and prayed. The temptation to look over her shoulder was almost overwhelming, but she resisted it. She was afraid that if she did turn, the very act would summon the sight of Malagant in pursuit, and she knew very well that they would be unable to outrun him.

The sparse vegetation gave way to the cover of trees, and her anxiety diminished slightly. Trunks flashed past, the light grew greener and darker, the path narrowing and weaving through the massive beeches, limes, and oaks. Rain started to fall softly, whispering down through the branches, misting Guinevere's face, covering her in a fine cobweb dew.

They rode on into the depths of the forest, and Lancelot eased the pace of the horse. In the rain, steam was rising from its flanks, and he could feel its quivering through the saddle. Ahead, a little off the path, he glimpsed a giant oak tree, its trunk wearing a thousand-year-old gnarled stoutness, its branches spreading like the structure of a cathedral. He tugged on the bridle and clucked his tongue to the horse, guiding it from the path toward the beckoning shelter.

Guinevere sat up, and her arms stiffened around him. "Keep riding," she said with alarm in her voice. "I want to get back to Camelot."

Lancelot shook his head. "It will be better to take a short rest."

"I don't want a rest."

"You're not carrying two people on your back."

She was silent. "I did not think of that," she said after a moment, her voice small.

Lancelot dismounted and then held out his arms to help her down from the saddle. Unthinkingly, she came down into them, and in the moment that they tightened to support her, she became aware that she was wearing nothing but her torn petticoat and that she was literally soaked to the skin, her flesh glimmering through the pleated linen. Lancelot was soaked, too, but she could still feel the heat of his body and her own, as if they were two halves drawing together to make one whole. His grip loosened and she pulled away from him, plucking ineffectually at the clinging chemise.

It had taken all Lancelot's control to let her go. But he could not prevent his body from responding, nor could he make himself turn away, although it was agony to look at her thus revealed. There had been women down the empty years of his life, many of them, and they had granted him brief oblivion with their bodies, but this was different. This was fire, and he had only to reach out his fingers and be burned. Or perhaps his hand was already in the fire, and it was too late. He wanted, he ached with wanting, but unlike Malagant, he could not wantonly take.

Guinevere raised her eyes to his. He saw the green flecks in their center, the little flakes of gold. He also saw the mirror of his own desire.

"Please." Her voice shook and she swallowed, her breathing rapid. "Please don't look at me like that . . ."

"As if everything were possible?" he said a trifle bitterly. His fists were clenched tightly at his sides to prevent himself from seizing her into his arms and opening her lips in the first of a thousand kisses. Abruptly he turned away and sat down at the base of the tree trunk that formed a natural seat. He pressed his spine against the grooved, knotted trunk and, throwing his head back, closed his eyes for a moment. In the aftermath of rescue he should have felt a soaring elation, but was aware only of a tremendous weariness.

Guinevere was still standing, that damned chemise clinging to the soft points of her body. He could feel her eyes upon him and sensed in her the wariness of the hunted doe. Perhaps she was right. He did not thrust himself not to make a kill.

The rain was falling harder now, no longer cobweb and silky, but with a steady heartbeat patter, drumming on the leaves, thudding on the ground—a comforting rhythm if a person had the shelter to enjoy it. Lancelot could hear the rain, but he could not hear Guinevere. He opened his eyes again and saw that she stood in the same place, as pale as a draped statue from the ancient times. His heart was like molten lead within his breast.

He beckoned to her. "Come closer to the trunk. The rain doesn't get through here."

She hesitated, raising her eyes to scan the downpour as if hoping it was only a shower. Then, biting her lip, she moved gingerly closer, but still kept a wide distance of personal space.

Lancelot shifted slightly, making room beside him. "Sit. You nearly died back there. Any moment now the shock will hit you."

Still she hesitated, and Lancelot saw that she would not yield to such dangerous closeness. Nor had he really expected her to. With an inner sigh, he stood up and gestured. "Sit," he said again, and then, "please."

She looked at him doubtfully for a moment, then with a silent nod of thanks, accepted his offer. She raised her knees and drew the tatters of her gown around her legs. Shivers began to ripple through her, raising gooseflesh on her smooth arms. Her teeth clicked together. Lancelot looked down at her and cursed the fact that there was not even so much as a wineskin in the horse's saddle roll, or a spare cloak.

He glanced up at the broad green leaves of the tree beneath which they were sheltering. The most that could be obtained was a drink of water.

Guinevere drew a shaken breath and looked up at him. "I have to thank you again," she said. "I hardly know how, and I dare not ask."

Lancelot's smile was more of a grimace. "There used to be an old custom—if you save a life three times, it becomes yours."

Guinevere shook her head. "I have never heard of it."

"Two down, one to go."

"You said that it 'used to be' a custom, not that it is now," she retorted, and then frowned. "What are you doing?"

"You'll see." He was busy with the leaves above their heads, twining and arranging. "There, that should be about right. Have a drink, you need it."

Guinevere looked at him, thoroughly mystified.

"Move your head a little to the right—yes, that's it. A little more. Now, open your mouth."

She did so, and he twitched the topmost leaf of the water chute he had made, sending a runnel of fresh rainwater cascading into Guinevere's mouth. She was not ready for it and choked and spluttered, missing most of it. A quiver of laughter, almost hysterical, ran through her.

"Do it again," she commanded Lancelot. "I wasn't ready."

Lancelot almost laughed, too, his own thoughts upon other occasions those words had been spoken to him with far less innocent connotations. He twitched the leaf again, and this time Guinevere caught the waterfall in her mouth. He watched the ripple of her throat, the delight on her face at so simple a pleasure.

"Again!" she cried like a child.

The spout of rainwater stepped down from leaf to leaf, then ran into her mouth in a crystal trickle. Once more she drank, then smiled at him, refreshed and renewed. "Where did you learn to do that?" she demanded. Rising to her feet, she stood on tiptoe beside him to study the workings of his leaf chute. It was simple and intricate at one and the same time, sturdy and delicate.

"I've lived most of my life out in the open. You learn the skills as you go along."

Guinevere looked at him. He was so self-sufficient, so confident and assured. She had seen his expertise on horseback and with a sword, against all the odds thrown at him. She had seen him defeat the gauntlet, and yet, this last skill seemed to her the greatest of all and, perhaps, the source of his confidence. Whatever the situation, he could look after himself. Her gaze fixed upon his hands where they still held the chute in place. They belonged to a craftsman, perhaps an artist, certainly not a warrior. "Don't you have a home?" she asked out of her thoughts.

His lower lids tightened, and his dark eyes were suddenly wary. "No, I don't have a home." He spread his hands. "Except beneath the sky."

"Have you never had a home then?" she probed.

"Not for a long time."

"That must be hard."

"Why must it?" he challenged, brusque now, his tone angry. "I'm my own master. I go where I please and I have nothing to lose." His mouth twisted.

"Why build a house and furnish it with love for the warlords to come and burn?" He broke off on the last word, his chest shuddering as he fought to control all that seethed within him. He had not spoken of it to anyone since the day it happened. He had ridden away and not looked back to see the piteous corpses of memory shackled in his wake.

"Is that how it happened?" Guinevere questioned softly.

"It was long ago." His throat was tight. "Long, long ago."

Guinevere nodded, understanding a little of the agony she saw in his eyes and his posture. "Every morning when I wake, I prepare myself to hear that Leonesse is burning."

"God save you from such a day." He gazed beyond her into the screen of dripping rain and the gentle gray greenery of the summer downpour. But the colors he saw were entirely different, composed of the opposite element—fire.

There had been so little time. The raiders had come ashore and were upon the village before anyone could prepare, least of all himself. His father had been lord of the manor, ruler of a small, contented domain, and Lancelot his newlywed heir on that fateful day. The high summer of a dry year it had been, and market day, the village crowded. He and his father had been strolling among the stalls with the women of their family. His mother, intent on obtaining a bargain as usual, his three sisters flashing glances at the young men through their lashes. His wife, Elaine, the sunlight on her barley blond hair, her face radiant with the first bloom of pregnancy. As always, attracted by the horses, Lan-

185

celot had left them to inspect a handsome bay colt that caught his eye, and so he was separated from them when the raiders launched their attack.

His father had hurried the women to the safety of the church, only to discover that it was not to safety but to death that he brought them. The raiders were pagans with only contempt for Christ. Lancelot could still remember lying on the ground by the horses, dazed and bleeding from a clubbing blow to his skull. The muffled screams, the roar of hungry flame. The memory assaulted him now and he had no defense. Naked, he faced it. Once more he saw the stained glass window depicting the Virgin Mary cradling the infant Jesus. Ethereal, not of this world. Bodies were silhouetted by the bright flames against the deep colors of the glass as the trapped villagers hammered upon the lead fretwork, striving to break out of what had become their funeral pyre.

He felt a gentle touch on his arm, and the flames receded enough for him to see Guinevere's concerned eyes raised to his.

"How old were you?" she asked.

He grimaced. "I was nineteen, not long married."

Her face filled with compassion and distress. "Your wife . . . ?" Guinevere did not know how to finish the question. Perhaps it was foolish to have asked it at all since the answer must be obvious.

"My wife, my unborn child, my parents, my sisters, everyone. They drove them into the church —no, that's wrong, they did not even have to drive them. Everyone thought that a Christian sanctuary was beyond violation—safe. But the raiders had never heard of that rule." He shuddered, seeing again the stained glass window, the writhing bodies, the bright flames beyond. Suddenly a woman's fist smashed through the glass and reached vainly out to the air, the fingers torn and bleeding. The raiders laughed and pointed. And then a massive fireball rolled over the church; the window exploded into a thousand shattered shards, and the screaming ceased. Except it never ceased inside his head.

"There was nothing I could do, nothing. I wasn't with them. I was in another part of the village, and the raiders had clubbed me senseless—to death, so they must have supposed, but I saw it all." He swallowed deep in his throat.

Guinevere took both of his hands in hers, wanting to show her sympathy as directly as she could. At first she had disliked Lancelot for his arrogance and lack of manners; but she had come to see that it was only a front, a defensive shield behind which the true personality sheltered, and now that shield was lowered for her.

"God save us all from such a day," she said in a voice filled with compassion.

"He didn't save me."

"Oh, but he did."

Lancelot snorted bitterly. "For what?"

"It's made you who you are—a man who fears nothing and no one. Surely you can use that gift for some good purpose." Her voice took on the passion of persuasion, seeking to draw him up out of his own personal abyss. "If not, you might as well have died in the church with the others."

"You don't know how many times I've wished that."

Probably every day of your life, she thought, but kept the words to herself. "But you didn't die," she said forcefully. "You survived, and we who survive bear a great responsibility both to the dead and to the living. Would your family have wished this way for you?"

His mouth tightened. She looked up into his face, seeing the suffering there, and wished that she could smooth it away on the tips of her fingers. But it went no further than the wish. To have made it fact was too dangerous. As a compromise, she stepped closer to him and squeezed his hand, imparting conviction and comfort. "We're not alone," she added, "none of us."

"Aren't we?" The bitterness was still there, and beneath it a deep, empty yearning.

Guinevere shook her head. "We love each other, or we die."

The atmosphere changed its quality. He was silent, but she could sense that it was not one of retreat from her beliefs or scorn. She had thrown him hope, and he was deliberating whether to take hold.

"We must each find our own way home," she continued, watching him. "But there is a coming home for all of us. I believe that with all my heart."

Lancelot had been holding his breath, but now he released it in a deep sigh. "Tell me what to do, and I'll do it."

There was a pleading, slightly puzzled look in his eyes now, as if a blindfold had been removed and he did not understand the terrain upon which he looked. "I cannot," Guinevere said gently. "Your life is your own."

"Then I give it to you."

Guinevere was unable to speak. He had stated the

words with such stark simplicity that she knew he meant them, and from a deeper part of himself than the one that had intimidated her in the forest a few weeks ago, desiring the kisses of a dairymaid. They had each traveled a fair distance since that moment.

"I cannot accept it," she said. "You forget—I'm to be married."

"And if you were free to do as you pleased, would you marry Arthur?"

The tensions of earlier had returned. She felt the heat of his stare and the answering heat it evoked in her own body. Arthur was noble and good, honest and wise, everything a ruler should be, and she had no doubts about her marriage to him or the love she bore for him. But this was different. The will could not command the more primitive rhythms of the body nor the part of the spirit that yearned.

"I am free," she said defensively. "As free as you are." And even as the words were uttered, she wished them recalled. How free was Lancelot? She had seen in his face that he was fettered by the past.

"Prove it," he dared.

The rain hissed softly down, drenching them, making a curtain between them and the background of the forest. Their awareness narrowed down to each other, to the heat shimmering within their drenched bodies. The smallest of spaces held them separate. A hairbreadth, a knife edge.

"How?" Guinevere was hardly aware of her own whispered word. Her body was fighting for mastery over her will and gaining the upper hand.

He returned her whisper, his breath upon hers. "Just for one moment, forget who you are. Let all the world go away, and all the people in it but you

189

and me. And for just one moment do what you want to do. Here. Now. With me."

And all the world to Guinevere did indeed go away. There was only the stillness, and Lancelot's burning gaze, drawing her will from her body and leaving her as boneless as a forest leaf. She trembled toward him and lifted her face. "Please," she said, and her voice was no longer even a whisper, but the barest stirring of breath.

A plea to take, or a plea to release, Lancelot did not know. He hesitated. The sight of her upturned face sent a pang through him so sharp that it was painful. He had never felt such hollow hunger before, and he was almost afraid of his own control— or lack of it. How could a starving man sit down at a feast and walk away after taking one small bite?

He stooped to claim, but Guinevere had felt his uncertain pause, and it gave her the time to pull back from the brink. "No, forgive me, I cannot," she said, and stepped away from him into the downpour. With eyes closed, she threw back her head and let the rain drench her burning body. The thin linen garment clung to her, revealing the pink tint of flesh, the swell of breast, lean flank, and long thigh.

Lancelot gripped the gnarled trunk while he fought his own battle. She could be yours, an inner voice told him. Do you really think she will fight you if you pounce upon her now? But much as he wanted to obey that voice, he held back. She might not fight him, they might find joy together, but it would be fleeting. Honor once tarnished never regained its sheen. And so he gazed upon her loveliness, desiring, and because love was more powerful than desire, he stayed his hand.

Beyond her, through the trees, he suddenly detected an indistinct movement; the blur of a human shape. He tensed and glanced toward the horse, judging the distance between himself and the sword in the saddle sheath. Other figures appeared between the trees, muffled in hoods to protect them from the rain. He saw the glint of armor beneath cloaks, but his tension eased. These were not Malagant's troops. They came from the wrong direction, and their garments were different. Within moments he had recognized the men as members of Camelot's royal guard. His part in Guinevere's rescue was finished.

"She's here!" the nearest man cried, and came striding toward them. "I've found her, she's here!"

Guinevere crossed her arms over her breasts and faced the hurrying, triumphant guard. Before he reached her, she looked over her shoulder at Lancelot with her soul in her eyes. Through the rain he saw love and desire, regret and resolve, and in that moment knew what he had won and what he had lost.

Chapter 14

"Thank God, thank God!" Arthur cried and swept Guinevere into a convulsive hug. "Are you hurt? And I swore I would protect you. Are you hurt?" Overwhelmed by his joy and relief, he covered her rain-streaked face with kisses.

"No, no, I'm unharmed," she reassured him, and trembled within his comforting arms. As strong as a rock, warm with love and compassion. Yes, unharmed, said a small voice at the back of her mind, but changed. Nothing could ever be the same.

They had brought her to Camelot's magnificent cathedral where Arthur had been on his knees praying for her safe deliverance. Outside, the rain still fell, screening the city in a silken gray veil, creating an air of poignance and mystery. She wore a guardsman's cloak over her torn, soaked chemise, but still she was cold. Shudders of delayed reaction made her teeth chatter.

"You're shivering," Arthur said with concern.

"We must get you to a fire—and dry clothing." He swallowed deep in his throat. "Through the dark night hours when I feared for your life, I wanted to die with you, but now I have you safe, there is a reason to live again."

Guinevere closed her eyes and leaned against him, fighting tears. Lancelot had said he would give his life to her. Now Arthur was saying much the same thing. Guinevere was overwhelmed by the strength of Arthur's emotion, by his very vulnerability. She wanted to tell him that no one's life should be in another person's keeping, but she was too exhausted to explain and too wary of hurting him by saying the wrong thing. And so she held silent. Arthur folded her close once more and then turned her, in the shelter of his arms, to lead her to the palace.

A fire blazed in the hearth, and the water in the bathtub set close to the fire was hot and scented with aromatic herbs. Aches and bruises were soothed, cuts and abrasions protested. Lancelot had both in plenty. A servant moved unobtrusively around the room, taking away his saturated garments for refurbishing, laying out towels to air.

Lancelot yawned. His eyes were heavy and he felt as if he could sleep for a week. He was aware of exhaustion of the spirit as much as exhaustion of the body. If he closed his lids, he saw Guinevere behind them, standing in the rain, the white chemise clinging to the points of her body. If he kept them open, he saw the wealth and power of the man who was to be her husband, his generosity. But Lancelot knew that Arthur's largesse would not extend so far afield as yielding Guinevere to another man. Lancelot had watched Arthur take her in his arms, had seen the streaks upon the High King's face that were nought of rain, and had known what he must do.

He completed his ablutions and, leaving the tub before he fell asleep in it, took one of the aired towels and rubbed himself dry. It would be a long time before he wanted to be wet again, he admitted ruefully. The servant brought a platter of food and a flagon of wine, setting them down by the hearth, then quietly departed. Lancelot donned the dry loincloth and a pair of clean breeches that had been warming near the fire. He wondered to whom they belonged. Probably one of the household knights, for the fabric was fine and soft, far more luxurious than he was accustomed to wearing, although once as a lord's son he had taken such garments for granted.

Lancelot gazed into the fire, watching the flames lick away at the core of solid wood, dissolving it to ash. He felt the reflection of the heat on his naked skin. Behind him he was vaguely aware of the servant taking up the fine embroidered shirt from the hearthside and moving behind him to help him put it on. Strange that when a man went up in the world, he lost the ability to dress himself.

"Thank you," he said without looking around. "You can go. I'm sure you have better things to do than wait on me."

There was a momentary pause and then a throaty chuckle. "You have given me back my life itself. The least I can do is give you the shirt on your back."

Lancelot swung around and discovered that the servant had been replaced by the High King himself, his face bright with joy.

Lancelot's expression was somewhat more wary. "There is no need, Sire." He took the shirt and pulled it over his head, discovering as he did so that he wanted to hide inside it until Arthur had gone away.

"Tell me what you want, and it's yours!" Arthur declared, and the hand that had held the shirt opened expansively, offering the world.

Lancelot pushed his head through the opening and shrugged the garment down over his body. He wondered what Arthur would do if he requested his true desire. "I want nothing," he said. "I did what any man would have done."

"You risked your life for another. There's no greater love."

This was worse than Lancelot had thought. He turned away, embarrassed, feeling as if he had been rolling in the dirt. "If only you knew," he muttered.

"Oh, but I do know." Arthur said with a half smile. "You've deceived me, but now I realize the truth."

"You know?" Lancelot's eyes widened. He could not fathom Arthur's attitude. The man appeared to be regarding him with approval, and that surely could not be right.

"You told me on gauntlet day that you lived only for yourself," Arthur declared, and his eyes sparkled with the relish of having sought and discovered a treasure. "The truth is that you care nothing for yourself. Look at you! No wealth, no power, no home, no goal. Just the passionate spirit within you that drives you on without respite. God uses men like you, Lancelot, because your heart is open and you hold nothing back. You give all of yourself, and we owe you more than we can ever repay."

Lancelot lowered his eyes and fiddled with his clothing, fussing and straightening, he who did not care what he wore or how he looked. It was obvious now that Arthur suspected nothing. He saw the best in everyone, expected the best, and Lancelot's discomfort increased. "If you knew me better, you wouldn't say such things."

"Wouldn't I?" Arthur opened his arms and drew the surprised Lancelot into a warm, wholehearted embrace. "Come, I take all of you, the good and the bad together. I cannot love people in slices."

Lancelot stood rigid for a moment beneath Arthur's onslaught, but he was genuinely moved by the trust and friendship being extended to him. He had been alone for so long, with taut barriers erected against the world. Now those barriers were under assault, and he could no longer withstand the onslaught.

"No more protests," Arthur added firmly, as he released Lancelot. He looked at the bemused younger man and smiled. "I am going to thank you in my own way. Eat and rest. We'll speak again tomorrow."

Lancelot wanted to say that he desired no thanks, that it would be for the best if Arthur let him alone, but the words would not come, and he stood in immobile silence until the king had left the room. Then he turned once more to stare into the heart of the fire. "I do not love in slices either," he said to the logs.

* * *

The rain ceased during the night, and a golden morning broke over Camelot, the sky a clear, new blue, the only clouds wispy and higher than the darting swallows that hunted insects on the wing. In the round council chamber, the sun slanted through the high windows and gilded the stone steps and magnificent table. The eternal flame burned in the brazier at its center, and the eleven knights of the assembly were arrayed at their places, waiting.

Arthur entered the chamber with Guinevere upon his arm. She had recovered well from her ordeal, and although her eyes were still a little shadowed, and there were bruises on her body from her battering in the underground river, she carried her head high, and there was a smile on her lips. Arthur looked at her with tender pride, filling his eyes with her regal beauty. When she would have left him to take her place among the scribes and clerks on the dais above the round table, he held onto her hand and brought her with him to his own place. Then he raised his voice to the knights.

"I have called you to the round chamber today, for I want to discuss with you a matter of great import." He looked around at the warriors, holding each one briefly with his gaze. "We owe Lady Guinevere's life to one man." He gestured to the servants who stood at the doors of the great chamber, and they drew them open.

A slightly bewildered Lancelot entered the room. He had been roused early from his bed by the servant who had tended him last night and informed that the High King requested his presence in the round chamber. There had barely been time to don his clothes, rake a comb through his hair, and drink the wine that was presented to him. He felt slightly unsteady now and wished that he had taken a moment to eat some bread, too.

Seeing the gathered men, their eyes upon him, seeing Arthur and Guinevere, he was uncomfortable. The High King had embraced him in private the night before and offered him the reward of whatever he wanted. Now came the public moment, and Lancelot would lief as not have endured it.

Arthur gave him a reassuring smile, which only caused Lancelot to grow more uneasy still. He was aware of the assembled knights regarding him with as much wariness as he was regarding them.

"What I am about to offer this man," Arthur said, once more turning to his advisers, "is his already. I believe that he comes to Camelot for a purpose, even if he does not know it himself." He left Guinevere and paced around to Malagant's place. "One seat stands empty."

The silence after he spoke was palpable. Shocked and worried glances were exchanged. It was the highest honor in the land to sit at the Round Table, and those already granted a place guarded the right jealously. Lancelot was a stranger, an unknown and perhaps dangerous quantity.

"You would make him a knight, Sire?" Kay asked, studiously avoiding Lancelot's gaze.

Arthur ignored his adviser, the force of his will bent upon Lancelot. "What I am offering is no life of privilege but one of hard service."

"We know nothing about him," Mador muttered sidelong to Kay, "although I have heard it said that he fights for money. And look at how reckless he was when he faced the gauntlet."

Arthur's eyes flickered toward the muttering knights. "But if you want it, Lancelot, it is yours, with all my heart."

"Sire, I think we should discuss—" Kay began.

"Enough!" Arthur thundered, his eyes flashing in a rare show of temper that once more brought silence to the Round Table. Then he twitched his shoulders, as if shaking off the irritation, and once more addressed Lancelot. "What do you say? Will you join us?"

Lancelot stood very still. A few days ago the answer would have come to his tongue without him even having to think, but then perhaps it would have been false. Things had changed so swiftly and were still changing. He felt as powerless as he had in the whirlpool of the underground river in Gore. He turned his eyes to Guinevere, who had been standing as silently as himself, her face pale and her lips held tight. Reasons to live were as manifold as reasons to die. He opened his mouth, but Guinevere was faster.

"My lord, may I speak on this matter?" She addressed Arthur, her voice slightly breathless, as if she had run to the decision.

Arthur gave a gesture of assent. "Assuredly you may, beloved, since this most closely concerns you, too."

She colored to the roots of her hair, and when she spoke, her hands plucked nervously at the folds of her gown. "I owe this man more than anyone here. He deserves any honor that you can give him, and more." She bit her lip. "But he does not belong in Camelot or anywhere else. He's a man who goes his way alone, and in that solitude and freedom lies his strength. If we wish to honor him—as I do from the bottom of my heart—let us honor him as he is, not as we would make him. Let him go, alone and free—with our love."

All eyes turned back to Lancelot. Guinevere lowered hers for a moment and then she, too, looked at him. Lancelot returned her stare. Solitude and freedom; the words sounded lonely, and he was not as fond of his own company as he had been. Solitary thoughts were insular ones.

"Well, Lancelot?" Arthur prompted.

Lancelot drew a deep breath. "Lady Guinevere understands me well," he acknowledged, "and even a few days ago I would have agreed with everything that she said. But here, among you, I have found something that I want more than freedom." His eyes lingered upon Guinevere. "I no longer know what life I'm to live, only that it would break my heart to leave you."

Guinevere looked away, her color still high, her lower lip caught between her teeth.

Oblivious to her reaction because all his attention was on Lancelot, Arthur said eagerly, "Bravo. So you'll join us?"

His gaze still upon Guinevere, Lancelot nodded once. "Yes."

Joyfully, Arthur embraced the younger man. "Then I bid you welcome. This is a new beginning. You will spend tonight before the high altar in the cathedral in contemplation and prayer. Tomorrow at sunrise you'll be born again as a knight of the Round Table."

Arthur's words rang around the room, picking up echoes, resounding in Lancelot's heart. For better or worse he had made the decision, and not out of casual curiosity but deliberate, intense will. And yet he felt like a man who saw the stars in the sky and yearned to hold one in his hand. No matter how high he climbed, how far he stretched, he would never attain his desire.

Chapter 15

*I*t was the blackest part of the night. The moon had waxed and waned; ragged clouds drifted across the stars. Hearth fires had been banked until dawn, and the only light in the streets of Camelot came from the lanterns of the city watch and the occasional citizen about on either very late or very early business.

Guinevere carried no torch, and no escort accompanied her swift, silent footsteps. She had put on her darkest gown, a midnight blue silk, and covered it with a black hooded cloak. Keeping to the shadows, she hurried across courtyards and down narrow connecting alleys until she came to Camelot's great golden cathedral. The building was as magnificent as the palace itself, perhaps more so, for it was older, more mellow and weathered. The light of men's prayers ascended heavenwards in soaring spans of filigree stone, a mingling of faith and power.

She avoided the main oak doors and entered the edifice by a modest side entrance used by the priests.

The darkness within the cathedral shimmered with the glow of hundreds of golden beeswax candles set upon the spikes of huge candelabrum or suspended on hanging wrought-iron crowns of light. Sanctuary lamps glimmered softly near the high altar, and as Guinevere moved lightly down the main aisle, she saw the man kneeling at the foot of the altar steps, his head bowed in prayer.

Her courage had brought her thus far, but now it almost failed. Her step faltered and she nearly turned around and fled. She should not be here, had risked too much already. On the eve of her marriage to Arthur, she was seeking out another man, one who ought to be cleansing his mind for his knighting on the morrow. It was foolish, it was dangerous. Guinevere clenched her fingers in her cloak and summoned her courage. Whatever the consequences, she had to speak to him.

He seemed to sense her presence, for suddenly he raised his head, and although he did not look around, she knew that he was feeling the disturbance in the incense-scented atmosphere. Guinevere went forward, her garments rustling softly upon the stone flags, and stopped before the altar, before the kneeling man. The candle glow picked out gold lights in his hair and flickered in his eyes as he raised them to her. Guinevere's heart turned over and her legs were suddenly weak. With Arthur she felt safe, cared for. But Lancelot had only to look at her, and her body melted. Taking a deep breath, she drew herself together. She had risked coming here for a purpose, and she would not have that purpose destroyed on the strength of a single look.

"Why?" she demanded of him, her voice low and

trembling. She flicked a swift glance around the cathedral, but they were the only two occupants. If there were priests or attendants about, they had chosen to leave Lancelot alone to his vigil at the high altar.

"You know why," he answered, his own voice low, a little husky.

Guinevere made as if to put her hand on his shoulder, then withdrew it, the movement incomplete. "Please, I beg you, leave Camelot. Tell Arthur you have changed your mind tonight, while there is still time."

Lancelot sighed deeply and, rising to his feet, faced her, holding her eyes. "I can't," he said simply. "I want to be wherever you are."

Tears filled Guinevere's eyes. His words were unbearable to her because she longed for him to say them, even while she knew that what he wanted was impossible. Sooner or later one of them would break.

"Please, don't," she whispered.

"Then what am I to say?" he asked. "Would you have me lie?"

Guinevere shook her head. "Say you're my friend, and say good-bye. There is no future in this."

Lancelot glanced away toward the altar and the soft glow of the candlelight while he sought for the right words. Then he looked at her once more. "Ever since I came to Camelot, I've told myself leave now, leave before it is too late. The night of your capture, I was alone on the city ramparts making the decision to ride away at first light. But now it is too late." A wry expression, half smile, half grimace, crossed his face. "All I think of is you, all I want in life is you.

Fifteen, sixteen barren years I have wandered. You said that for everyone there is a moment of home-coming."

Guinevere heard her own words in his mouth and knew that her judgment was flawed. She had thought that she could handle these moments in the cathedral chapel, but she had been fooling herself. "You know how it must be," she said with a note of fear in her voice.

He was relentless. "Then tell me that you don't love me."

She avoided his eyes, and their merciless ability to see straight through her. "I don't . . . love you," she forced out. The saints in their stained glass windows witnessed her lie with impassive faces. The candles flickered softly, and the scent of incense hung in the air and was drawn into the body with each breath.

"Look at me and say that."

Guinevere's heart was pounding. Although she stood in the sacred silence of a church, she felt as if she were in the midst of a battlefield or a violent thunderstorm. The atmosphere was charged with a tension greater than that which had gripped her half naked beneath the rain-drenched trees of the border forests. She swallowed and faced Lancelot. Twice she started to speak, and both times she stopped. In a holy place, a lie was a profanity, especially to your own heart.

Lancelot reached out and unclenched one of her hands from the folds of her cloak. He took it within his own. "Your own body says you lie," he said softly. Drawing her hand close, he laid a kiss upon her palm. "I'll leave Camelot now, this moment, if only you will come with me."

Guinevere almost said yes. Her heart screamed at her to give him that answer. To be with him, their home the back of a horse and the open road. Ah God, she thought, if only I was indeed a dairymaid. But she wasn't. She was Guinevere of Leonesse, soon to be High Queen of Camelot, and she had a duty beyond herself and this beautiful, vulnerable man. And so the words remained unspoken, and she withdrew her hand from his, her palm tingling from the salute of his lips.

"This is our chance of happiness, we get no other life," he said, and still he held her with his eyes, trying to bring her with him.

Guinevere held her ground, emotionally torn, but knowing which path she had to tread. "No, this is not how happiness comes. I must do what I believe to be right. Let happiness come or not, as God wills."

"God?" The word rang around the cathedral and the candles fluttered. He swallowed whatever else he would have said and just looked at her with love, desire, and pleading.

Afraid of losing her resolve beneath such a stare, Guinevere turned and walked quickly away, almost breaking into a run.

Lancelot heard the thud of the door closing behind her. He raised his eyes to the stained glass window beyond and above the altar. In the candle-light darkness, the lead outlines of the figures were dusty and indistinct.

Slowly, he knelt again and bowed his head in prayer, but he found that the words *Thy will be done* caught in his throat.

* * *

Sunlight shattered through the great glass window of the cathedral's east end and filled the air and the ground with glorious splinters of color—ruby and amethyst, cobalt and topaz. Confined within a tracery of lead, the figure of Christ in glory glowed forth upon the congregation, hands raised in benediction. There were some who held that the face of the Lamb of God bore a striking resemblance to that of Arthur in his youth.

A trumpet sounded a haunting series of notes that echoed around the vaults and spans of the cathedral and drifted up through the great hammer beam roof like a prayer toward heaven. As silence descended in their wake, Arthur stepped forward into the shimmering reflection of stained glass light and looked down upon the bent head of the man who knelt at his feet. The sword of his kingship was in Arthur's hand, and the sun rippled along the blade, gilding the steel with rainbow colors.

Arthur touched Lancelot lightly upon each shoulder with the flat of the weapon in the genuflection that conferred knighthood. "Arise, Sir Lancelot," he declared.

Lancelot did so, and the crystal colors of the Christ window shone down upon his face, too. Arthur sheathed the sword and raised his right hand to lock Lancelot's in a powerful clasp. "Brother to brother. Yours in life and death." The words rang out for all to hear, potent and fierce. Then Arthur stepped away and Agravaine took his place, repeating the clasp.

"Brother to brother. Yours in life and death."

One after the other, the knights of the Great

Council swore the oath and accepted Lancelot amongst them. Even Kay and Mador, who had protested the advancement, spoke the words in sincerity without a hint of rancor. It was the High King's will, and they would not block him on his wedding day. Let it be a gift to celebrate his marriage.

Lancelot had been prepared for something of a pageant to mark his passage into knighthood and a place at the round table, and now found his expectations cast awry. Although everyone was adorned in their most sumptuous garments and jewels, the ceremony itself had been direct and simple. A promise of loyalty to the death. Through thick and thin, conferred by the touch of a sword. The power of the fierce handclasp tingled through his blood, and despite his effort to stand back and view the ritual with the eyes of a wary observer, he found himself involved, stirred to the very heart. Almost without knowing it, he filled his lungs and responded to all of them.

"Brother to brother. Yours in life and death."

His knighting was the first ceremony of the day. The second, the climax, was to be the marriage of Guinevere and Arthur, hence the crowded cathedral and the winking of jewels on rich silk and velvet gowns. Soberly dressed himself in the blue and silver colors of the royal guard, Lancelot took his place among the other knights of the council. They formed a guard of honor along the main aisle, while Arthur himself waited with the priest at the altar for his bride.

Lancelot stood as rigid as a statue, proper and perfect, as if nothing in the world could touch him and he was indeed made of stone. It was the only way to endure the next hour of his life.

A golden rectangle of sunlight marked the open doorway of the cathedral, and into it stepped Guinevere. Illuminated like an angel in one of the high stained windows, she stood there for a moment, a vision in tints of gold and cream and white. A nimbus of sunshine burnished the filaments of her hair and lit the brown with highlights of bronze and gold and red. A single trumpet sounded her presence, and a deep silence fell upon the gathered throng. A child with a reed basket walked slowly down the aisle, strewing scented pale rose petals upon the flagstones.

Guinevere drew a single, steadying breath, and then set her foot within the cathedral and made her way slowly and proudly toward the high altar. Lancelot felt her approach. The very air seemed to move and shimmer. He had been determined to look straight ahead, to give no sign, but his resolve wavered beneath the vision she presented, her hair unbound, the silk wedding gown clinging to the supple curves of her body. So near and yet so far. He stared at her with all the hunger in his soul. Briefly her eyes flickered to his, made an even briefer response, and then she was past him, walking regally on to the waiting bridegroom. Lancelot tightened his jaw and stared into the middle distance once more, feeling bereft.

At the altar steps, the brimming joy in Arthur's eyes elicited a nervous smile from Guinevere. She was still not sure in her heart that she was doing the right thing, but in her mind she was certain. This marriage was for her father, for Leonesse, for Arthur and Camelot. And it was for herself, too, for her own good. So why did she ache so even while she smiled?

The priest made a gesture with the flat of his palm. Beside her Arthur knelt, and she bowed her head and knelt with him.

The wedding bells were still clamoring joyfully across the city, peal after peal declaring the union of the High King to Guinevere of Leonesse. In the square a huge fair was in progress, with jugglers, fire-eaters and sword-swallowers to entertain the crowds. The covers on the gauntlet had been removed, and the young men once more dared its revolving balls and bladders in vain attempts to emulate Lancelot's performance.

Within the palace the atmosphere was somewhat more formal. Before the feasting and celebration could begin in earnest, the knights of Camelot had to swear homage to their new queen.

Dwarfed by its ornate carving, Guinevere sat on a raised throne with Arthur at her side, while one by one, his officers made their pledge to her. Agravaine was the first, his blue eyes bright and earnest as he knelt to her.

"I swear to love and serve Guinevere, my true and rightful queen, and to protect her honor as my own."

The words bore a similar ring to the "Brother to brother" of Lancelot's knighting, but there was more of courtesy about them and less of raw power.

Guinevere met Agravaine's eyes and smiled gravely. He rose to his feet, bowed, and made way for Patrise to do the same. Guinevere's gaze drifted to Lancelot waiting his turn at the end of the line, the last man. His face was without expression, the way it had been in the cathedral before that brief, anguished glance. Why couldn't he see it, she wondered a trifle desperately. Why couldn't he have ridden out last night? This way both of them would be torn and torn and torn until nothing but shreds remained.

". . . my true and rightful queen, and to protect her honor as my own."

Guinevere drew herself together and managed to smile at Patrise. Her right hand covered her left, where the new wedding band of Celt gold gleamed on her finger, symbol of eternity and belonging. Each knight swore his oath and passed on to his place at the Round Table, until only one man and one place remained. Guinevere steeled herself.

Lancelot stepped forward and knelt at her feet as he had knelt at God's altar the previous night. But instead of bowing his head as the others had done, he looked directly into her eyes. His look bore the piercing keeness of a sword edge, and it went straight through her heart.

"I swear to love and serve Guinevere, my true and rightful queen and to—"

He was interrupted by a sudden, urgent pounding on the outer doors. All eyes turned toward the noise, and a gesture from Arthur sent servants hurrying to open them.

The sight on the threshold catapulted Guinevere to her feet, her face draining to white. "Jacob!" she cried, and flew down the steps to the door. Her servant was supported by two soldiers, for he had not the strength to stand on his own. His face was bruised and bloody, and his breath came in horrible shallow rasps.

"Forgive me, my lady," he gasped, and there was blood in his mouth. "Ill news—Malagant—has taken—Leonesse." Red drops spattered his tunic, and his head slumped. "Save us—from burning."

"Jacob?" Guinevere's voice rose with concern and alarm. Her servant did not respond. Gently the soldiers lowered him to the ground, and one of them looked at her with pity in his eyes.

"He is dead, my queen," he said. "I think it was only his spirit that brought him this far to you. His body was finished long ago."

A sob rose in Guinevere's throat, but she choked it down. There could be tears later, in private. Now she had to be strong for Jacob, for Leonesse. She looked to Arthur. "You heard what he said, about Leonesse?"

Arthur curved a protective arm around her shoulders. "Yes, I heard. There'll be no delay. The council is already assembled here, the army is stood to arms. We can be on the road to Leonesse before nightfall." To the guards he said, "Bear this man to the chapel and bring a priest to attend him. I want him accorded all honor in death."

"Yes, Sire." The soldiers set about their task. Arthur began issuing orders to his captains, Lancelot among them. Guinevere watched him fastening his scabbard to his belt and remembered him saying *"God save you from such a day."* But God had not. Indeed, she doubted that God had anything to do with the bringing of this terrible news. And then Lancelot raised his head from his task and their eyes met, hers full of anguish, his of understanding.

Chapter 16

For three days and three nights, Camelot's great army marched toward Leonesse. The weather held calm and the roads were good. Nor were they troubled by outriders and harriers from Malagant's force. The occasional scout was sighted, but they kept their distance, their task being to report back on Arthur's movements to Malagant. Arthur had his scouts out, too, but they reported the way ahead clear, no sign of the enemy whatsoever, lest it be in the occasional burned farmhouse or barn.

It was dusk of the fourth day when the men of Camelot crested the last hill and looked down on the fertile valley of Leonesse. The loop of the river reflected the sunset and drew the eye to the silent town. Arthur drew rein on the hill, and Guinevere rode up beside him on Moonlight. She gazed down on the familiar scene. The woods to the south, the meadows before the town, the rolling hills to the north.

Only a few months ago she had stood on this same

hill and gazed with love and fierce pride upon her town and its busy, contented populace. Wheat-colored stone and red-tiled roofs, orchard groves and sun-splashed courtyards. "Leonesse," she whispered, her heart aching. At least Malagant had not seen fit to burn it yet as he had burned the homes of those living deeper in the countryside. But what was his purpose in staying his hand, unless it be a trap?

Arthur, too, was staring intently at the distant town walls, his mouth tight within his trimmed silver beard. He shifted in the saddle as if in response to his irked thoughts. "The bridge is unguarded," he remarked. "And the gates are open."

"What do you think Malagant intends? Could he have fled at our approach?" There was more hope than conviction in Guinevere's voice.

"I believe not. Malagant has his pride like any man," Arthur said thoughtfully. "And it was he who threw down the first challenge. If he has retreated, it is to serve his own ends, not make things easy for us." He swung around and sought Sir Kay among their escort. "We will make camp for the night."

Kay rode out of the ranks. There was anxiety in his eyes. "Where, Sire?"

"There." Arthur pointed ahead to an expanse of open grassland, dusky green in the gathering twilight. The ghostly shapes of grazing sheep dotted the landscape, their bleats filling the air with a soothing rustic sound completely removed from the tension of war.

Kay's studied the fields with an experienced soldier's dismay. "It is too exposed, Sire. How are we to defend—"

Arthur said nothing. A look was enough, and Kay

subsided. "Sire!" he saluted and, tight-lipped, reined away to give out orders.

Kay said nothing untoward as he issued the command to make camp, but his stiff expression and brusque voice told their own tale to the other knights. Tents were pitched throughout the field, and cooking fires lit. Around the edges of the great encampment, teams of soldiers lifted long frames off wagons and hauled on the ropes attached, erecting them into high watchtowers. Preparations for the possible conflict went forward apace.

Lancelot's first reaction at the command to set up the tents was similar to Kay's, but he quickly shrugged aside his doubts. Arthur was far too experienced a general to make such an obvious error unless it had a purpose. They said that he had won his first battle against invaders from across the great sea when only fourteen years old, and not once since that time had he been defeated.

Bluff and counterbluff, Lancelot thought as he tended Jupiter. Malagant was hiding somewhere and hoping that Arthur would descend upon Leonesse. Now Arthur was attempting to draw Malagant out of his concealment. Lancelot made a fuss of his mount and ensured that he was comfortable. The last three days had been hard on both man and horses. If there was to be a battle soon, then a respite now was essential. With a final slap on the sleek, black neck, Lancelot left Jupiter to his ration of oats and hay and went among the soldiers. He was a member of the High Council now, and he knew that his presence would hearten them.

He paused at a cooking fire and accepted a bowl of

vegetable broth from one of the soldiers who was stirring a simmering iron cauldron with a huge wooden ladle. The soup was hot, and Lancelot sipped it with relish while he gazed around at the bustle. Nearby two men were honing their swords on large oiled grindstones and easing their tension by joking loudly with each other. A fletcher was busy feathering the flights of arrows, using goose feathers and bluebell root glue. Last-minute adjustments and repairs to armor were being made, men finding tasks for their nervous hands. Monks and lay workers were laying out surgical instruments and preparing stretchers and bandages. The soldiers eyed such necessary work nervously and crossed themselves when they had to pass the surgeon's post, offering up a prayer that they would not find themselves stretched upon one of the operating trestles.

Lancelot watched all this, feeling a part of it, and yet still apart. A newcomer, a stranger still. *Brother to brother.* A smile, part irony part humor, crossed his face. Finishing the broth, he returned his bowl to the soldier at the cauldron, thanked him, and moved on toward the king's tent on the crest of the hill. A smaller tent was pitched beside it, and within he heard the low murmur of female voices. His stomach jolted him when he recognized Guinevere's, and like a raw adolescent, he longed for her to emerge just so that he could lay eyes on her. For an instant he hesitated, but other captains and adjutants were entering Arthur's tent. Not wanting to call attention to himself, he followed them within, pausing on the threshold to hold the flap open for a scout who had just ridden in from reconnoitering Leonesse.

Arthur was seated at a trestle table, the knights of

his council around him. A map was spread before him, its edges held down by stones, and Arthur had been using his dagger as a pointer.

The scout knelt before the king, then rose to give his report. "The town's empty, Sire."

Arthur nodded as if the squire's words were confirmation of what he expected to find. His scarred warrior's hands toyed with the dagger. "Did you go in?"

"No, Sire. But all the gates are open. There's nothing moving there, neither army nor people. I saw no ravens or kites beyond the usual. There has been no killing."

The word *yet* hung unspoken in the air, and the men exchanged glances.

"Well done," Arthur nodded to the scout. "Go and find food and drink, then report back to me in an hour. I have more work for you yet. The rest of you, gather 'round and listen."

Arthur's plan was simple, a borrowing and embellishing of Malagant's own strategies. "We fight fire with fire," he told his captains. The words had unpleasant associations for Lancelot, and he withdrew at the first opportunity to prepare himself for the coming battle.

He walked around the perimeter of the great encampment, checking that the sentries were all alert at their posts, and the guards on watch in the high towers. Orders issued forth from the command tent, and the men in camp set about obeying them with thoroughness and speed.

Lancelot returned from the outposts and wended his way through the busy troops toward the horse lines. An escort of royal guards crossed his path and forced him to an abrupt halt. The royal banners of Camelot and Leonesse fluttered on the tip of the leading man's spear, blue and silken gold. "The queen comes," he declared. "Make way!"

She was making the rounds of the fighting men, talking to them, building up their courage. The sound of her voice sent a pang through Lancelot. The sight of her slender, upright figure was almost more than he could bear. Being near was too much and not enough.

Guinevere finished talking to a fletcher seated at a fire, and turned to move on. Her gaze caught Lancelot's through the torchlit night. Neither body nor expression acknowledged his presence, but he saw his own longing briefly reflected in her eyes before she lowered them and moved on.

"I love you!" he wanted to cry after her, but the words stayed jailed inside his head. For her sake that was where they had to remain.

Guinevere was shaken by the way her body had leaped in response to Lancelot's look. She had thought that marriage to Arthur, the pronouncing of the sacred vow, would make a difference to the way she felt. In a way it had. She was even more protective of Arthur now, his pride and his feelings. She knew how vulnerable was the man beneath the kingly exterior. But by the same token, her love for Lancelot had not diminished. He was vulnerable, too, more scarred by life than Arthur, and it was hard to hurt him again and again by cleaving to another man. Arthur fulfilled the needs of her mind, her own vulnerabilities, but if she faced herself with the grim truth, it was Lancelot she desired as a lover. When Arthur looked at her, she was filled with a warm glow of security. When Lancelot looked, her body burned.

Walking quickly, as if she could outstrip her thoughts, she returned to the command tent. Arthur was staring down upon the myriad campfires, twinkling like stars in the open field. The evening breeze was scented with meadow grass and woodsmoke. Guinevere paused beside her husband and, of a sudden impulse, slipped one arm fiercely around him, clinging on to her security. It was good and right. It had to be. Forget the other, think only of Arthur and Leonesse.

The vehemence of her embrace both touched and amused Arthur. He kissed the top of her head and set his own stronger arm around her waist. For now they were married only in name. He could have commanded a wedding night in his tent beneath the stars, but the canvas was too thin, and there were too many ears to hear and eyes to see what he desired to be a private joy. Just himself and Guinevere, not a king and a queen, but a man and a woman. His arm tightened slightly as he gazed out over the encamped men. He knew with a soldier's gut feeling that they were going to win this war.

"What is it, my lord?" Guinevere asked, and turned a little to gaze up at him, her arm folded through his, his broad palm spread upon her waist.

Arthur shook his head. The feeling in his gut was of victory, but his bones were cold, as if ghostly footsteps had trodden across his soul. "Nothing," he murmured. "An old soldier's melancholy." He squeezed her waist and kissed her temple. "Summer nights and lovely young women do not best prepare a man for battle."

"I did not mean to bring you grief."

"Malagant would have struck sooner or later, whether I had you or not," he said with a shrug. "But I would be lying if I did not admit that I wish it was later."

Guinevere leaned back against him, absorbing his strength, her soft hair against his bearded cheek. "I wish it, too," she murmured.

All was still in the darkest hours before dawn. The moon had set; the brightest stars had tumbled beyond the rim of the horizon. Only embers glowed in the fire pits dug by Arthur's army, and the cresset lamps and horn lanters no longer glowed from within the pale canvas tents. A breeze fingered eerily through the camp, stirring the grass, rippling the limp banners and lifting an unlaced tent flap. The grazing sheep beyond the perimeter bleated incessantly to each other. The sentry in the tall watchtower stood motionless.

Asleep at his post, Ralf thought with contempt. The soldiers of Camelot had developed soft underbellies during the years of Arthur's so-called peace. Old fool. Malagant's captain gently touched a healing scar on his lip, and then gave a command to a waiting adjutant. The man saluted and went to relay the order. Within moments, the sheep began moving toward Arthur's tents, driven by the dark-clad soldiers crouch-running among them. And behind the first troops, more came crawling over the grass, weapons at the ready. The sheep began to run, their cloven hooves pitter-pattering on the soft turf, their bleating more urgent now. Behind Ralf, rank upon rank of mounted marauders awaited the signal.

Teeth and eye whites glinted. So did the dark sheen of sword steel and crossbow quarrel.

Ralf's horse swung and plunged, sweat creaming its dark hide. "Now!" Ralf cried, and signaled a trumpeter to blow a blast that resounded like a horn of the apocalypse upon the silent encampment. The sheep stampeded and scattered in terror, and the men among them charged into the heart of Camelot's sleeping army, intent upon its annihilation.

Wave after wave of riders swept into the camp, slashing and shooting. Tents were ripped open, and sleeping mounds cut to ribbons on the saw blades of the deadly ripswords. All was confusion, a darkness of hurtling movement lit by flashes of bright flame.

Ralf drew rein and brought his horse to a stamping halt. His gaze swept the scene, and a cold trickle of alarm ran through him. Where were the screams of agony? the staggering wounded? Not a single one of Arthur's soldiers had snatched at a weapon to fight back. He jerked his mount around to one of the burning watchtowers and looked at the dead guard sprawled at its foot, an arrow in his breast. Fire licked at the corpse, and even as Malagant watched, the hood on its head rolled back to reveal that the face inside was naught but a ball of straw, pinned to the body by a crude wooden stake.

A stone fist squeezed Ralf's gut. He wrenched on the reins and raised his voice in a bellow of warning. "Fools, they are not here, there's no one here! You are battling with dummies!"

He was not the only one to shout the alarm. Other soldiers were rapidly discovering that their victims were no more than rolled-up blankets and old clothes given the semblance of human shape by wood, twine, and straw.

In the near distance, flickers of light blossomed in the darkness as torches were lit, one from the other in a chain. Link upon link the brilliance grew until it formed a mighty loop.

"They've fallen for it." Lancelot grinned at Agravaine as he kindled his own torch from the one in the knight's fist and passed on the gift of fire to Patrise at his other side.

"They will fall for much more before we have done with them," Agravaine growled, and tightened his scarred knuckles on his stallion's reins. "And they'll never rise again. He looked sidelong at Lancelot. "There are many rumors about you, but all vouch for your prowess with a sword."

"And for once you hope that the rumors are true?" There was a smile in Lancelot's eyes and a wry twist to his mouth. Agravaine returned the smile.

"About the prowess, yes," he said.

The knights of Camelot began their advance upon the camp where Malagant's troops were milling in confusion. Stately at first, as if taking part in a parade, their armor glowing a fiery red, reflections glittering on harness and groomed horse hide. Saddle to saddle, knee to knee, they paced in step with each other, proud and magnificent. Brothers in life and death. And with the same fluid, stately grace, Arthur raised his sword on high and struck at the stars with the shining blade. His lungs expanded, and the night was filled with the force of his voice.

"Charge!"

A war bugle sounded the attack, the brazen notes almost deafening Lancelot. He slackened the rein and used his spurs. Jupiter surged, matching stride with Agravaine's chestnut. The ground shook beneath the thunder of the iron-shod hooves. Faster and faster, rank upon rank, blazing like a comet across the dark field. Rising up from the grass as if they had grown out of the soil, Arthur's foot soldiers joined the charge, their swords drawn and shields held high.

The knights hit Malagant's confused forces with devastating force. Swords clanged upon shield, were parried by other swords, or else ripped through leather and flesh. Now came the screams of agony that Ralf had expected to hear, but they were being uttered by his own men.

A crossbow bolt whizzed past Lancelot's ear. He cut down the man who had fired it in a single, smooth blow. Beneath him, Jupiter never faltered. To either side of him, Agravaine and Patrise kept pace, their own sword arms rising and falling. They were like three reapers in a field of wheat, and they were unstoppable. Cut and thrust, slash and parry. Red firelight and the crimson baptism of blood.

Even as the knights carved a swath through the enemy, a squad of Ralf's reinforcements came bursting out of the darkness and slashed viciously into Arthur's foot soldiers. The fighting broke out with renewed vigor, and the screams of wounded men tore through the night.

Arthur sat on his horse apart from the battle, commanding a small rise so that he had a clear overview of the fighting and could direct men to where they were needed. The sight of Agravaine,

Patrise, and Lancelot cutting down all who blocked their path did not miss his eye. He knew the two established knights for superb swordsmen, but Lancelot was easily as good, if not better. He was not as powerfully built as Agravaine and Patrise, but he possessed a tensile strength, and lightning speed that had their own devastation.

Arthur's study was interrupted as two mounted soldiers galloped up to him.

"The archers are in place, Sire," saluted the first one.

Arthur nodded briskly. "Hold them until I give the signal."

"Sire!" The soldier spurred his mount away.

"The left wing's falling back, Sire," informed the second messenger.

"Then pull back and regroup in order. Find Agravaine. Tell him to charge."

"Yes, Sire."

Arthur turned to a third soldier who had ridden up. "Is the center holding?"

"It is, Sire."

"Good. I want the second battalion to support the left wing."

The man saluted and galloped off. Arthur watched the battle go forth with renewed concentration, one hand resting on the sword hilt at his hip. He had served a long apprenticeship in the field. More than forty years of experience mantled his shoulders now. He did not doubt that it was enough to defeat Malagant of Gore. Further up the hillside, prepared for a swift escape if the impossible should occur, were Guinevere and her escort. He could feel her with him, her anguish and determination as the two armies fought over her beloved Leonesse. He wondered if she in her turn could feel him. *It will be all right,* he reassured her in his mind. *Malagant cannot win. I love you.*

And across the valley on the far hillside, Malagant too sat motionless on his mount, tracking the movement of troops with impassive eyes. He raised one arm, and a fresh squadron of marauders thundered down the hillside into the fray. They struck it like a wave crashing on a rock and were splintered to individual fragments, riding high, and falling back into the darkness. Screams rose like spindrift through the night.

Arthur's hand clenched upon his stallion's reins, and the dark roan tossed and cavorted. The left wing steadied and held. The knights continued to thrust a spearhead into Malagant's troops; Agravaine, Lancelot, and Patrise forming the tip of that spear, tempered steel, unbreakable.

Hooves thundered. Another messenger rode up to Arthur and breathlessly saluted. "They're breaking, Sire!" he panted. "The enemy is breaking!"

Arthur nodded, but no gleam of triumph entered his eyes. Too often battles were lost at the very moment when their generals believed them won. "Hold the center," he commanded, and his expression was severe, his voice forceful with emphasis. "Do not give chase. Stay in your ranks."

The young man bowed and turned back to the fray.

"The first batallion has regrouped, Sire," announced another equerry. Blood trickled from a minor cut on his cheekbone, and his horse was lathered up.

"First batallion forward. Sound the advance," Arthur said incisively. "Watch that left flank!"

"Sire!"

Arthur's blood sang. A part of him wanted to draw his sword and pound down into the battle among his knights, know the joy of the brotherhood once more. But another part held the impulse at bay. He was the High King, and the responsibilities on his shoulders were too heavy to carry into battle. Knowing what was at stake, he held to discipline, his mind as cold and clear as the waters of the river Avalon.

From his own hillside vantage point, Malagant knew that all had not gone according to plan. Arthur's luck in battle was still holding. "My time is coming," Malagant said to himself. It was not by way of self-reassurance, but an affirmation of the destiny he had always acknowledged for himself. "I will hold the High Kingship in my two hands by right of conquest."

Out of the fire-shot darkness Ralf rode up to him, his face streaked with tears of blood and his sword hand crimson to the wrist.

Malagant arched a brow at his senior captain. "Is the battle won?"

Ralf grimaced. "Almost, my prince."

Malagant cracked a grim smile. "As bad as that?"

Ralf licked his lips, not knowing how to respond to his lord's dark humor.

Malagant pulled his horse away down the hill and faced a second, huge army—his reserves. He could pitch them all against Arthur now and pin his hopes on a final, all-out assault or he could make a tactical retreat. It was the latter he chose. Arthur had the bit between his teeth. The likelihood was that these men would be cut down, too, by that damned squad of royal guards. Besides, Malagant did not know how many troops Arthur himself had held in reserve.

He raised his arm on high and waved toward the far hills, giving the signal to pull out. Time was on his side.

Down in the valley, Agravaine left the remnants of the battle and rode up to Arthur. Heaving with exhaustion, glowing with triumph, he bowed his head to his king. "They're running, Sire. Do we hunt them down?"

Arthur pursed his lips and stared with narrowed eyes toward the hill that had been occupied by Malagant's command post. The torches no longer burned upon the crest. "No," he said after a moment. "Let them go; they've taken a bad mauling. Our concern now is Leonesse."

The knights regrouped around Arthur. Sergeants and adjutants reassembled the men under their command and formed them into ranks ready to march upon the town of Leonesse. Monks, surgeons, and their attendants worked among the battlefield casualties, binding, stitching, administering the last rites. Those who could walk or ride moved out with the main army toward the town.

Bugles sounded. Battle banners rippled in the night wind. Dawn was pink on the horizon as Guinevere came galloping down the hillside on her white mare to join Arthur for the march.

She rode toward the cluster of knights, Arthur at their center and, with a feeling of weak relief, saw Lancelot among them, unharmed. Even through her fear for Leonesse had run a fear almost as strong that she would lose the two men who meant most to her in the world.

The knights parted to let her through and she thanked them, her manner preoccupied. The town itself had not burned, but she had yet to speak to her people. Her white mare nudged past Jupiter. Knee touched knee. She saw Lancelot's controlling hand on the black's rein, and remembered his fingers grasping hers in the cathedral, the brush of his lips across her palm. Their eyes met briefly, and then both of them looked away. She joined her husband and fixed her thoughts upon Leonesse.

Agravaine looked sidelong at Lancelot and dismissed the suspicion that had momentarily clouded his mind. The new knight was staring into the middle distance, and the only look in his eyes was one of battle weariness. Absurd to think that he should have looked upon the queen with anything more than passing courtesy, or that she should have answered him, when obviously all her care was for Arthur and Leonesse.

Chapter 17

Dawn was a pink flush in a liquid green sky when the army of Camelot paced cautiously through the wide-open gates of Leonesse. His senses on edge, Lancelot stared around as they moved between dark buildings and up the cobbled street leading to the central square. The war bugles had fallen silent, and the only sounds were the clop of horseshoes and the tramp of boots.

"Holy God," muttered Agravaine, crossing himself. "The place is deserted." His eyes flickered. "Where are all the people?"

Lancelot did not answer. A feeling of dread crawled up his spine and pulled at the roots of his hair. It was as if he was in the underground river once more, beaten and battered, unable to control his own destiny. On all sides he saw the signs of Malagant's vindictive occupation. Doors swung open, half torn from their hinges. Furniture was smashed in the street, simple tables and chairs of no value except to their owners. The shops and businesses had been looted. Shelves were empty, their contents either stolen or wantonly tipped upon the floor and ground underfoot. And among the houses and the shattered possessions, not an inhabitant was to be seen, living or dead. Their own echoes rebounded to mock at Arthur and his men.

The column entered the main square and drew to a halt. Guinevere stared frantically around, her complexion ashen. "Where are my people?" she demanded, her voice cracking. "What has he done to them?"

Lancelot studied the main square, the church on one side, the palace walls on the other. The dread wriggled on his scalp like ribbons of ice. On the ground, lying in the dust before the church, was a child's straw doll, battered and trampled by the hooves of Malagant's cavalry. His gaze flickered from the doll to the church, to the beauty of a stained glass window caught in the brilliance of the rising sun. The colors were so sharp that they cut him to the heart. His eyes misted over. He saw another church, another window; melting heat, screams of pain and terror; a hand punching through the glass in a final desperate spasm that had ignited a fireball and destroyed his world.

"No!" The cry tore out of him now as it had all those years ago, filled with denial and frantic terror. He leaped down from his startled horse, ran to the church, and threw himself at the great iron-studded doors. A mighty beam had been hammered across them, bolting them shut, just as the doors of that other church had been bolted.

"No, No!" Lancelot sobbed and battered himself against the door. Memory was so strong that he seemed to smell the smoke and hear the screams. And although he knew he could not save them, that he was too late, still he battered on the doors and tore at the securing beam until he ripped his nails to the quick and his fingers ran with blood.

A swift gesture from Arthur sent others running to help Lancelot shift the beam. From the other side now could be heard the sound of hammering fists and cries for help. The sounds increased Lancelot's striving to a frenzy. He did not feel the splinters that stabbed his hands, or the bruises sustained by his shoulder and arm as he made of himself a human battering ram. All he heard were the cries for help; all he saw was a tower of fire. He was not even aware of the moment when the beam gave way and the great oak doors swung inward. The sudden releasing of force drove him to his knees.

A child ran out into the street, then stopped and stared at the gathered might of Camelot with wide eyes. His mother followed, fearfully trying to grab him back into her arms, And then she, too, stopped and stared. Her eyes lit upon the blue and gold banners, and then upon Guinevere.

"Oh, my lady!" she cried with joy and relief. "My lady, you came for us!" She ran to Guinevere's saddle and kissed the hem of her gown. Beginning to cry herself, Guinevere leaned over to clasp the woman's hands.

"You're safe now. Malagant will never come again!"

The imprisoned people of Leonesse poured out of the church and threw themselves rejoicing upon Arthur's troops. A mood of pensive tension was replaced by one of utter euphoria. Arthur was submerged under a welter of hugging, kissing people, so that he was almost in more danger of losing his life than he had been during the battle with Malagant. Guinevere, laughing even as tears streamed down her face, was spun from embrace to embrace until finally she found herself in Oswald's arms.

Her old adviser hugged her tenderly, and she kissed him on both cheeks. "Oh, Oswald, I'm so glad to see you!"

"And I you, never more," he answered somewhat wryly, and as they parted, moved on to be embraced by a smiling Arthur.

"You're safe, old friend, thank God for that," Arthur declared.

Oswald shrugged. "Oh, I'm so old now that no one thinks it worth the trouble of killing me."

"Malagant would," Arthur said darkly before turning to receive the good wishes of yet more townsfolk.

Outside the church, Lancelot stood beneath the decorated stone arches of the doorway. Drenched in the sweat of effort, his body weak with exhaustion, he unburied his face from his bleeding hands and stared at the scene before him with a mingling of astonishment and disbelief. Children were racing around the square, capering for the sheer pleasure of being free after so long cooped up inside the church. Women were smiling and crying, men too. The entire vanguard of Camelot's army had been overwhelmed by celebrating townspeople. The church's stained windows were intact, glowing with nothing more sinister than the light of a new day.

Slowly, dazed with emotion, he staggered to his

feet. A woman wearing a patched apron grasped one of his scratched hands and pressed a kiss to his reddened knuckles. "God bless you, sir. God bless you," she said with tears in her eyes.

Bemused, Lancelot could only gaze at her speechlessly. A tug at his leg drew his attention down to a small boy who was staring up at him out of huge blue eyes. Freckles spattered the bridge of his snubbed nose, and he could not have been more than five or six years old.

"Can I go home now?" he asked Lancelot seriously.

Lancelot swallowed. His throat was so tight that it was difficult to answer. "Yes," he croaked. "Yes, home now." Salty heat burned his eyes. As the little boy ran across the town square, in the direction of the houses beyond, Lancelot turned away, assailed by a feeling of grief so strong that it overpowered all other emotions. His own child had died unborn. He could not join the celebrations; he desperately needed to be alone.

Pushing his way through the crowd of laughing, dancing people, even shouldering aside those familiar to him, he sought the sanctuary of a dark, open doorway in the palace wall. Uncaring where he was going, only that it be alone, he blundered through the doorway like a candle-blinded moth and entered the palace garden. The medicinal scent of herbs wafted on the breeze as he brushed the plants in his stumbled passing. In the gathering light the morning chorus of birds filled the air, and the turf glittered with dew. The path ended at an apple grove. The sacred trees of Avalon. Lancelot could go no further and sank to his knees in the deep grass between the gnarled trunks. The morning was beautiful and new, but before he could embrace it, he had to release the ghosts from the past.

Sobs shuddered his body as the long-buried grief poured out of him, wordless, inconsolable. He had not wept on the day that his home and family had burned. He had told himself that mourning would not bring them back. Nor would it, but he saw now in the midst of the storm that it was the only way to be healed. He had been wounded too deeply for too long. Curling over, hugging himself, he surrendered to grieving for all that had been lost so long ago.

Dawn brightened in the sky. Lancelot lay in the grass, inhaling its sweetness. His clothes were damp from the dew, but they would dry soon enough. He was beyond such discomfort for now. The moving of the soul was of far greater moment. He saw things with a clarity that was almost too painful to bear, for they had been locked in the dark for so many years. Nineteen years in the world, and almost as many in limbo.

Doves cooed and fluttered in the cots at the side of the grove, the sound soothing and redolent of summer. He listened, letting the peace flow over him. Soft footsteps sounded on the path, and the air moved. He looked up and saw Guinevere coming toward him. The light of dawn shone upon her, so that she glowed like a figure from a stained glass window. A golden nimbus of sun-caught hair filaments glowed around her head, and her face was radiant. He stared at her, more than half in a dream. Never had he seen her look so beautiful, never had he felt love so deep, so strong, and never had he known so clearly what he must do . . . but not yet.

She knelt down beside him in a rustle of robes and gently touched his face. "You have been weeping," she said.

"I have been finding myself." He reached up and took her fingers in his, kissed them, and lowered them. They looked at each other but said nothing. Feelings ran too deep for speech to encompass them. The moment was precious and fragile, to be held and treasured.

As if from far away the church bells began to ring in the square, a joyous peal to celebrate the liberation of Leonesse. The sound carried across the palace and floated into the garden, masking the softer cooing of the doves.

Lancelot released her hand. "Listen," he murmured. "They're calling you home."

She shook her head, a tiny frown on her brow. "In a while." she said, and in her face he saw mirrored his own reluctance to break the magic of the moment. It would never come again. And yet they could not remain. People would soon be looking for their queen, and too many questions would be asked.

"I have no home but where you are," he said, more than half to himself. "And that's the one place I cannot be."

They fell silent again while the bells pealed and pealed and the morning brightened around them. A small sigh was drawn from Guinevere. She knew that she had to go. Lancelot did not rise with her. She could see him still clinging to the tranquility of the garden.

He looked up at her. "It was the church," he said.

"When they all ran out and danced in the square, they set me free, too."

"Yes, I know."

He smiled and gazed at the doves fluttering in an oblique bar of first sunlight. "I would follow the path of my heart if I could." He did not look around, and Guinevere realized that he was giving her the grace of time to leave. For a brief instant she hesitated, and then she raised her dew-damp skirts above her ankles and left the sanctuary of the garden for the safety of the palace.

Guinevere stood at the window of her old, familiar chamber, the one that had been hers since her entry into womanhood. It was comforting to be surrounded by the trappings of her former, less-troubled life. But it was only a visit, and perhaps a farewell. She had changed and was still changing. The carefree young woman had become a queen and a wife and had discovered the bittersweetness of love.

She stared out the open window at the early morning brightness. Outside, her people were picking up the threads of their lives and weaving them back into some semblance of normality. The wounded were being brought in from the battlefield for proper tending in the town. Arthur would be there, speaking to the men, giving them encouragement. He always put others before himself; he deserved all the loyalty and support she could give him.

Guinevere turned from the window and found her maid, Elise, waiting upon her. The young woman's eyes were dark-circled with lack of sleep, and she was swaying where she stood. Guinevere was immediately contrite.

"Go to bed, Elise. There is nothing that I want or cannot fetch for myself."

"My lady, it is not right that I should retire before you," the maid protested.

Guinevere smiled bleakly. "I wasn't always a queen, Elise. Do as I say, go to bed. I'll retire myself as soon as I have spoken with the king."

Elise dipped a graceful curtsey. "As my lady wishes. Goodnight, my lady . . . I mean good day, my lady."

Guinevere's smiled warmed slightly. "Sleep well, Elise."

The door clicked gently shut behind the maid. Guinevere continued to stare out the window while she tried to make order of her confused thoughts and emotions. She was exhausted herself, but the energy of triumph had buoyed her up until now. She stifled a yawn behind her hand and thought about going down to find Arthur. But what if she found Lancelot instead? Did he still linger in the apple grove, the salt tracks of tears on his face? Her heart turned over with the turbulence of her love for him.

A group of townspeople passed beneath her window on their way home. One of them doffed his hat and flourished it to her. "God bless you, my lady."

"God bless us all!" Guinevere cried down to them. Behind her she heard the sound of the door opening and wondered if her maid had returned, perhaps for her cloak or the casket of hairpins. "Elise?"

The door clicked softly shut. "No," said a male voice, the timbre slightly hoarse.

Guinevere gasped and spun around, a rush of

color flooding her cheeks. It was as if thinking of him had summoned his presence. If the garden had been dangerous, her private chamber was an even greater risk. He took a few steps forward and then halted. She saw that he was dressed for a journey, his cloak fastened at his breast and a water skin slung over his shoulder.

Guinevere swallowed and fought for the composure that he seemed to have acquired. "What are you doing here?" Her voice quavered and she swallowed again.

Lancelot's stare was intense, as if he would draw her soul from her body and take it into his own. "I think you know," he said. "It is time for me to move on. I've come to say good-bye, and to wish you well and to . . ." His voice faltered, revealing that he was not as composed as she had first thought.

So, it had come, she thought. Once she had bid him go from her. Now that he was about to do so, she could not bear it. "It has been a long night," she said unsteadily. "You've not slept. Perhaps you should wait until tomorrow."

He shook his head, and there was a determined set to his jaw. "I've time enough for sleep. I'll be far away from here by nightfall."

Her hands were shaking. She clutched the folds of her gown and held her head high. "Where will you go?"

"I don't know." He shrugged. "Westward. Wherever the road leads."

"And will you be coming back this way?"

"I—I don't think so."

"Never?" She choked the word.

He lowered his eyes and fiddled with his gauntlets for a moment. She looked upon the planes of his face, the downcast lashes, the dark tumble of his hair, and had to bite her lip to prevent a cry of pain. He raised his head, and she saw her own anguish reflected in his eyes. "Never. I know what I must do now." He gestured with his graceful swordsman's hands. "I've never believed in anything before, but I believe in Camelot. I can serve it best by leaving."

"I—"

"Tell the king I'll always remember that he saw the best in me."

"And what shall I tell myself?" Guinevere asked, her voice low and hoarse as she strove for the control to let him go with dignity and generosity.

He said softly, a world of heartache in the words, "That there was once a man who loved you too much to change you."

Without being aware, Guinevere took several steps toward him. The space between them became touching distance. I'll—I'll not forget him. I sheltered under a tree with him once, in the rain. I loved him then . . . and I always will.

Lancelot was trembling, too. Now that she was closer, she could see the rapid heartbeat in his throat and the shine of tears in his eyes.

"Bid me good-bye," he said gruffly, "and let me go."

"I can't," Guinevere answered brokenly. "The words don't come."

"Then give me your hand."

She unclenched her right one from her gown, not the left that wore her wedding ring, and he took it in his. Turning it over, he raised it to his lips and laid a kiss in her palm. She cupped her fingers against his cheek, feeling the roughness of stubble, the tenderness of skin, the warmth and strength of him. Then he released her hand and, drawing himself up, made her a formal bow of parting.

Guinevere quivered. The touch, so fleeting, was not enough to last her the lifetime for which they must be parted. "Lancelot," she whispered, gazing up at him through a blur of tears. "Lancelot, I owe you a kiss."

He hesitated. She saw the desire leap in his eyes and the denial form on his lips, and her own curved in a small, poignant smile.

"I'm asking you."

He gazed upon her, and his longing overcame the good intentions he had had of saying farewell firmly and walking away. "No, my queen," he said.

"Not a queen, not now, with you." She raised her face toward his as she had done beneath the oak tree in the rain, and returned him the words he had once given to her. "Just for one moment . . . let all the world go away, and all the people in it, but you and me."

He spoke her name like a wish and drew her into his arms. Their eyes met and held, making the moment last forever, and then he bent his head and she raised on tiptoe to meet him, and their lips joined. It began gently enough, but they had waited too long and lived through too much for the gentleness to be enough. The passions of despair, white hot desire, and fierce love could not be contained in decorum. Her fingers tangled in his hair, she pressed herself against him, and he closed his eyes and groaned, his spread hands tightening upon her waist and spine, while the kiss went endlessly on.

In the midst of inspecting Leonesse's defenses and gauging improvements, Arthur suddenly remembered that he had promised to breakfast with Guinevere, give her a report on the state of the town as a whole, and let her know how matters were progressing. Accordingly, Agravaine in tow, he changed direction.

"Probably she has given up on me and retired," Arthur said wryly as he strode toward the palace.

"I am sure she understands your burdens, Sire."

"Only too well, Agravaine." Arthur chuckled. "She can see through me as if I were glass." It was not a complaint. The knight noted the lithe bounce in his lord's stride. Since Guinevere had entered his life, Arthur had shed the years and regained much of the luster of his youth. Marriage to Guinevere had changed Arthur for the better. It remained to be seen what marriage to Arthur would do for the lovely young queen.

In Guinevere's antechamber her maids were both dead to the world. Arthur moved softly so as not to waken them and crept to the door of the inner room. "I fear I'm too late," he said, and setting his hand on the latch, opened the door.

His breath froze in his chest, and his body turned to stone. Behind him, Agravaine sucked a sharp breath through his teeth. And near the bed, Guinevere unlocked her lips from Lancelot's and turned to stare at the intrusion. In the moment before her expression changed to one of horrified shock, Arthur saw the heavy lids, the kiss-swollen lips, and the dazzle of love for another man. Never, ever, had she looked on him thus. Arthur's heart became stone, too, and he felt it crack into a thousand pieces. Too late, indeed!

For an eternity no one spoke. Somehow Arthur managed to breathe, although every movement struck through his chest with the pain of ice. "Agravaine, fetch the guards," he commanded.

Agravaine hesitated, obviously worried and uncomfortable. "Sire, I—"

"Do it!" Arthur's voice was a frozen snarl.

"Yes, Sire."

Arthur stared at the two of them, still only inches apart. Then he turned and walked away, his step that of a man who had received a mortal wound.

Chapter 18

Arthur stood alone in the Round Table chamber, his mantle thrown around his shoulders, beads of rain dotting the rich wool. Candles burned fitfully in the corona lucis above the great table, their flame agitated by a draft from the hard equinox wind that was blustering against the walls of the palace.

The army had ridden in earlier that evening, fresh from their triumph in Leonesse, but much subdued. Victory had been won, but their king had tasted defeat. Arthur paced slowly around the great table, stopping at each place. He could hear the voices of his knights, see the pity and blame in their eyes.

"She betrayed you and Camelot."

"She was too young, too beautiful."

"The law must take its course."

Arthur shuddered and shook his head in denial. "Am I to lose everything?" he asked the cold air. "Is that how it has to be? Ah God, I cannot bear it!" He threw himself down in his chair and put his head in his hands. "I loved her," he moaned. "I loved her."

Rain slashed against the windows, and several candles guttered and went out. "God forgive me, did I love her too much?"

His mind filled with the vision of Guinevere walking down the nave of the cathedral on their wedding day, the light from the stained windows decorating her path with jeweled lozenges of color. The smile on her face, her graceful bearing. He had had no reason to doubt her. She had laid her hand within his and given herself into his keeping without hesitation. And in return he had given her every last iota of his love and his trust.

The image in his mind was overlaid by another one, this time from a waking nightmare. He saw her in Lancelot's arms, her body pressed intimately to the younger man's, not an inch of space between them. Lancelot's hands at her waist, in her hair, Lancelot's mouth upon hers in a lover's kiss.

"Why," Arthur whispered through the bars of his fingers. "Why?" His head jerked up, twisting from side to side, and the final cry was a howl of pure rage and grief. *"Why?"*

The stone walls were thick and the room was cold. Lancelot had been granted the warmth of a wrought-iron brazier, but it had gone out long since, and he had not bothered to replenish it. He had been Arthur's prisoner for perhaps a week, but in all that time he had not seen the king. Solitary confinement had been his lot since Arthur had discovered him with Guinevere locked in that damning embrace. He had been closely guarded on the journey back to Camelot, hemmed around by dour-faced guards, shunned by the men who had sworn him an oath of brotherhood. But then he had sworn an oath to treat Guinevere's honor as his own, and in their eyes, as well as Arthur's, he had broken it.

Was Guinevere confined, too? He suspected so. Probably not as harshly as this, but nevertheless her every move would be watched. *Oh my love,* he thought, *this should never have happened to us.* And yet he could not regret the feel of her lips and the pressure of her warm, slender body against his own. It should have been forever, not just a brief, stolen moment, for which they were both now paying the price. He leaned his head wearily against the wall and closed his eyes. Sleep would not come, he had wrestled with it too often to think it would, but he could at least rest his eyes and see Guinevere's image imprinted on his lids.

The sound of footsteps echoing on stone caused him to open them and turn his head in the direction of the door. He heard the scrape of the guard's boots and the thump of a spear shaft on the flags as the man stood to attention.

"Unlock the door," commanded Arthur's voice.

"Sire!"

Metal jingled and a key grated in the lock. Arthur dismissed the man and pushed into the room, closing the door behind him.

Lancelot's heart began to pound. He rose quickly to his feet. Arthur looked dreadful. His eyes were red-rimmed and sunken, revealing that he too had slept very little, and the skin was slack and dull over gaunt bones.

"My lord, I—"

"Be silent," Arthur said with chilly authority. The very lack of emotion in his voice revealed how much he was suffering. "I want none of your glib persuasions."

Lancelot's jaw tightened. He had known that this confrontation must come. Now it was here, he set himself to endure, his spine rigid.

Arthur advanced into the room and planted himself before Lancelot. "Did you come to Camelot to betray me?" he demanded.

"No, my lord, I—"

"You desired her—you pursued her," Arthur cut him off, and his voice began to scald with bitter rage.

Lancelot held his ground and met Arthur's gaze square on. It was his only hope. "The queen is innocent, my lord."

"Innocent?" Arthur laughed harshly. "I saw her in your arms, her lips on yours!"

"You saw all there has ever been between us and all there ever will be." Lancelot dug his hands through his hair in a despairing gesture. "I've fallen in love with a woman I can never call my own. That's all my crime and all my punishment."

Color stained Arthur's cheekbones, and his body trembled with fury. "You presume to pronounce your own punishment?" he snarled. "Your crime is treason, and the sentence for treason is death."

Lancelot swallowed. Having hidden from his own emotions for more than twenty years, he was not skilled to cope with Arthur's raw, jealous rage. "I never meant to hurt you, my lord," he said inadequately.

"Then what did you mean to do?" Arthur choked. "I trusted you. I loved you. And you betrayed me.

Didn't you think that would hurt me? Or perhaps you did not think at all, except with your loins!"

Heat stained Lancelot's face and his own anger rose. There was a grain of truth in what Arthur said, but no more, and that among a thousand other grains of different meaning. Fair but unfair. He made the effort and kept his voice level as he replied. "All I wanted in life was to be with her, and yet I was leaving Camelot alone. It was our farewell that you witnessed. I would not have returned this way again."

The color drained from Arthur's complexion until he was a pasty gray. "Am I to be grateful for your leavings?" he demanded hoarsely, his eyes staring. "You leave me nothing—nothing!"

Lancelot looked miserably at the older man trembling before him. Every time he opened his mouth, he seemed to make the damage to Arthur's pride worse. "My lord—" he held out a pleading hand, entreating the king to see with rational eyes, but that, too, fell on stony ground.

"No more! I'll hear no more!" Arthur's voice cracked. "You'll be charged with treason under our laws. Defend yourself to the court. And the law will judge you!" He turned on his heel and slammed out the door. The key turned decisively in the lock, Arthur's footsteps retreated at a near run, and Lancelot was once more alone.

He groaned and slumped on the narrow bed with which he had been provided. Defend himself? How could he do that when Arthur was the law of Camelot? Would it be so bad to die? He grimaced. For a foolish old man's jealousy, for a foolish young man's ardor, for a single kiss, yes, it would.

There was more to Arthur than this vindictive

bitterness. It must pass. . . . All things must pass. He stared bleakly at the wall and watched the daylight run its course on the glowing tawny stone.

Guinevere sat in the silence of her chamber and stared at the flames licking the logs in the hearth. She was wearing a gown of charcoal gray silk shot with patterns of woven gold, a somber, queenly garment and a reminder to herself of the position she held. Time and again she had relived that moment with Lancelot, knowing that if she had her time over, she would have let him leave without that all-damning kiss. Nothing was worth this confined silence or the pain she had seen in Arthur's eyes as he turned from her. And yet it was only one kiss, and Arthur had more of her than she had ever yielded to any man—everything except her heart.

The sound of the lock being turned in the door curtailed her ruminations, and she turned toward it with conflicting expressions of hope and despair on her face. There was no road out of her predicament, save that it lay over a bed of thorns.

The door opened. She caught a glimpse of the guards on duty outside, and then Agravaine entered the room, the usual enthusiasm in his blue eyes now quenched and somber. He inclined his head to her. "The king asks for you, my lady," he said in formal tones, and she could see how uncomfortable he was. Agravaine was one of Arthur's best fighting men, but he was not a diplomat or a deep thinker. He lived life by a soldier's gut instinct, and he was obviously out of his depth.

"At last." Guinevere rose to her feet. Perhaps

Arthur had calmed enough for her to be able to reach him and mend the breach. "Elise," she commanded, and picked up her small hand mirror to check upon her appearance. The maid hastened to her mistress's side and helped her with her toilet while Agravaine stood to one side and looked stiffly on.

"You think me vain, sir?" she inquired with a sidelong look.

Agravaine reddened. "No, my lady." His eyes met hers and then flicked away to the middle distance.

"I know that you were with him when . . . when he found me bidding farewell to Lancelot, but whatever you think of me, I love Arthur. He is my husband and my king. I will strive to be worthy of him. There, I'm ready." She laid the mirror back down on her coffer and moved with slow dignity to Agravaine's side.

He cleared his throat and led her to the door. Elise began to weep and was immediately comforted by Petronella. Guinevere felt like weeping herself, but she clung to her composure. After all, came the bitter thought, I am a queen.

When they reached Arthur's chamber, Agravaine halted outside and banged the door once, hard, with his clenched fist. Then he opened it for Guinevere but did not enter himself. Guinevere drew a deep breath and stepped over the threshold. Behind her, Agravaine drew the door shut. The latch clicked and she was alone with Arthur.

He stood on the far side of the room, his back to her; and when he heard the door close, he raised his head and spoke without turning around, as if he could not bear to face her. "I must know the truth. I ask you not to lie to me, even if you think you will hurt me."

Guinevere held the breath she had drawn and waited.

"Have you . . ." Arthur struggled. "I must know. Have you given yourself to him?"

Color flooded Guinevere's cheeks. She breathed out. "No, my lord." And remembering the storm of that final kiss, she knew that it was only by the grace of God that she could answer thus.

"Do you love him?"

She bit her lip. The truth, he had said, even if it would hurt him. "Yes," she replied, her voice low-pitched, almost inaudible. But he heard her and turned around. The look of anguish on his face made her catch her breath for pity. Instinctively she reached out to him, but he avoided her, his face twisting in pain.

"How did I fail you?"

Tears blazed in her eyes. "You have never failed me, my lord."

"I saw your face as you kissed him."

Guinevere's mind darted, seeking the words that would lessen the tension building in the atmosphere. A week had not served to lessen his rage and grief but rather with brooding to increase it.

"Love has many faces," she said. "I may look on you differently, but not with less love."

He let out a choked breath, as if he had been struck in the soft space beneath his heart. He knew what she was saying, and it fulfilled his secret dread. If she could kiss Lancelot with passionate abandon, then what was left for him, the cuckolded husband?

The role of the father she had lost? But she was far more to him than a daughter.

"When a woman loves two men," he said wearily, "she must choose between them."

"I choose you," she said firmly, looking directly at him. "As I have always done."

"Your will chooses me. Your heart chooses him."

"Then you have the best of it," she said desperately. "My will is stronger than my heart. Do you think I put so high a price on my feelings? Feelings live for a moment, and then the moment passes. My will holds me steady to my course through life."

He searched her face, seeing in it the fierceness and honesty that had first attracted him to her. "As mine does me," he acknowledged. "And yet all I have to do is look at you, and everything I have ever believed in fades to nothing, and all I want is your love."

Guinevere took a step closer. "You have it."

He arched a black eyebrow. "Do I?"

"My dear lord, I—"

"Then look on me as you looked on him!" he snarled. And he, too, took a step closer so that they were face to face, and there was nowhere for her to hide or prevaricate. For an instant she met his dark stare, but it was too fierce, too demanding of the truth, and she could not hold it. Unable to face him a moment longer, she turned away in failure and put her hand across her eyes.

"How could you do this to me?" Arthur demanded, lashing out in renewed pain.

"I swear to you, I've done nothing," Guinevere said without turning round.

"No," Arthur snarled savagely, "you're innocent,

but you kiss him like a lover. You've done nothing, but you let him into your bedchamber at night alone. God help me, any more of this innocence and I'll go mad!"

This was worse than Guinevere had ever imagined. The Arthur she thought she knew, the kindly, benevolent figure, had been swallowed up by a jealous, vindictive being, against whose venom she had no defense. She had wanted to ask him what he had done with Lancelot, but seeing his mood now, she knew that she dared not.

"I'll do whatever you tell me, my lord," she said in a forlorn voice.

Arthur let out a deep sigh and turned to pace the room like a caged beast. "I don't know what to tell you. I don't know what to think or feel anymore." He stopped and stared at a wall hanging depicting a scene of carefree lords and ladies picnicking beside a river. "I no longer see my way ahead." There was a long silence while he gained control of himself. The mantle of kingship fell once more around his shoulders, and he turned to face Guinevere with bitter pride.

"I have been given so much in my lifetime," he said woodenly. "Only fools dream of the one thing they cannot have."

Guinevere hung her head, the burden of guilt crushing her spirit. Hurting Arthur was the last thing she had ever intended when she came to Camelot. If only—. She stopped herself and clenched her fists at her sides. If only was a fruitless game to play. "Forgive me," she whispered, tears spilling down her cheeks.

Arthur was unmoved by the sight. "What have I to

forgive?" he said with a shrug. "I dreamed a dream of you. It was a sweet dream while it lasted."

Guinevere swallowed the sobs that were choking her throat.

"Agravaine, escort the queen back to her rooms," he commanded harshly.

"Yes, Sire." His expression blank, Agravaine bowed and fell into step beside Guinevere.

Arthur then slumped, his eyes squeezed tightly shut and his fists clenched.

Chapter 19

A meeting had been called in the round chamber, and all the knights were required to attend—all except one, and he was guarded in isolation. Agravaine glanced around at his brother knights and saw his own concern mirrored on their faces, although no one spoke their thoughts aloud. The specters of dishonor and betrayal were already too close for comfort. Arthur had been impossible since discovering Lancelot and Guinevere in each other's arms. At first he had refused to speak about it, and then, later, when he did, there had been no reasoning with him. Agravaine could not condone what Lancelot and Guinevere had done, but neither could he condemn out of hand. He did not believe that they had deliberately gone behind Arthur's back, and he knew that they were both full of remorse that the king should ever have seen that embrace. Lancelot had been on the point of leaving. It was Agravaine's opinion that Arthur should let him go. Without Lancelot's disturbing, charismatic presence, Guinevere would cleave to Arthur. In all other ways she had shown herself to be a sensible, practical young woman. Agravaine knew that several of the others felt that way, too. But persuading Arthur would be difficult.

There was a brief fanfare and the doors of the great chamber swung open to admit the king. As one, the knights rose and saluted him. Arthur strode rapidly to his place, his expression frowning and grim. Agravaine's heart sank.

Arthur glared around the array of knights. "May God grant us the wisdom to discover the right, the will to choose it, and the strength to make it endure," he said in a tone that suggested that the words were spiked with broken glass.

"Amen," declared the knights, and once Arthur had taken his seat, they sat down, too.

Arthur stared at the flame burning in the table's center brazier, and then he looked around the table at his knights. His eyes paused on the empty place. First Malagant, then Lancelot. He did not think he would seat anyone there again for a long, long time. "I have reached a decision," he said. "This business must be settled, and straight away, for the good of all concerned. I was mistaken in Lancelot. You warned me, and I did not listen. As a man, I may forgive, but as a king, I must see justice done."

Agravaine listened and wondered if Arthur could see inside the words he was speaking. It was as a man torn by pain that he was making an issue of a matter that could be dealt with quietly. Unless there was blatant adultery, it did not touch upon the well-being and security of the kingdom. "Does Lancelot admit guilt, Sire?" he asked.

Arthur narrowed his eyes. His hands tightened on the arms of his chair. "Whatever he has to say in his defense can be said at the trial."

Patrise exchanged a dismayed glance with Agravaine. "The trial, Sire?"

Arthur looked coldly at Patrise. "There will be a public trial at noon tomorrow in the great square."

"In the great square?" Kay said, his expression one of horror.

All of the knights stared at Arthur as if he had lost his wits. Agravaine gnawed his lower lip. He, of all of them, was closest to the king and had been with him when Lancelot and Guinevere were discovered; but until this moment he had not realized how mortally wounded Arthur actually was. "Would it not be better to settle the matter in private, Sire?" he ventured. "It seems so—"

"You think the honor of Camelot a private matter?" Arthur thundered, half rising from his seat, his face a congested, dusky red. "Am I to hide in dark corners as if I am ashamed? Let every citizen see that the law rules in Camelot!"

There was a terrible silence as Arthur subsided in his chair. The king never lost his temper; the king never bellowed his will at his knights.

"Does anyone else desire to speak?" The red-rimmed eyes blazed around the table, daring them to open their mouths. "No? Well then, I declare this assembly closed. We convene again tomorrow at noon."

In silence the knights bowed and departed. Agravaine paused, wondering whether or not to speak, but Arthur waved him away with a brusque gesture. "Let me not doubt your loyalty, too," he muttered.

Agravaine gave up and strode out after Kay and Patrise, closing the great doors behind him. Alone, Arthur hung his head and wept.

The morning dawned bright and clear, a crisp day when it would have been a joy to ride through the turning leaves of the forest in search of game, or walk along the lake shore, watching the fishermen. Instead, the fine weather was to bear witness to the public trial of Lancelot and Guinevere.

All around the town square, tiered benches had been set up, and the population summoned to bear witness. What they were being required to see, they were not quite sure; and there was a constant low buzz of speculative conversation as the people left their homes and gathered to wait for events to take their course. A wooden platform had been built out from the palace steps, and upon it sat the knights of the High Council in their official robes. Seated in their center upon his royal throne was a grim-faced Arthur. Today he wore his royal crown, a gem-encrusted circlet that had been passed down through the bloodline since before the time of written memory. The gold gleamed on his brow and emphasized his authority.

A little to one side was Lancelot, flanked by guards, obviously a prisoner, although he was not bound. He held himself with quiet dignity, and when Arthur glanced his way, he met the king's gaze straight on. Across from him, also closely guarded, was Guinevere. Her face was wan, but her head was carried high. She would face this without flinching, and Lancelot's heart went out to her.

At the front of the platform, Mador stepped forward, unrolled a parchment scroll, and in a ringing voice began to read out the charges.

"Guinevere, Lady of Leonesse, Queen of Camelot, and Lancelot, Knight of the High Council, are hereby charged, in their own persons and in collusion one with the other, with dishonor to the realm, violation of the king's rights under law, and common adultery. These crimes constitute an act of treason against the kingdom of Camelot, and the penalty under law is death."

There was a collective gasp of shock from the crowd and a ripple of movement as neighbor turned to neighbor, exclaiming.

Mador faced Lancelot, his voice booming out over the audience. "Sir Lancelot may speak to the charges."

"What I have to say is for the king alone," Lancelot replied steadily.

Mador glanced questioningly at Arthur. After a moment's pause, the king gave a brusque nod of permission. "Let him speak."

Lancelot crossed the space between them to stand at the foot of the throne on which Arthur sat in his dual role of king and judge. The knights on either side withdrew several paces, affording a modicum of privacy. Lancelot bowed, and then, as he raised his head once more, he held Arthur's cold and angry eyes with a direct look.

"My lord, you said to me once, if you must die, die serving something greater than yourself. If my life or death serves Camelot, take it. Do as you like with me. You have been given the power to do great good. Use it well." The last words were those with which Arthur had challenged him after the gauntlet, and now, running a different kind of gauntlet, Lancelot threw them back at the king.

Arthur tensed, his knuckles showing white on the arms of the throne. Stare met stare in a bitter duel. But for Arthur, the time to back down had come and gone.

"Have you anything more to say to me?" he asked harshly.

"No, my lord."

"Then let the trial proceed." Arthur's eyes disengaged. Lancelot's did not. He returned to his place and faced Arthur, and it seemed to the king that the accused had become the accuser.

"Sir Lancelot may speak to the charges," cried Mador.

"I have nothing to say." Quiet though it was, there was contempt now in Lancelot's tone, and color stung Arthur's cheekbones. He gestured tersely at Mador to continue.

"Sir Lancelot's innocent, I know he is," Peter, the stableman, said hotly to his brother Thomas.

Thomas was a sentry in the royal guard, and today he was on duty at the causeway gatehouse. Most of the population was in the square attending the trial of the queen and the Round Table's new knight. Peter had been unable to stomach the sight and, after one glimpse of the proceedings, had ridden out to the walls to bring his brother a flask of wine and a loaf of bread.

Peter propped his feet on the trestle, examined the

loose sole on his boot, and took a drink from the flask. "No smoke without fire," Thomas said.

"In that case Arthur would have had to arrest every man in Camelot," Peter retorted. "Don't tell me that you don't think she's beautiful."

"Yes, but I've never been close enough to kiss her. That's what they're saying he did, probably more besides. They were out all night in the forest, weren't they?"

Peter restrained the urge to throw a fist in his older brother's face. Thomas was too big and burly to hit with impunity. "Lancelot was leaving. I know. I helped him make preparations. Jupiter was all saddled up. I never thought to call our king a fool, but I do believe he has lost his wits."

"More personal than his wits," Thomas pronounced, biting into the loaf and tearing the crust with strong, white teeth. "He's been hit below the belt, where it most matters to a man of his age with a pretty young wife."

Peter scowled at his brother. "Well, it's not true, I know it isn't."

"Why don't you go and testify on his behalf, then?"

"Who'd believe me? They're all like you," Peter said scornfully.

Their discussion was curtailed by the sound of horses advancing over the causeway at full gallop. Thomas jerked his boots off the trestle and shot to his feet, unbalancing his chair. Half tripping over its legs, he grabbed his spear from the corner and peered out of the lancet window. Peter ran to his brother's side and, craning on tiptoe, saw a carriage rattling across the causeway toward them, escorted by a troop of horses. The riders were wearing the colors of Leonesse, and they were in a tearing hurry.

"What's happening, what's wrong?" Peter demanded.

"How should I know?" his brother snapped, and left him to shout orders to the other guards under his command. Peter hesitated for a moment, then righted the chair and pounded down the stairs after Thomas. God pray that Malagant had not returned to harry Lady Guinevere's people again.

"Open the gates!" roared the leader of the escort in urgent tones. "Open the gates, we come from Leonesse! We bring witnesses for the trial!"

Thomas had reached the lowest window in the tower by now, and he leaned out to shout down. "The trial's already started."

"Then hurry and open up. The queen's good name depends on this evidence!"

"All right, all right!" Thomas snapped. He descended the final steps and emerged to examine the leader of the troop and the carriage through the portcullis. Within the carriage depths, as far as he could tell, were two of the Leonesse elders. The leading rider fidgeted impatiently, and his sweating horse stamped and rolled its eyes.

"Open up!" Thomas shouted to the guards in charge of the portcullis winch, and beckoned with his hand.

The iron gridded door began to rise in its slots, and the horsemen rode into the city, followed by the carriage.

"If you hurry you'll—" Thomas began, but that was as far as he got. The troop leader withdrew the crossbow that had been concealed beneath his cloak and fired down directly into Thomas's exposed breast. Thomas fell without a sound. His second-in-command was hit, too, and crumpled in the dust. The back of the carriage flung open and a heavy tree trunk shot out, followed by six of Malagant's marauders, their dark armor covered by the bright surcoats of Leonesse. Tied in their seats by thick cords, gagged by cloth, the elders were powerless to do anything.

Peter, who had been peering out of the lower window and had seen everything, howled at the winch guard to lower the portcullis. Feverishly, the man began winding, but it was already too late. Malagant's men pushed the oak trunk upright, and as the portcullis wound down, one of the spikes jammed in the wood, and the entire structure ground to a halt with a shuddering thud. Camelot's defenses were null and void.

There was a table in the room covered with an embroidered linen cloth, and Peter dived under this and hid, his teeth chattering together in fear and shock. He heard footsteps scuffing up the stairs and the door barged open.

"No one here," a deep voice growled. "Go up onto the battlements. Secure them next."

"Sir!"

The footsteps disappeared at a run. Peter did not move. He saw what had happened to Thomas and knew that if they noticed him, it would be his fate, too.

The surprise of the attack had been so complete that there had been no chance for the gate sentries to sound the alarm. Already, Malagant's advance troops were moving to secure the city walls. They met with little resistance, for almost all of the guards had been drafted to the town square to keep order and bear witness to the trial.

Now, unchallenged, Malagant's army rode along the causeway at the speed that made them so frighteningly formidable—the elite raiders who had burned so many of Leonesse's border villages. And riding at their head was Malagant himself, his cropped black hair too short to ruffle in the breeze that was snapping the banners on Camelot's walls. One by one, those banners came down, and Malagant's hard mouth curved in a savage smile. One man's beginning was another man's end.

In the town square, entirely ignorant of the danger that was stalking them, the crowd listened to Mador address their king.

"Is it the High King's wish that the queen be questioned by this court?"

"It is the High King's wish that the law take its course," Arthur said neutrally.

There was a drawn-out silence. All eyes except Arthur's turned to Guinevere. Color flooded her pale skin, but she held her chin high and let the populace see that she was not afraid.

The silence was broken by the sounds of tramping boots and the clatter of horseshoes on cobbles. The citizens began turning on their benches, craning their necks to discover the source of the disturbance. On the platform Agravaine raised his head and, with a feeling of cold shock, saw the figures on the rooftops and battlements. Dark leather and steel, short-cropped hair. These were soldiers neither of Camelot nor Leonesse. His hand went to his sword hilt.

Mador, ever the official and a stickler for protocol, strove to continue the proceedings. "Do you deny the charges?" he demanded sternly of Guinevere.

She did not reply, for her own gaze was following the soldiers gathering above and around the town square. The arena was swiftly becoming a trap.

"Who goes there?" Agravaine challenged. He took a pace forward, his expression sharp with concern.

Mador opened his mouth as if to protest, then closed it again, his own eyes going to the roofs. The sound of horses was much closer now, and the running footfalls of heavy boots. Something was wrong, something was desperately wrong.

"Where are the guards?" Patrise glared around at the ordinary soldiers of Camelot, scattered among the bewildered citizens. Those escorting Guinevere and Lancelot tightened their cordon around the captives as if suspecting that this was some kind of escape attempt.

"Up on the roofs!" Agravaine thundered impotently. "Who goes there? Answer me!"

Mador abandoned his scroll and drew his sword. "What's going on?" he asked with frustration. "Are we under attack? Is it a ploy to ruin the trial?"

Patrise shook his head and there was a look of disbelief in his eyes. "The city gates," he said. "They are coming from the city gates. How could we have been so blind?"

"I don't underst—" Patrise's words were cut off by the deafening blare of a dozen battle horns. Arthur thrust himself to his feet and stared toward the sound with the wide eyes of utter astonishment. Here in the heart of his domain he was under attack.

The notion froze him where he stood. His heart told him that it was impossible, but his eyes saw the truth.

Down the main thoroughfare leading from the square to the city gate rode a mass of armed men, and at their head was Malagant, astride a black horse, his eyes aglow with mocking triumph. In stunned confusion, the people of Camelot watched the advance of the dark array. No one knew what was happening. It was no use looking to their own knights and soldiers for guidance, for they were as stunned as the citizens.

Malagant's gaze roved scornfully over the gathering. He drew his sword and, rising high in the saddle, caushed his mount to rear up and paw the air. He punched the drawn weapon on high and roared out his own name. "Malagant!" The cry echoed and rebounded off the walls and the rooftops, circling like a bird of prey. And as the ripples faded, he was answered. On the rooftops and balconies, men rose up at his bidding, black silhouettes against the bright sky, and responded to his call with their own blood-curdling war cry.

"God save us," muttered Agravaine, and stepped nearer to the king.

Lancelot stared up at the dark army crowning the battlements. The crossbows were out, and most were trained upon Arthur. If one did not hit, then another would. There was no escape. Behind the crossbow men was an outer ring of soldiers bearing flaming torches. It was full daylight; they did not need them to guide their way or keep them warm. It was evident that they intended Camelot to burn.

Malagant raised his voice. It was harsher and more powerful than Mador's, as if imbued with the smoke of all the towns and villages he had destroyed in his search for power. "Nobody moves, or the great Arthur dies!"

Horrified silence greeted his words. Arthur gazed around, taking in the crossbows aimed directly at his body and the ring of torches beyond. He could see the dawning terror on the faces of his people, and there was nothing he could do to help them. He was powerless, his men held at bay by the deadly threat of those crossbows. He had gathered everyone in the square, determined that they should witness his justice as he took his revenge on the person he loved most in the world. And this was what it had brought him. Without the consuming desire to punish, his vision would have been clear and Malagant would never even have reached the causeway.

"May God forgive me," he muttered, too low for the smirking Malagant to hear. But Lancelot heard and looked at him sharply.

Malagant gazed around the great square, and there was relish in his voice as he raised it to address the cowering people.

"My men control the city gates and every exit from this square! On every roof I have soldiers with burning torches! I have only to lift my arm and your golden city burns to ashes. I am the law now!" He shook a bunched, exultant fist.

Arthur squared his shoulders and walked slowly forward. "My people are unarmed, I am unarmed," he said almost wearily. "If it is me you want, then here I am."

"No!" Guinevere cried, reaching out, but Arthur

had already stepped beyond her, and if he heard her, he gave no sign.

Malagant laughed aloud in contempt and gestured to the crowd. "Do you hear him? Do you hear the great King Arthur of Camelot? Look at him! A man waking up from a dream. The dream is over! This is reality!" He pointed with his sword to the dark-clad troops menacing the square on all sides. "Did you truly believe that Camelot was a land of brotherhood?" he sneered. "I will tell you the truth, Arthur. Camelot is a land of wealth and privilege, protected by a highly trained professional army." His upper lip curled. "No need to be ashamed of that. The strong rule the weak. That's how your God made the world, although you will tell it differently."

Arthur looked steadily at Malagant on his great black warhorse. "We are all born weak and helpless," he said, and now his voice was strong and filled with purpose. He could feel the energy flowing through his body now, and he met the mocking black eyes without fear or hesitation. "We will all grow old. God makes us strong only for a while so that we can help each other."

"God makes me strong so that I can live my own life and be subject to no law save those I make," Malagant retorted. He swung his horse and pointed his sword at random at a man in the crowd. "You! Arthur says to you that you have been born to serve other men!" The sword tip pointed to the next man in the row, and the next beyond him. "And to you, and you as well. Serve others, he says." Malagant leaned over his saddle, his obsidian eyes narrow and bright. "Tell me, when do you live your own freedom? Freedom from Arthur's tyrannical dream, freedom from Arthur's tyrannical laws!" He gestured at the knights on the platform. "Freedom from Arthur's tyrannical God?"

Arthur listened to Malagant and watched the frightened, shocked response of his people. With every moment that passed, he grew more certain of what Malagant intended. He had known for some time that the Lord of Gore desired Camelot for his own. The scornful comments were born of jealousy. What Malagant wanted, he took. And what he could not have, he destroyed. A sudden pang went through Arthur. Perhaps he understood Malagant because the man's emotions were his own. Arthur's gaze went to Lancelot. The man should not be standing there on trial for his life. It was at the whim of an envious king, not the law of the land, that he was accused of treason.

"My God," murmured Arthur. Had he really been so blind that it had taken Malagant's invasion to make him see the light? He grimaced at Malagant, posturing upon his great warhorse. "Is this the way it has to be?"

Malagant had paused for effect. Now he drew another deep breath and once more addressed the crowd. "All I ask of you is obedience. You obeyed Arthur. Now you will obey me!" He swung himself off his horse and tossed the reins to an equerry. The crowd fell silent as Malagant approached the platform steps and confronted Arthur. A solitary child wailed, and its terrified mother hastened to silence it.

Malagant and Arthur stared at each other. There was no fear between them. Malagant's eyes were hungry, Arthur's resigned. On the platform behind him the knights and guards stood frozen, scarcely breathing. Malagant's gaze cut briefly to Lancelot, and then to Guinevere, as if assessing what he would do with them as soon as he had the opportunity. Then, his attention again on Arthur, he drew a line in the dirt with the toe of one black, polished boot.

"Your day is over, Arthur. I want your people to see you kneel before me so that they may know who truly rules them now." He raised his sword to the cathedral bell tower and gave a signal to two of the black-clad marauders positioned there. "The bell will ring three times. You will kneel at my feet by the third bell, or you will die."

Arthur stared impassively at Malagant. He knew full well that it did not matter whether he knelt or not. Malagant would still have to kill him. A captive or exiled king would be a rallying point for rebellion, and while he lived, Malagant could never truly call himself ruler of Camelot.

The great bronze bells swung in their housings, and the clappers struck a resounding note. Arthur stared out over the ranks of his people, taking in their faces. The elderly, the mature. The young men and women who had been infants when he had first come to Camelot's throne and were now clutching infants of their own and watching the proceedings with frightened eyes. Malagant spoke of freedom, but it was the freedom of death.

The bells spoke a second time, and Malagant tapped the flat of his sword against his thigh. "Too proud to kneel to me, Arthur? You think you can serve your people better dead?"

Arthur shrugged. "I've no pride left in me. What I do, I do for my people and for Camelot."

The bells tolled a third time, the note long and sustained, as if time had stretched out to give Arthur a few more moments of life. He thought of the joyous tones pealing out on his wedding day and glanced once over his shoulder at Guinevere in love and farewell. Her eyes were bright with unshed tears. Arthur smiled at her, all rancor gone. "I loved you, I still love you," he said, and then turned to address his people and the man who would enslave them.

"Forgive me for what I am about to do. This is my last act as your king. You must not be afraid. All things change. I am Arthur of Camelot, and I command you now—" He paused in his descent of the platform steps, his eyes upon Malagant's hungry face. Malagant took a step backward, giving Arthur all the room he needed to bow down.

Arthur gazed down at the groove in the dust and suddenly flung his arms high and wide, his voice roaring out across the square,

"Stand and fight! Never surrender. Fight as you have never fought before!"

Malagant's triumphant expression became one of incredulous fury. He stepped even farther back and at the same time made a decisive chopping motion at his crossbowmen. Aim was taken, triggers squeezed, and blue-black bolts sped through the air.

Arthur smiled into Malagant's face.

"Camelot lives on!" he cried. The last word was punched from him as he was caught in the crossfire of the flying bolts and jerked off his feet. The force of the volley flung him in the air, his arms spread wide in the symbol of a crucifix.

"No!" screamed Guinevere, "Please God, no!"

She tore away from her guards, ran to Arthur, and was the first to reach him and see the wounds inflicted by the fire-hardened tips of the steel bolts. "Arthur, dear God, don't die! A surgeon, someone bring a surgeon!"

Upon the platform, swords rasped from scabbards and pandemonium broke loose. The townspeople began rising up from the benches, but instead of running away or yielding Malagant their obedience, they started to attack Malagant's troops.

Astounded, Malagant stared from Arthur's bleeding body to the fracas in the crowd. "What are you fighting for?" he demanded in genuine perplexity. "You can keep your city. Why lose everything when all you have to do is bow to me?"

The fighting only intensified. Malagant's face hardened. "Damn you, Arthur," he spat at the dying man, and flung his arm wide in a signal to the men on the rooftops. "Burn the city!" he howled. "Burn everything so that not a stick remains!"

His troops waved their torches in answer, black ribbons of oily smoke rippling away from the orange of flame, and then they set about the task of torching the buildings. It had been a dry summer, and houses swiftly caught light. Tongues of fire licked up walls and curled around wooden balconies. Roofs became beacons displaying the path of Malagant's ambition.

The palace guards surrounded Arthur and Guinevere, forming a barrier. She cradled him in her arms, tears pouring down her face. A grim-faced surgeon examined the wounds and shook his head over the damage inflicted.

"Destroy them all!" Malagant roared, mad with

rage. His horse circled and plunged, striking out with deadly forehooves. And Malagant struck out too, his blade shining with reflected firelight.

The knights of the High Council drew their swords, and working in concert, each defending the other, started to battle their way through the mayhem of hand-to-hand fighting toward Malagant, determined to cut him down. Lancelot's guards joined the fray, leaving him alone on the platform. A marauder spurred past him, his ripsword rising and falling like a bludgeon, people falling beneath the deadly blade. Lancelot recognized Ralf, Malagant's chief adjutant. Lancelot's first instinct was to go to Guinevere and Arthur, but there was nothing he could do. First the battle had to be won. There was time enough for all else later. And if it was lost, it would not matter.

He leaped down from the platform and was immediately challenged by a marauder. Lancelot's fist flew out and caught his attacker's sword arm, then continued the punch to the point of the man's unguarded chin. Lancelot's left hand shot out to capture the falling sword. Armed now with a weapon, he was unstoppable. He performed a warrior dance through the chaos, stepping lightly, cutting to kill, his concentration honed upon the charging, shouting figure of Ralf.

Ralf jerked his horse around. Gore dripped from the edge of his sword, and his dark armor was spattered with blood. Lancelot leaped across his path, barring his way. The move was so swift that for a moment Ralf was taken aback. The surprise, however, lasted no more than a split second. He was too experienced a fighting man for that. Uttering a yell, he came at Lancelot, intent on cleaving him down the middle.

As if he were playing the gauntlet, Lancelot waited his moment. He let the terrifying blow descend, and then, almost when it seemed too late, he slashed upward with his own sword and caught the serrated notches in Ralf's with his edge. A twist of the wrists, a jerk of the upper arms and shoulders, and Ralf was levered off the horse and deposited on the ground with a jarring thud. The animal reared and plunged. Lancelot swung himself up into the empty saddle and drew the reins in tight to control the beast. He had no need to deal with Ralf. Malagant's captain would never rise from the ground again. Already he was surrounded by an enraged mob of townspeople, and one of them had torn the ripsword from his hand.

Without looking back, Lancelot rode through the fray toward Malagant, intent on destroying him. The knights, under Agravaine, had driven Malagant's lieutenants back across the square. Their order was less than perfect, and their leader was partially exposed. Lancelot kicked his horse onward, maneuvering it toward Malagant's open flank.

As if possessed of a sixth sense, Malagant turned. He saw Ralf's horse, and then he saw the man astride. Their eyes met and held across the diminishing space in a mute acceptance of combat. Malagant turned his stallion to meet Lancelot's and raised his sword on high. For a moment neither man moved, each assessing the other, calculating. Then Malagant made a mocking thrust, large and slow. A child could have parried it. Lancelot saw the scorn, saw that the move was designed both to throw him off his guard and to anger him. It did neither. He responded to it in a similar vein, making a labored parry. Then he feinted a deliberate return thrust at the last moment, turning it into his lightning-fast strike. There was the shriek of steel upon steel as Malagant whipped up his defense and blocked a blow that would have slashed him open from collarbone to navel. It was the first time that Lancelot had ever met an opponent with the speed to block him, and for a vital instant he was too surprised to follow through. Malagant's blade flashed. Lancelot parried. The blow jarred his arm, but in his turn, he was fast enough to prevent injury. They were evenly matched, and it was going to be no easy task for either man to defeat the other.

On the ground, Malagant's men struggled to protect their leader, while the knights fought to keep the enemy footsoldiers from slashing at Lancelot. Strike and counterstrike rang out, hard and swift, without mercy. Both men were straining for breath, and there were longer spaces between each clash of sword. Not only were they matched in speed but in endurance, too.

Suddenly, Malagant swung away, breaking contact. For an instant, Lancelot thought that he had had enough, that he was running, but even as his mind told him not to be so stupid, one of Malagant's crack troop of mounted marauders attacked on Lancelot's other flank. Lancelot swerved and ducked to avoid the oncoming blow, but his horse falsefooted, and although not wounded, he was topped from the saddle. He rolled as he hit the ground, thus avoiding serious injury. Malagant rode in at him with the intention of crushing him beneath the flailing hooves of his stallion. Lancelot ran in close to Malagant's horse and, crouching low, made a swift slashing motion with his sword. Malagant twisted in the saddle to strike, his mouth an open snarl. The snarl became a yell of alarm as he began to topple sideways, his saddle girth cut clean through.

Evenly matched once more, the two men resumed their fight. Now they were in the thick of it, and as well as dealing with each other, they had to fight off other attackers, too. And still neither could gain the advantage. Lancelot's breath sobbed in his lungs; his sword arm was hot and aching. They had fought each other across the square and were now close to the trial platform, deserted now, a long streak of blood where Arthur had fallen. Malagant leaped up the steps and cried aloud to rally his men.

"Malagant! Malagant!"

There was a ragged answering howl, far less assertive than it had been earlier. Quite simply, his men could not spare the breath. Red stars of effort bursting in front of his eyes, Lancelot leaped onto the platform in pursuit of Malagant.

A look of impatient disdain on his face, Malagant faced Lancelot and raised his sword. Once again the blades met with devastating speed. The lightning parries rang out, mingling with grunts of effort. Sweat stung in Lancelot's eyes, blurring his vision. He blinked hard to clear his gaze, and in that moment, Malagant struck. Lancelot's swift reflexes were not swift enough, and the tip of his enemy's sword opened up a long superficial gash down Lancelot's flank.

In a different man, the wound might have signified

the end, but to Lancelot it was a goad to spur him on, the incentive he needed to push his will beyond his body. The blood ran hot down his side, stinging and burning. There was an exultant glow in Malagant's black eyes. Little did he know that he had just looked upon death.

Lancelot braced his wrist and focused all his being in one rapid, tremendous blow.

Malagant's sword cartwheeled through the air, and as Malagant stood unguarded, Lancelot punched forward, driving his sword deep into Malagant's chest. "God loves a winner," he panted in savage mimicry of Malagant's own words. The blade had gouged through a rib and resisted his attempt to wrench it free, and so he left it where it was and scooped Malagant's sword from the ground.

Malagant stared down at the hilt protruding from his body, quivering with each driving pulse of blood, then he looked into Lancelot's implacable eyes. There was denial and disbelief in his own. He struggled to pull the weapon from his body, but it was beyond his strength. His legs buckled and he fell back into Arthur's empty throne, his stare locked upon eternity.

When Malagant's soldiers saw their lord dead upon Arthur's throne, they lost heart and yielded. Soon all of Malagant's once brave army had surrendered to the people of Camelot.

The pity was, Lancelot thought, looking around at all the slaughter, that it had come too late.

Chapter 20

Lancelot strode down the corridors of the palace toward the Round Table chamber. Outside the clamor had died away. He could faintly hear Agravaine's voice raised in command as he took control. In a moment he would go back out and help the other knights, but there was something he had to do first.

He pushed open the chamber doors and discovered Guinevere cradling Arthur in her arms, pressing his war-scarred hand to her cheek over and over again, her face wet with tears. Lancelot hesitated, unsure whether to advance or retreat.

At the sound of the door opening, Guinevere turned her head and saw him standing there. "There's no more we can do," she said in a choked voice. "His wounds are beyond stitching."

Lancelot saw that linen cloths had been bound around Arthur's wounds, but already they were soaked with blood. Everyone knew and feared the deadly force of the crossbows of Gore. The wonder was that Arthur was still alive and conscious. The king's face was gray with impending death, but he still had the strength of will to fix his gaze on the man at the door.

Nailed by that look, Lancelot advanced into the room and knelt at Arthur's side.

"My lord, I bring you good tidings. Malagant is dead and his troops have surrendered. The fires are being doused even as I speak." He took Arthur's other hand in his.

Arthur nodded imperceptibly. His throat worked as he strove to speak. "I did not doubt it," he whispered. There was a moment's silence while he mustered his strength. "Lancelot . . ."

"My lord?"

"Is my . . . sword still by my side?"

Lancelot touched the ornate hilt of the weapon. "Yes, my lord."

"Take it into your keeping."

Lancelot looked at Guinevere, then back at Arthur. A great honor was being conferred, but with it came a great responsibility. And he dared not hesitate, for Arthur was already on borrowed time. Without thinking, acting on the instinct that made his swordplay so deadly, he reached down to the hilt and lifted it from its scabbard.

The ghost of a smile touched Arthur's lips as he felt the sword leave him. "My last and truest knight." His voice was now no more than shallow breath. "You're the future . . . the future of Camelot . . ."

Exhausted, he sank back. Guinevere gave a small

cry. Fearing that he had died, she took him in her arms and held him tight, unheeding of the blood that stained her gown. She kissed his face, his beard, his lips.

Arthur's lids flickered, and his glazing eyes met hers and saw the tears of love and grief. "Sunlight," he said, his voice suddenly strong. "I feel it now. . . . My love." The last word faded to a sigh, and his head slumped in Guinevere's lap. She huddled over him, weeping.

Lancelot stood up. He looked at the sword in his hand, the sword of Camelot, given to him by a dying king whose greatness the world would never see the like of again. And yet that king had entrusted him with the royal sword. Slowly, reverently, Lancelot sheathed it.

They came, the people of Camelot. Hundreds upon hundreds, they gathered at the lakeside to bid farewell to their king. The sky was pale with cloud, a halo of brighter white pinpointing the position of the sun, and a chill breeze ruffled the surface of the water.

Moored to the bank was a raft fashioned of felled young birch trees. The branches had been broken up and tied into bundles of kindling, and these had been stacked around a core of dry furze. Upon the furze was spread a pall of violet blue silk, the final resting place of Arthur, High King of Camelot. The royal guards in their blue and silver livery stood to attention in a great semicircle on the shore. Close to the raft itself were the members of the High Council, the effective government of

Camelot. Faces were stern, but hearts were full of emotion.

Guinevere, somber in a black velvet bodice and a skirt of the royal purple silk, knelt at Arthur's side, her hand over his clasped icy ones as she looked for the last time on his face. It was serene in death, as if a troubled thought had never crossed the wide brow.

Across from her, Lancelot, as bearer of the royal sword, performed the office of covering Arthur's body with another swathe of the purple cloth, leaving only his face exposed.

"It is time," he said gently to Guinevere.

She glanced around at the watchers upon the shore and nodded. Leaning over Arthur, she kissed his cold brow, and then eased to her feet. The hem of her gown was wet, but she did not feel the heaviness of the moisture.

Lancelot drew the royal sword and cut the barge's mooring rope. Small ripples shuddered through the water and in their impetus, the barge began to drift away from the shore. The current of the tidal lake caught the funeral boat and began to tug it away toward the sea.

Among the royal guard, a cordon of archers fitted flaming arrows to their bows and, at a signal from Agravaine, launched them into the sky. Some missed their target, but most fell onto the barge. The furze and dry kindling caught light at once, and flames crackled skyward, the smoke rippling like incense, and sparks fizzing like orange fireflies.

Lancelot held the royal sword on high, presenting the hilt toward the water. One by one, the knights drew theirs and followed suit. The sun gleamed through the clouds and the crosses on the sword hilts flashed in a last salute to the fallen king. And it seemed to those who stood on the lakeside, watching the burning barge, that they heard Arthur's voice on the wind.

"Camelot lives on."